Changeling Press, LLC

ChangelingPress.com

Preacher (Dixie Reapers MC)
with Ryker & Badger
Harley Wylde

Harley Wylde

Preacher (Dixie Reapers MC)
with Ryker & Badger
Harley Wylde

All rights reserved.
Copyright ©2019
Preacher (Dixie Reapers MC) ©2019 Harley Wylde
Ryker (Roosters 2) ©2019 Harley Wylde
Badger (Roosters 5) ©2019 Harley Wylde & Paige Warren

ISBN: 9781792994067

Publisher:
Changeling Press LLC
315 N. Centre St.
Martinsburg, WV 25404
ChangelingPress.com

Printed in the U.S.A.

Editor: Crystal Esau
Cover Artist: Bryan Keller

Table of Contents

Preacher (Dixie Reapers MC 5)

Harley Wylde

Kayla: My twin brother, Johnny, practically disappeared when he started prospecting for the Dixie Reapers, and if I wanted to see him, then it meant going to the compound. I'd never been inside the clubhouse, wasn't supposed to go there, but sometimes the devil on my shoulder prods me into doing things I shouldn't. Johnny made it sound like there were drugs being snorted left and right and orgies, but that wasn't what I found that night.

I never expected to fall for a heartbroken man I could never have, a man much older than me. But that night, Preacher took me in his arms, claimed my virginity with a passion that left me seeing stars, and I knew that I'd made the right decision. Even if it did come back to bite me in the ass two months later. When I'd walked through the door that night, I'd never counted on being fucked by a super hot biker, and I definitely didn't expect to end up pregnant!

Preacher: When I lost my family, before even prospecting for the Dixie Reapers, I'd closed off my heart and vowed to never let another woman in. A quick fuck here and there with the club pussy kept me sane, but no one would ever mean anything to me. Then the most tempting woman I've ever met gave me a night I knew I'd always remember, right before she disappeared. When she turns up two months later, I find her in the arms of one of the prospects.

Fury hits me first, then she knocks me on my ass when she tells me she's pregnant. With my kid. I turned away from God all those years ago, gave up being a minister, and signed my life over to the Dixie Reapers. I don't know that I believe in a higher power anymore, but maybe it's time I start praying again. Because giving this woman everything she needs, being the man she deserves, is going to take one hell of a miracle.

Dear Reader,

Thanks to all of you who asked for Preacher's story -- and here it is! Preacher, like all the Dixie Reapers MC books, is a stand-alone story, but if you'd like to read the series in chronological order, Preacher takes place between Torch and Rocky. Preacher is not as long as the other books in the series, but I tried to make it just as hot. I can't begin to tell you how much I love these characters, not just in this story, but in the entire series. They hold a special place in my heart, and I hope they will offer you a bit of enjoyment.

The feedback I've received on this series has been amazing, and I appreciate each and every one of my readers. Venom, Torch, Rocky, and Bull have been Amazon bestsellers, and that's thanks to all of you. If you have a moment to spare, I would love it if you'd take a few seconds to leave a review. It doesn't have to be long. Just something to let other people know what you liked or didn't like about the books. Reviews not only help other readers, but I love to hear what my readers think. I hope you found the story entertaining and enjoyed that gooey feeling you get when characters get their happily-ever-after.

If you'd like to be notified of future books, you can sign up for my newsletter or follow me on Amazon. Thank you again for taking a chance on my Dixie Reapers and Preacher!

Until next time...

Chapter One

Kayla

I wasn't supposed to be here. Johnny had warned me away, telling me that the compound was no place for a girl like me. I nearly snapped his head off and reminded him I was a grown-ass woman and not some child. He was all of two minutes older than me, but acted like he was thirty and not nineteen. My twin brother was a pain in the damn ass, but I missed him. We'd done everything together, until he'd decided to prospect for the Dixie Reapers, then overnight, he was gone. All his time was tied up with club business, and he no longer came home to visit. He'd walked away from me, and it hurt like hell, especially since he damn well knew what life was like at home.

I didn't have a car, and walking all the way to the compound hadn't been fun, but as I approached the gates, I felt my stomach twist and turn. I'd met a few of the prospects from the times I'd shown up to see Johnny, but I'd never met the patched members, and Johnny wanted to keep it that way. He'd told me that what went on in the clubhouse wasn't something I ever wanted to be a part of, and I'd avoided the place all this time, but as I heard the music blasting from inside I wondered if the temptation would be too great.

The hem of my denim skirt rode up, and I tugged it back down as I neared the gate. The prospect on the other side was one I'd met once or twice. He always leered at me and gave me the creeps, but so far he'd kept his hands to himself. His gaze caressed me in a way that suggested he'd like to do far more than look, and I tried to hold back my shiver of revulsion at the mere thought of his hands on me. It wasn't that he was bad looking, but he definitely gave off a creeper vibe.

"You here to see Johnny?" he asked.

"Yeah. Thought I'd surprise him."

"Oh, he'll be surprised all right. He's inside," the prospect said, tipping his head toward the clubhouse. "But then, you aren't allowed in there are you? Too pristine for a place like that."

"I'm not pristine," I snapped.

I might be a virgin in the strictest sense, but I was far from angelic. I'd never technically had sex, even though I'd given a few blow jobs and fooled around, but I'd used my trusty vibrator to take care of my virginity. I'd heard it would hurt, and no way was I trusting a guy with something like that. Especially not since the guys I knew were selfish and fumbling. No finesse whatsoever.

"Just remember that you were warned." The gate slid open, and he motioned toward the clubhouse. "Enter at your own risk."

That sounded like something the creepy guy in horror movies says right before the heroine does something incredibly stupid, like enter a house full of mass murderers, or choose the darkened pathway filled with deformed, dying trees instead of the brightly lit path. This was just a clubhouse full of bikers, one of whom was my brother. How bad could it be?

I stepped through the gate and made my way across the lot to the building with *Dixie Reapers* across the top in neon, and slowly climbed the steps. The noise from inside was even louder now, and I pushed open the doors, not sure what to expect. The way my brother talked, I half-expected naked women and orgies going on out in the open. My gaze scanned the room, but I didn't see my brother -- or any orgies. The place was packed wall-to-wall with men and women in leather cuts with Dixie Reapers stitched across the back. Other than some smoking and drinking, I didn't see anything wild going on. Not that those things were wild, but to hear Johnny tell it, all kinds of shit went down in here. They just looked like your average group of adults having a nice time.

No one paid me any attention as I moved farther into the room, but the fact I was the only one not sporting one of those leather cuts made me feel a little out of place. At least I'd worn my black top and not the red one I'd picked up first. Still, I didn't exactly blend, even if some of the women present looked to be my age or close to it. I'd learned enough from Johnny to guess those were the old ladies. He seemed rather fond of the President's woman, and I wondered if I'd ever get a chance to meet her. To hear Johnny tell it, the woman was up for sainthood. I didn't think anyone could ever be that perfect.

At the end of the bar, a man sat alone, a line of shot glasses in front of him, and an old worn Bible nearby. I hadn't taken the club for being religious, but then this man didn't seem quite like the others. He wore the same cut as everyone else, but as I studied him, I realized he was more somber. There was almost a haunted look to him, as if he were trying to drown his demons in whiskey, or whatever he was drinking. I felt this pull, as if I were supposed to get closer to him.

Slowly, I made my way across the room and slid onto the stool next to his. He didn't even so much as glance my way, but I could tell from the way his mouth tensed that he was more than aware of my presence, and didn't seem to care for it. I didn't know what he was trying to run from, and it was honestly none of my business, but I'd found that sometimes people just needed to be reminded they weren't as alone as they thought. Despite the fact the room was full of people, not a single one had come to sit by him. Maybe he'd chased them off, or maybe they left him alone because of the vibe he was putting out. Neither was going to deter me. Someone as sexy as he shouldn't be drowning their sorrows. Not alone anyway.

The guy behind the bar came over, a swagger to his step and a cocky smile on his face. His cut said Prospect, but thankfully he wasn't someone I knew. The minute my brother found out I was here, he'd likely escort me back to the gate and send me home, which was the last place I wanted to be. The guy leaned on the bar, his arms folded so that his biceps bulged. I assumed I was supposed to be impressed, but he looked just like every other asshole in my neighborhood who wanted in my pants. *Not happening, buddy.*

"What can I get for you, beautiful?" he asked, his lips tipping up on one side in a way I supposed most would find sexy. It wasn't making me drop my panties, that was for sure. I was completely immune to guys like this one.

"Rum and Coke," I said.

The guy next to me snorted.

"What?" I asked, turning my attention his way.

When his gaze clashed with mine, the breath in my lungs froze. Dark hair and a close-cropped beard were sexy enough, but damn... The man's eyes were truly things of beauty. I saw blues, greens, golds. Maybe even a hint of gray. Those were the kind of eyes a woman could get lost in, the kind of eyes that would make her do something really stupid.

"You ever actually had a rum and Coke?" he asked, his voice deep and smooth.

"Maybe."

He smiled a little. Not a full-out smile, and not even a smirk. It was almost like his lips had turned up without his permission because it was gone almost as fast as it happened.

"Why don't you give her a *Sex On The Beach*?" the guy next to me said.

The Prospect leered at me. "Oh, I'd be delighted."

I couldn't help but roll my eyes. "Just the drink, thanks."

I could tell he wanted to say something, but he refrained, walking off to fix my drink. I focused on the guy sitting next to me again, and noticed his cut said *Preacher*. Since he had a Bible nearby, I wondered if that's how he'd gotten the name. I didn't think an actual preacher would be sitting here drinking alcohol. But then, I didn't really know any religious types.

"I'm Kayla," I said.

"Preacher."

He went back to looking at his shot glasses, which were empty now. Now that he'd spoken to me, no way was I letting him go back to his brooding silence. He was probably older than I'd first thought, but that only made me curious. I was used to guys my age, who didn't know what the hell they were doing. But a guy like him? I was willing to bet that he knew exactly how to treat a woman, both in and out of the bedroom.

"Why aren't you partying with everyone else?" I asked.

"Weddings aren't really something I like to celebrate," he said.

"Don't believe in marriage?"

He held up his left hand, a gold band on his ring finger. "Already met my one and only. And someday I'll get to see her again."

See her again?

"Did she move?" I asked.

"Yeah." He glanced my way. "To heaven."

Way to put your foot in your mouth, Kayla.

"I'm sorry. I wouldn't have pushed if I had known. It must be hard being here without her."

He shrugged. "It's been twelve years, but it doesn't get any easier."

Holy hell! She'd died twelve years ago, and he still wore his wedding ring? Talk about commitment! I couldn't even get a guy to go past the first date, and here he was, a widower for over a decade, and he still carried his wife in his heart. Part of me wanted to cry over the pain he must feel from losing his wife, but the other part thought it was touching that love like that still existed outside books and movies.

"She must have been really amazing," I said.

"She was." I got a genuine smile that time.

The Prospect returned with my drink, and another line of shots for Preacher. We talked and drank for over an hour until both of us were well on our way to being drunk.

If anyone asked later, I'd say that's how I ended up in their meeting room, or whatever the hell they called it, with my skirt shoved up and my panties ripped off me. Yeah, definitely the alcohol, and didn't have a damn thing to do with raging hormones and a hot as hell biker who needed a little comforting.

Johnny was going to kill me when he found out.

* * *

Preacher

The gorgeous woman who had listened to me talk about my wife, and had seemed genuinely interested, was exactly what I'd needed. I didn't know precisely when she'd ended up in my lap, or at what point I'd started kissing her, but it wasn't long before we were stumbling down the hallway. I pushed her into the room we used for Church. If Torch knew, he'd kick my ass, but I never took women to my home. It made them think it was something more than it was.

I couldn't remember the last time I'd been this damn turned-on, though. It should have scared me, the feelings tumbling around inside me, but I shoved them down and just focused on the pleasure. Her curvy body pressed tight to mine, and damn if it didn't feel like her hands were branding me everywhere they touched. She fumbled with my belt, and a moment later she had my pants unzipped and her hand was diving into my underwear and wrapping around my cock.

I pulled her top off and dropped it onto the table, then leaned back a little to admire the view. The scrap of black lace that cupped her breasts was probably the sexiest thing I'd ever seen. Pulling up her skirt, I saw the panties matched, and I had this insane urge to keep them as a souvenir. Kayla's hands were tugging my pants and boxer briefs down until my cock was freed.

She dropped to her knees and licked her lips, her gaze fastening on mine, as she leaned forward and gave my cock a long, slow lick. I groaned and sank my fingers into her hair, urging her to do it again. Fuck but that felt incredible! It had been a while since I'd been with anyone, but I knew it hadn't felt like this.

"Open, baby. Wrap those lips around my cock," I told her.

Her lips parted, and I thrust inside. Her mouth felt like heaven as I stroked a little deeper each time. She looked hot as fuck on her knees, my cock in her mouth. Those sultry eyes of hers were nearly my undoing as she stared up at me.

"You can take more, can't you, sweetheart?" I asked.

She hummed, which I took as an agreement. Kayla deep-throated me, taking every fucking inch of my cock, not gagging so much as once. It was like she was made for this, made to be fucked. I gripped her hair tighter and fucked her mouth, not stopping until I came. She swallowed, and then kept sucking even after I didn't have anything left to give. I was still hard as granite, which hadn't happened since... No, I wasn't going to think of *her* while I was fucking Kayla. It wasn't fair to either of them. With any other woman, I wouldn't have cared, but Kayla... She didn't seem like the others I'd fucked for a quick release. She listened, and she seemed to understand my pain. This wasn't a quick screw to let off steam. It was something more, which was downright terrifying.

I pulled free of her mouth and helped her to her feet. I normally fucked the women from behind, so I didn't have to look at them, but I wanted to see her wide, expressive eyes as I pounded into her sweet pussy. Tearing her panties from her body, I urged her onto the table and spread her legs wide. My cock slid along her slit, and it felt so damn good. I closed my eyes a moment, just savoring the feel of her against me. Then my senses returned long enough to put on a condom. I hadn't fucked without one since my wife died, and I wasn't going to start now, no matter how tempting Kayla might be.

I slowly pressed inside her, gritting my teeth at how fucking tight she was. I'd never known a virgin who could suck cock like she could, but the way she gripped me had me wondering if I was her first. I nearly stopped, but she felt too damn good. She moaned and leaned back on the table, popping the front clasp on her bra and cupping her breasts. *Christ!* I sank balls-deep into her, only pausing a moment. The fact she wasn't in any pain, and I hadn't felt anything tear inside her, gave me a sense of relief that I wasn't going to fuck up her first time.

She lifted her hips a little, letting me slide in even deeper, and my control snapped. I gripped her hips tight as I plunged into her again and again, fucking her with a passion that had long been absent from my life. Her sweet cries just added fuel to the flames, and I wouldn't have been able to stop if I tried. I wanted her, needed her. I'd not allowed myself to feel a connection to anyone in so fucking long, but with her, even if it was just a few minutes, I completely lost myself in the moment. I didn't shut down my emotions. It wasn't mindless fucking, but something more.

"Rub your clit, baby. Let me feel you come on my cock," I murmured.

Her small fingers circled the little bud, and I felt her pussy clench down. It wasn't long before she was coming, crying out my name as her body tensed and her pussy tried to milk me dry. I fucked her until every drop of cum had been pulled from my balls, and even then I wasn't ready to pull out. She clasped me tightly as she panted for breath, her eyes still glazed and hazy from her release.

"That was so worth the wait," she said softly.

I didn't know what the hell she meant, and my brain was too sloshed with alcohol to puzzle it out. I knew I hadn't met her before, so how could she have been waiting for this? For me? I pulled free of her body and helped her stand. Her lips pressed against mine in the gentlest of kisses, then she fixed her skirt, refastened her bra, and pulled on her shirt. With a sassy smile, she kissed me once more, longer and deeper than before, and then she walked out the door. I waited a few minutes, trying to gather my thoughts. A good ten minutes passed before my mind began to clear, and I decided to clean myself up. Whatever had just happened, I knew that it was different from anything I'd experienced in the last twelve years. I'd already met my one and only, but Kayla had touched a part of me I'd thought long dead. If I'd known she was going to disappear, I might have moved faster. Especially when I realized the fucking condom broke.

Fuck my life.

I disposed of the rubber, zipped up my pants, and started for the door, pausing when I saw a scrap of black lace on the floor. I picked it up, inhaled her sweet scent, then stuffed the ripped panties into my pocket. I hadn't wanted to keep a woman's panties since the night I'd first slept with my wife. I'd analyze later why I wanted to keep the damn thing, then I went back to the main room looking for Kayla. The little minx was nowhere to be found. I didn't know who she'd come with, or why she'd been here at all, but I wasn't ready for her to go. There wasn't room in my life for a steady woman, and there never would be, but it didn't mean we couldn't enjoy each other's company a little more.

I stepped out onto the porch and scanned the area. No sight of her. The Prospect at the gate was smoking a cigarette as I approached, and he straightened when he saw me. I didn't care much for the little shit, but one of the members thought he had potential. I personally didn't think he was going to patch in. There was just something about him that had always set me on edge.

"What can I do for you, Preacher?" he asked.

"Did you see a woman come out of the clubhouse? Maybe five or ten minutes ago?"

"Yeah, she took off. Why? Did she do something wrong? Want me to go after her?"

The light in his eyes told me that he had other reasons for wanting to go after Kayla, and I wasn't sure I liked it. She wasn't mine, would never be mine, but she sure as fuck didn't belong to some punk ass Prospect either. I'd had my doubts about this one, and I'd told Torch and Venom as much. Carter. That was the little shit's name. I'd seen the way he treated the women when he thought no one was looking, and that wasn't going to fly as long as I was around. It was one thing to use the sluts to let off a little steam, but it was another to treat them like trash.

"She didn't do anything wrong. I just wanted to spend some time with her."

He grinned. "Yeah, she's a hot little thing. I'd love to get those legs of hers wrapped around me."

I grunted and walked off so I didn't give in to the urge to hit the little bastard. I had no business feeling that way about a woman I'd just met, one who meant nothing to me. But there was that little voice at the back of my head, the one I didn't like most days. *But she's different.*

Yeah, she was different. And different was very, very bad.

I'd ask around and see who knew her. Maybe she was a friend of Isabella's or Ridley's. If I had to guess, they were close to the same age, which made her too damn young for me. Then again, my Pres was in his fifties, and he'd claimed Isabella. Fuck, he'd damn well married her, and seemed more than happy. Maybe age really was just a number in the grand scheme of things.

When I went back into the clubhouse, I scanned the crowd and quickly found Ridley and Venom. They seemed surprised when I approached them, and I wondered if I'd been too much of a reclusive bastard lately.

"Preacher," Venom said, slapping me on the back. "Enjoying the party? The ceremony was perfect. You haven't lost your touch."

I grunted, not giving a shit about the wedding. Yeah, I was still technically an ordained minister, but I'd given up on God a long-ass time ago. The day he'd let my wife die, I'd turned my back and walked away. I didn't even touch my fucking Bible anymore, unless the club needed something. Like this wedding tonight.

"Do either of you know a Kayla?" I asked.

Ridley's brow furrowed, and she shook her head. "No. Should I?"

"I thought maybe she was a friend of yours. Are Torch and Isabella still here, or did they already take off to celebrate on their own?" I asked.

"With the looks he's giving her, they won't be around much longer," Venom said. "But Isabella is across the room."

I glanced that way and saw the blushing bride. "Thanks."

By the time I pushed through the crowd and reached Isabella, Torch looked about two seconds away from tossing her over his shoulder and walking the fuck out. She smiled when she saw me, and the next thing I knew, she'd thrown her arms around me and was hugging the shit out of me.

"Thank you so much," she said. "It was the best wedding ever!"

"You're welcome. I actually came over for a reason. Do you know anyone named Kayla?" I asked.

"The name sounds familiar, but I can't place her," Isabella said. "Did she do something wrong?"

Why the fuck did everyone assume Kayla did something bad? She was too fucking sweet to get into trouble, unless that trouble included a drunk widower and a broken condom. I needed to find her and make sure she was okay.

"I met her here tonight, and I was just trying to figure out who she knows."

Torch turned his piercing gaze my way. "Some woman you don't know was here?"

"I know her now," I muttered.

"Who's manning the gate?" Torch asked. "This event was family only."

"Carter," I said, trying not to sneer as I said his name.

Torch grunted. "I'll have a word with him tomorrow. For now, I think it's time I get my beautiful bride out of here."

"Congratulations, both of you," I said, then blended back into the crowd.

I still had no idea who Kayla was, or how to find her. My gut churned as I thought about never seeing her again, but I'd fucked up. If I'd stopped her from walking away instead of standing there like an idiot, then I'd know more about her.

She probably thought I was just another asshole, using her for her body.

I had this horrible feeling that I was never going to see Kayla again, and for some reason, that really bothered me. Fuck it. She was gone, and there wasn't shit I could do about it right now. I'd have a few more drinks, then call it a night. I could battle my conscience tomorrow.

Chapter Two

Kayla

I shouldn't have been a chickenshit and run out like that, but I hadn't thought Preacher would want me to stick around. Weren't bikers the fuck-and-leave type? At least when it came to random women like me. He'd needed comforting, and I'd offered it, but that didn't mean he wanted to hang around and cuddle afterward. If anything, I'd imagine he'd be fucked in the head each time he slept with a woman who wasn't his wife. So, I'd given him the space he likely needed, and since he hadn't exactly come after me, I was probably right to leave.

I felt the stickiness between my legs and tried to fight down the panic rising inside me. He'd put on a condom. I distinctly remembered him doing that, but something must have happened to it. I knew condoms weren't foolproof, but... Butterflies rioted in my stomach as I thought about the possible consequences I'd face. Surely I wouldn't get pregnant the first time I had sex, right? That shit only happened in books and movies.

The walk home was long, and I hunched my shoulders, trying to disappear as I walked down the broken sidewalks of my neighborhood. Once upon a time, it had been a nice place to live. A really fucking long time ago. Ever since my parents were kids, it had been crackhead and prostitute central for our small town. I think that was a large part of why Johnny had left, and I couldn't really blame him. He deserved a shot at a better life. If he'd stayed, he'd likely have been dealing drugs on the corner, or have been killed in a drive-by. I knew the life he'd chosen wasn't exactly safe, but at least he had a group of guys to watch his back. He wouldn't have had that around here.

The dilapidated house I shared with my mom and her latest boyfriend was just up ahead, and I quickened my pace. It wasn't safe to be out here dressed like this, especially since I'd lost my panties tonight. Guys in this part of town thought they could have whatever they wanted, and anyone who cried rape usually paid the price. I'd been lucky that nothing bad had happened to me so far. I knew a lot of that had to do with Johnny. He'd kept me safe all my life, even when my mom's latest and greatest would get handsy with me. But I was on my own now, which meant I had to be smart.

When I got into the house, I locked the front door and paused, listening for any sounds. I could hear my mom and her current boyfriend going at it in her room, the smell of pot heavy in the air. The living room was littered with beer bottles, and I knew they were likely drunk too. Bad things happened when Ray was high and drunk. I quickly walked straight back to my bedroom, trying not to make a damn sound to alert anyone of my presence.

Johnny had installed two deadbolts on my door, and a chain, and I locked all three every time I was in my room. The first time I'd woken to one of my mother's boyfriends looming over me in the middle of the night, jerking his cock off as he leered at me, I'd freaked the fuck out, and then Johnny had beat the shit out of the guy. I'd found all three locks on my door when I'd gotten home from school that day. Johnny had skipped class to make sure I was taken care of, but then he was always doing things like that for me.

I stripped out of my clothes and pulled on my pajamas. As much as I would have loved a bath or shower, no way I was chancing it tonight. If Ray had consumed as much beer as I thought he had, and if pot was thrown in to the mix, then I wasn't safe outside my room. He was one of the worst of all the guys Mom had brought home over the years. He didn't even hide the fact he wanted me, rubbing his cock in front of my mom as he stared at me. I didn't trust him, and sadly, I didn't trust my mother either. If Ray gave her an ultimatum, like he got to do whatever the fuck he wanted to me or he was walking out, she'd hand me over on a silver platter. He supplied all her drugs and booze, and no way was she giving that up.

The cheap cell phone Johnny had given me started ringing, and I quickly answered. He was the only one who ever called me, and I needed to hear his voice. I'd gone to the compound tonight, needing my brother, but I hadn't even stuck around long enough to find him. Not after...

"Why the fuck were you here tonight, Kayla?" he barked into the phone.

"I needed to see you."

He got quiet a moment. "Everything okay? Did Ray... he didn't touch you, did he?"

"No. Not for lack of trying on his part."

"Kayla, you can't just show up unannounced at the compound. You could get me into serious trouble, you know that? This is the best thing I've got going for me, and I don't want to screw it up."

Tears pricked my eyes at his harsh tone. "I'm sorry."

"If it's not Ray, then why the hell were you here? I've told you this isn't the place for you to party."

"You think I was there to party?" I asked, my heart feeling heavy. Did Johnny not know me as well as I'd thought he had? We were twins, two halves of a whole, and yet… "I've never been a party girl, and you know it, Johnny."

"Are you safe?" he asked.

I glanced at the locks on the door. "For now."

"If you weren't here to party, and it's not Ray, then why did you need me?"

"It's Joe."

The silence on the other end lasted so long I'd thought for a moment he'd hung up.

"Joe-motherfucking-Banner?"

"Um, yeah. He's been recruiting pretty heavy around here."

"Jesus fucking Christ. You're not joining his stable, Kayla."

"I wasn't planning on it," I muttered. "But… he said if I don't, then he'll find a way to make me. I'm scared, Johnny. You know what he did to Vera. He fucked her up so bad she doesn't even look the same anymore, and before she was even healed all the way, he had her working the streets."

"I'm on my way. Pack a bag, something small with just the essentials."

Pack a bag? Where the hell did he think I was going? It wasn't like he could let me stay at the compound with him. He'd already told me there were only two types of women there. Old ladies, or club sluts. And since I wasn't one of the first, and had no intention of becoming the second, there was no place for me there. Even if the most beautiful eyes I'd ever seen did flash in my mind for a moment. No way Preacher would ever lay claim to me. He was still married to his dead wife, and just because we'd fucked didn't mean anything. I knew I was just convenient for him tonight, and that was fine. At least my first time with a guy had been on my terms.

"Kayla, did you hear me?" Johnny asked, and I realized I hadn't said anything.

"Yeah. I'll get some stuff together."

"I'll tap on your window when I get there. Don't leave that fucking house."

He hung up, and I stared around my room. I didn't have much, but I still had my backpack from high school. I pulled it out and dumped a handful of clothes inside. Three outfits and the other important stuff like panties and such. My brush was on the dresser, and I shoved that into the bag too. My hand paused on the locks to my door, and I listened to make sure Ray was still occupied before I crept into the hall bathroom to retrieve my small bag of makeup and my toothbrush. I grabbed the box of tampons I kept under the sink too.

After my bag was stuffed as full as I could get it, I changed into something comfortable, and then sat on the bed to wait for Johnny. I heard his motorcycle roar into the driveway, and my body tensed. It didn't take but another minute before he was tapping on my window. I lifted it and stared out at my twin, the only person who had ever been there for me my entire life. He held out his hand, and I gave him my backpack, then he helped me climb out the window.

"Where are we going?" I asked.

"I'm putting you on a bus," he said. "You're getting the fuck out of this town before it ruins your life."

I froze mid-step. "Leave?"

He turned to face me. "Kayla, I can't protect you all the time anymore, and you're obviously not safe living at home. Mom doesn't give a shit what happens to you, never has and never will. And I'm sorry, but you're just not tough enough to live here without ending up spreading your legs for Johns or dead in a ditch."

"Thanks for the vote of confidence."

"You're my baby sister… "

"By like two minutes."

"Whatever. The point is that I don't know how else to protect you. So I'm sending you away. I have enough money for a bus ticket out of here and then hopefully enough to get you established in a new place. I made some calls. A buddy of mine has a studio apartment over the garage where he works. He's going to let you rent it for three hundred a month, utilities and trash included."

"I don't have three hundred dollars, Johnny."

He pulled a wad of cash out of his pocket and stuffed it into the front of my backpack before zipping it. "Now you do. There's about seven hundred there, but it should hold you until you can find a job. I'll take care of the bus ticket when we get to the station. And Kayla… whatever you do, don't come back."

My eyes burned as I fought hard not to cry. "Does that mean I won't see you anymore?"

"Not for a while. I'll try to come visit when I get a chance, okay? But you need to do this. This is your chance to change your life."

He took me by the hand and led me over to his bike. After he swung his leg over the seat, I climbed on behind him, slinging the backpack over my shoulders. I didn't know where I was going, or what I'd do when I got there, but I knew he was right. I needed to get away from this place. I'd been lucky so far, but eventually that luck would run out.

But you know what they say about running from your past? It always catches up to you…

* * *

Kayla
Two Months Later

The money my brother had given me was long gone, and I'd found a job working nights at the local diner. It was hard work, on my feet for sometimes ten or twelve hours day, but the tips were decent. I had a feeling that had more to do with the fact my shirts were fitting a little snugger across my breasts than usual. I'd gone up at least a cup size, and they hurt like hell. At first, I'd thought it was my period finally coming, since the damn thing was several weeks late. But nothing had happened.

One of the girls I worked with, a single mom who was two years younger than me, suggested I might be pregnant when the smell from the grill had sent me running to the bathroom to puke my guts up. I'd laughed it off, until I'd really thought about it. I was late, my boobs were getting huge, and I was throwing up because of a smell? Yeah. I'd gone straight to the pharmacy after that shift and bought every kind of pregnancy test they had. Every last one had come back positive.

It had scared the shit out of me, and I hadn't known what to do. Preacher had a right to know he was going to be a father, but I wasn't certain if he'd even want to know. A guy like that, still hung up on his dead wife? I couldn't imagine my news being welcome. So I'd kept it to myself. My frequent bouts of nausea had triggered some questions at work, and I'd finally had to tell the manager I wasn't sick with the flu, but I was pregnant. He'd shrugged and gone back to his paperwork, just happy to know I wasn't spreading germs to all our customers.

My shift was ending, and my back felt like it was damn well breaking. I'd worked a double when someone had called in sick, and now I was going to pay the price. Yeah, the tips were welcome because who didn't need extra money? But my body was protesting. I knew I'd go home, shower, and likely crash before I'd even had a chance to eat. We ate for free while we were working, so I'd had two meals since I'd come on shift, but my stomach was already growling again. I was either constantly wanting to stuff my face, or I was hugging the toilet.

I clocked out and gathered my things before heading back to my tiny apartment. It wasn't anything special, but it was mine. My brother's friend, Jeremy, was actually a really great guy. He hadn't hit on me once, had always been polite, and he checked on me periodically to make sure I didn't need anything. I hated to admit that Johnny had been right to send me away. Now I had a chance at a good life, and even if I had to work my ass off, this baby would have the kind of home I'd never had. At least my place was clean, even if the furniture was threadbare.

Climbing the metal stairs that ran up the side of the garage, I could feel the fatigue pulling at me. I put one foot in front of the other, practically dragging myself up the next step by pulling on the handrail. My keys were already clutched in my hand, and I unlocked the two deadbolts before I pushed the door open. The scent of the lemon cleanser I'd used that morning teased my nose, and I reached inside to flip on the light. I'd no sooner cleared the door than something heavy slammed into my back, sending me sprawling on the floor.

A weight covered my body, and a hand slammed over my mouth. Panic welled inside me. My heart started racing, and I wished like hell I'd paid more attention to my surroundings. How the fuck had he managed to get up the stairs behind me without making any noise?

"Thought you could get away from me?" he asked, his lips near my ear.

My eyes went wide as I recognized who was on top of me. And I knew in that moment, I was completely screwed. I didn't know how he'd found me, or why he'd bothered, but all those lewd looks I'd dealt with were going to become something much, much worse.

His hand skimmed up my thigh, shoving under the skirt I'd worn to work. I started thrashing on the floor, kicking my feet, and trying to bite the hand over my mouth. *This isn't happening!*

"That's it. I like it when they struggle."

I could feel the bulge in his pants press against me, and then he was kicking my legs apart. I fought harder, slamming my hands on the floor, and doing anything that might draw attention to what was happening. I didn't know if Jeremy was still downstairs, but there were times he'd slept in his office. I hoped like hell this was one of those times. I managed to kick over the table near the door and heard the crappy wood splinter on contact.

Carter started to unzip his pants, and tears streamed down my cheeks. I never stopped fighting, never stopped trying to break free. Even when he tore my panties, I still fought. But just as suddenly as he'd attacked me, his weight was lifted off my body, and I heard something slam into a wall. Gulping in huge breaths and crawling as far away as I could, I finally turned and saw Jeremy beating the shit out of Carter.

The Dixie Reapers Prospect fell to the floor, his face a bloody mess and one of his eyes swelling shut. Jeremy kicked him in the ribs while he was down, then sent a knee into the asshole's nose, not only breaking it, but knocking Carter the fuck out. He slumped to the floor, and Jeremy made his way over to me.

He knelt and slowly reached out a hand, almost as if he were afraid to scare me more. "Please tell me I fucking got up here fast enough."

"You did," I said, wiping the tears away. "He was just about to... but he didn't."

Jeremy nodded. "I'm taking you home. When we get to town, I'll call your brother, and he can meet us somewhere."

"You're throwing me out?" I asked.

"I'm sending you home, where you belong," he corrected. "Johnny has always been your knight in shining armor, and I don't know why he stopped now. But I think you need your brother right now, maybe more than ever before."

"I can come back?"

He smiled a little. "I'll leave the apartment vacant for a week or two, to see if you come back here. But I think you need to pack your things. Once Johnny hears what happened, he's not going to want you to be quite so far away anymore. And Kayla... you should tell him about the baby."

My eyes went wide. "How... "

"You didn't tie off your trash very well. Some of the sticks fell out in the dumpster. Saw them when I hauled out the garage trash. I figured if you wanted me to know, you'd say something. Just tell me that you want this baby and some asshole didn't force himself on you."

"It was consensual," I said. "But he doesn't know. I'm not sure I can ever tell him."

"That's your call to make. But your brother needs to know everything, all right? He can't protect you if he doesn't know the entire story. And not just what happened now, but about that baby."

"All right. Just let me get cleaned up, and I'll pack my things."

"I'll wait here and make some calls. I'll get one of the mechanics to open for me tomorrow."

I went into the small bathroom and splashed water on my face before I started packing. I'd been so excited about having a real shot at a decent life, and now I was going back? I didn't understand why Jeremy thought I wouldn't be safe here. Yeah, Carter had found me, and he'd almost… I shivered. But that could have happened no matter where I was living. I'd seen the look in Carter's eyes often enough to know something like this might happen one day. I'd tried to tell Johnny, but he'd blown me off, saying Carter was like a brother to him and would never hurt me.

After I packed the last of my things, and looked around the apartment one last time, I let Jeremy lead me down to his truck. My hometown was only about two hours away. Johnny had made sure I was close enough that he could easily visit whenever he had time, but maybe if I'd gone farther, Carter wouldn't have come after me. I didn't regret the past two months because I'd grown a lot during that time. And now I knew that I could make it on my own.

The two-hour trip flew by, and soon we were pulling into the parking lot of an all-night diner a few miles from the Dixie Reapers' compound. Jeremy sent me inside with some cash and orders to get a slice of pie. I dragged my tired body into the diner and claimed a seat at a booth in the window. Jeremy had his phone pressed to his ear, and I knew he was talking to Johnny. When he finally came inside, I couldn't tell if the conversation had gone well or not, but that question was answered soon enough when Johnny came roaring into the parking lot on his Harley.

It was good to see him, but the fierce look on his face told me this wasn't going to be a pleasant reunion. And so I waited patiently for him to come in, to have a seat, and then I started telling him everything. From the night I spent at the clubhouse, and what happened with Preacher, to Carter trying to rape me. And lastly, I told him I was pregnant. He looked a little shell-shocked at that last part, and beyond furious over what happened with Carter. I spared him the details, but the anguish in his eyes was enough to tear me apart. Whatever I'd thought of my brother since he'd joined the Dixie Reapers, it was obvious that he loved me.

"Where's Carter now?" he asked.

"I arranged for someone to contain him," Jeremy said. "Figured the Dixie Reapers would want to take care of him."

Johnny nodded before focusing on me again. "I think it's time for you to meet the President of the Dixie Reapers. I'm not set up for company since I share my space with the other prospects, but Torch will probably find a spot for you. And he needs to know about Carter."

"All right," I said softly.

His gaze dropped to my belly. "And Preacher needs to know about that kid. I know you think he won't want anything to do with either of you, but I think you're wrong."

I could tell there was something he wasn't saying, but I didn't want to press him. I rode with

Jeremy to the compound, and as we pulled through the gate, my palms started to sweat and nausea welled in my throat. I knew I was seconds away from puking and nearly dove out of the truck when it came to a stop.

Johnny rubbed my back as I threw up the slice of pie, then he curled an arm around my waist and led me into the clubhouse. I didn't know what to expect when we went inside, but it wasn't for Preacher to nearly lose it and attack my brother.

Chapter Three

Preacher

I'd gotten tired of sitting on my ass at home, staring at the TV like some mindless idiot, but I wasn't really feeling the vibe of the clubhouse either. More than one club slut had put her hands on me, and my dick wasn't the slightest bit interested. I hadn't fucked anyone, unless my hand counted, since the night I'd met Kayla. For the first time in twelve years, I didn't wake up from dreams about my wife, fighting the urge to cry into my fucking pillow because I missed her so damn much. No, I woke up hard as a fucking post after dreaming about how tight Kayla had been, or how fucking fantastic her mouth had felt wrapped around my dick. I felt a little guilty, almost like I'd replaced the woman of my heart with some random woman. Except, Kayla didn't feel like a random woman. And maybe that just fucked up my head even more.

I still didn't know where she was, or who she was for that matter. She'd never given me her last name, and the few people I'd asked hadn't shared any information with me. I had a feeling that punk ass Carter knew something, but he wasn't saying a word. I didn't know if he was looking out for Kayla, or for himself. The way he'd looked that night when I'd brought her up, I had a feeling he was keeping quiet for his own reasons and none of them good. There was something seriously creepy about that guy, but I seemed to be the only one who felt that way. I didn't like the thought of him becoming my brother when he patched in, but unless I could sway some more people my way, he would likely get voted in. He did his work and kept his mouth shut, I'd give him that.

I sipped on my beer and attempted to look like I actually wanted to be here. Truth was, I didn't much care where I was right now. I was miserable at home, miserable here... It ate at me that Kayla had run off, and I had no way to find her. The longer she was gone, the more I realized that somehow we'd connected that night, in more than just a physical way. I'd sworn to never get attached to another woman, and yet I'd done it anyway. We'd only talked for maybe an hour that night, and what had happened after that was over all too soon. But in those moments, I'd felt closer to her than I had to anyone since...

"Where the fuck is that punk-ass Prospect?" Tank grumbled as he settled on the stool next to me.

"Which one?" I asked.

"Carter. I have a job I need done, and no one seems to know where he is. According to Ivan, the guy took off two days ago and hasn't been seen or heard from. I checked with Torch, and he didn't get permission to take off like that. Last anyone around town saw him was this morning. He was at some second-rate hacker's house. Wire's wording, not mine. Whatever he's up to, he didn't want us to know what was up. I'm waiting to hear back from Torch on whether or not we need to question the hacker."

At least I wasn't the only one who didn't like the little fuckstick now. Maybe I didn't have to worry about him patching in after all. If Torch was pissed, then he'd likely be out on his ass once he came back. Good riddance, as far as I was concerned.

The Prospect manning the bar tonight, a favorite of Torch and his old lady, pulled a cell phone out of his pocket, frowning at the screen. I went back to focusing on my beer, not needing to get involved in anyone's drama. The kid had a way with the ladies, and it wouldn't surprise me if some hook-up was trying to get back in his pants. I felt Tank tense next to me and looked up just in time to see the kid go deathly pale, then vault over the bar and go running for the door.

"What the fuck was that?" I asked.

Tank shrugged. "I don't know, but I'm thinking it's not good."

An engine turned over in the parking lot, and from the deep growl, I knew the kid had just hopped on his bike. It wasn't like Johnny to leave a post, though, and apparently I wasn't the only one who was more than a little intrigued. Tank slid off his stool and started for the door, but before he could get outside, we could hear Johnny peeling out of the compound and taking off down the street. He was a good kid, so I hoped whatever the fuck was going on that it wasn't that serious.

Tank reclaimed his stool, but I noticed he glanced toward the door every few minutes. I couldn't blame him for being worried. It wasn't like Johnny to just disappear like that. Everyone knew that he was a favorite of our President and Isabella.

He wasn't gone more than a half hour, maybe a little longer, when he returned. But he wasn't alone. My heart started pounding, and I felt fury engulf me as he walked in the door with his arm around Kayla. She was pressed tight to his side, and looked so damn pale and exhausted. I didn't even realize I'd stood until I was right in front of the kid, ready to take a swing.

"Get your fucking hands off her," I said, my voice more growl than anything.

Kayla's eyes went wide, and she paled even further. I watched as she swayed and her eyes rolled back in her head. Johnny cursed, and I reached out and snatched Kayla into my arms as she started to slump to the floor, giving the kid a glare that had made men cower in fear. Johnny just stared at me with raised eyebrows.

"What the fuck did you do to her?" I asked.

"Nothing."

Torch, Venom, and Tank came over.

"Pres, I had planned on this introduction going a little differently," Johnny said. "This is my sister, Kayla. And I think we need to talk."

Sister? I looked down at the woman in my arms. Now that Johnny had said that, I did see a resemblance between the two of them.

"My baby sister," he said, smirking at me.

Fuck. *Baby* sister? Johnny was only nineteen. Was Kayla even legal? I felt a little dazed, but remained upright with Kayla clutched against my chest.

"By two minutes," Johnny said.

Oh, thank Christ. I breathed a little easier. Wait. They were twins? How had I not known that Johnny had a twin sister? Hell, had anyone known?

"Church," Torch said.

"There's something else," Johnny said, focusing on me. "I didn't do a damn thing to Kayla. But you did."

"Me?" I asked. She'd wanted me that night. Had she told Johnny otherwise?

"Yeah." He patted my shoulder. "Congratulations, Daddy. You knocked her up."

My breath froze in my lungs as he smirked and walked off, following Torch and the other officers. Knocked up? Kayla was pregnant? With *my* kid? Holy hell. My knees felt like they might buckle, but I took one step, then another. As I cleared the clubhouse door, Bull followed.

"Where are you taking her?" he asked.

"Home."

"You gonna claim her?" Bull asked.

Fuck if I knew what I was doing. What I did know for certain was that Kayla belonged with me. I ignored Bull and walked to my house. Torch had given me a four-bedroom home less than a mile from the clubhouse. I'd told him at the time that it was a waste of space because I only needed one bedroom, but he'd insisted. Now it looked like I'd be using at least one of those other bedrooms. A kid? The thought left me dizzy.

I'd tried to have kids with my wife, had tried for years, but we'd never been successful. I'd always thought I was at fault, that maybe I had a low sperm count or something. I'd offered to see the doctor, but she'd always told me that we'd get pregnant when we were supposed to. But it had never happened, and then she'd been taken from me. The moonlight glinted on my wedding ring, and I stopped in the middle of the road for a moment. I waited for panic to set in, for the intense pain and sorrow I felt every time I thought of Rachel. It didn't come.

I looked up at the sky and wondered if she was looking down on me. If there was a heaven, I knew that's where she'd be. She'd been so perfect, so sweet. And she'd died far too soon. The stars shone brightly overhead, and this sense of peace filled me. A slight breeze blew and ruffled my hair, like a light caress.

"All right, Rachel," I said. "I can take a hint."

My wife would have never wanted me to turn my back on Kayla or the baby. That much I knew for certain, and as much as I'd thought about the woman in my arms over the past two months, I knew that she wasn't the same as the others I'd fucked and walked away from over the years. Mostly because she'd never been far from my thoughts.

When I reached my home, I carried Kayla inside and went straight to the master bedroom, which was on the first floor. All the other bedrooms were upstairs and shared a bathroom. My bed was still mussed from earlier in the day, and I gently laid her down. I removed her shoes to make her more comfortable, then got a damp cloth from the bathroom and lightly pressed it to her cheeks and forehead.

Her eyes slowly fluttered open, and I gave her what I hoped was a reassuring smile. Must not have worked because she bolted upright and gave me a panicked look. Her chest rose and fell rapidly, and I worried that she'd hyperventilate and pass out again.

"Easy, baby. Do you want some water?"

"Where am I?" she asked.

"Home."

Her eyes went wide, and she stared at me.

"Were you going to tell me?" I asked. "That you're pregnant."

"No. Maybe. I don't know." She relaxed a little, and her breathing slowed. "I honestly didn't think you'd want to know. You're still married to your dead wife and don't have room for me and a kid. I can raise the baby on my own."

I made sure I had her attention as I slid the wedding band off my finger, then placed it in the bedside table drawer. It was the first time I'd taken that ring off since the day Rachel had placed it on my finger. It didn't feel as horrible as I'd thought it would, not at all like I was getting rid of her. I knew she'd always be a part of me, but it was obvious that I had responsibilities now and couldn't pine after Rachel forever.

"What are you doing, Preacher?" she asked.

"Call me Nick." I smiled. "The mother of my child should know my real name."

"You don't seem all that upset," she said.

"The condom broke. I tried to go after you once I realized what had happened, but you'd vanished. I asked several of my brothers who you were or where you'd come from, but no one knew. The prospect, Carter, seemed to know something, but he wasn't talking."

She went deathly pale again at the mention of Carter's name.

"I think I'm going to be sick," she muttered before she scrambled out of bed and went running to find the bathroom.

I followed and held her hair as she threw up, rubbing her back, and wondering if this was a pregnancy thing, or a fear thing. It was obvious Carter's name had scared the shit out of her, and I wanted to know why. If the little asshole had threatened her in some way, he would answer to me.

"Let's get you rinsed off in the shower and tucked into bed," I said. "We can talk more tomorrow. You look like you're about to drop."

She weakly nodded and let me undress her. I stripped out of my own clothes, then got into a hot shower with her. My body reacted to the sight of all those soft curves of hers, but I wasn't about to take advantage. After I cleaned her up, I dried the both of us, then helped her brush her teeth. When she was finished, I carried her to bed, sliding in next to her.

Kayla curled against my side with her head on my chest, and she let out a breathy sigh.

"This is nice," she murmured. "No one's ever held me like this before."

"You mean you've never cuddled in bed?"

She hummed. "You were my first. My only."

Her words trailed off, more of a slur, but they ricocheted around my brain. First? Only? Jesus Christ. She really had been a virgin that night, and I'd taken her on the damn table like a common whore. And knocked her up too.

There was definitely a lot for us to talk about. But morning would be soon enough.

* * *

Kayla

I felt the warmth of sunlight on my face before the brightness registered. I'd slept harder than I ever had before, but that might have had something to do with the hard, and very naked, body that I was plastered against. I looked up and realized that I hadn't dreamt about being in Preacher's arms. No, Nick's arms. But if I hadn't been dreaming about that, then I likely hadn't been dreaming about Carter either. Or rather having a nightmare about him.

I lifted the covers and checked my body, but thankfully I didn't seem to have any marks from my struggle with him. Although, if I had, Nick likely would have said something last night. And probably come completely unglued when he found out I was almost raped. At least, the way he'd come after Johnny just for having an arm around my waist, I was going to assume that he would be angry over what happened to me. I didn't understand why he'd reacted the way he had. We'd had a one-night stand, and while I was pregnant with his baby, he hadn't known that at the time.

His left arm was thrown over the top of his head, but I noticed the wedding band he'd been wearing was gone. I'd thought that part wasn't real either. Had he really removed it? For me? None of this made sense, and I was starting to feel incredibly confused. I didn't know the man lying next to me, not really. Yeah, we'd talked for a while that night before he'd led me off to a secluded room and changed my life forever. And not just because the sex was incredible, but because he'd left a little something behind.

I'd been scared to death of being a single mom, but I'd known that I would make it work. It might have been hard to figure out the logistics of working nights and having a baby in my life, but plenty of other women did it and so could I. Oh, hell. Did I even still have a job? Was I going back? Jeremy had made me pack everything, but that didn't mean I was actually staying here, right?

"You're thinking too much," Nick said, his voice a deep rumble.

I looked up at him again and found him watching me. "Sorry."

"How do you feel?" he asked, giving my hip a squeeze.

"Better." I really did feel better. Well, as long as I didn't think too hard about why I was back in this damn town. Then I'd probably freak the hell out.

"Have you seen a doctor yet? About the baby?" he asked.

"No. I don't have insurance, and before I could see if there was a free clinic nearby, Jeremy insisted I come back here."

His eyes narrowed. "Jeremy?"

"My brother's friend. I was staying in an apartment over the garage he owns."

He sat up, leaning back against the headboard, but pulled me along with him so that I was still pressed to his side. It should have felt awkward, being naked in bed with him like this, but oddly I found it comforting.

"Why did you leave town? Or were you just here visiting your brother?" he asked.

"I lived here, with my mom and her boyfriend." I pressed my lips together, not wanting to admit where I'd been living or why I'd left. I'd never been embarrassed before over where I come from, but Nick was different from anyone I'd met before. He might be a biker now, he hadn't always been one. He'd shared a home with his wife, had been a minister in a local church. He'd led a respectable life.

"Why did you leave?" he asked again.

"There's a pimp in my neighborhood who was pressuring me. The last woman who told him no nearly died and ended up working for him anyway. When I told Johnny what had happened, he got me out of town."

The intensity of Nick's gaze left me a little dizzy.

"What's his name?" he asked, his voice deceptively soft.

"It doesn't matter. I'm not going back there. I don't think."

"Fuck no, you're not going back!" His arm tightened around me. "You're staying right here with me."

"Here?" I asked, looking around the room. It was probably the nicest bedroom I'd ever seen, and I'd be willing to bet the rest of the house was the same.

"Did you think you would show up here, tell me you're pregnant, and I'd let you walk away?" he asked.

"I didn't tell you I was pregnant," I muttered.

"No, that would have been your brother. You should have come to me, Kayla. Was I such an asshole that night that you felt you couldn't tell me we were having a kid?"

"It was a one-night stand, Nick. You didn't make me any promises, and I knew you still loved your wife. Love, I mean."

"Kayla, there will always be a place in my heart for Rachel, but she's not the one I've been thinking about the last two months. I wasn't lying last night. I looked for you. I asked half a dozen brothers if anyone knew you, even asked Carter, but no one would say anything."

"Carter?" I could feel the blood drain from my face, and if I'd been standing, I'd have landed on my ass on the floor.

"Hey," he said softly. "What's wrong? Did that asshole do something to you?"

"It doesn't matter."

"Like fuck it doesn't!"

"Nick, I... I didn't come here because I'm pregnant." If I didn't tell him, I had no doubt Johnny would run his mouth. "Jeremy drove me here last night because Carter showed up at my apartment."

Nick moved so fast he was a blur, but he was suddenly looming over me, his hands braced on either side of me. His jaw was so tense I worried he'd crack his teeth.

"I'm fine," I assured him. "Jeremy heard me struggling and got to me in time."

"In time to stop what, exactly?"

I swallowed hard and tried to look away, but Nick turned my face back toward him. His gaze softened, and he gently pressed his lips to mine. His kiss was sweet, and just what I'd needed right then.

"Talk to me, baby. What did Carter do?" he asked, his voice calmer than before.

"He knocked me to the floor and tried to... " Tears pricked my eyes, and my heart ached as I remembered what had happened in vivid detail. "He unzipped his pants and was about to rape me when Jeremy came upstairs to check on me."

Nick flung himself off the bed and roared his rage as he began pacing the length of the room. His hands dug into his hair, and he looked about two seconds away from committing murder. My brother had always protected me, but I'd never had anyone get so angry on my behalf before. Part of me liked that Nick seemed to feel so strongly about my well-being, and the other half was afraid of just what he might be capable of. Yes, he'd been a minister, but those days were long behind him. Now he was very much a Dixie Reaper, and I didn't think for one minute they walked the straight and narrow.

"I'm going to fucking kill him," Nick said, growling as he slammed his fist into the wall. The drywall caved in, and I winced.

"Johnny was going to talk to your President last night and let him know what happened. Jeremy made sure Carter was detained, in case the Dixie Reapers wanted to take care of the matter, seeing as how Carter was one of yours."

He snorted. "Not mine. I never liked the little shit."

"You're not going to do anything stupid, are you?" I asked, earning me a glare. "All right, maybe stupid was a bad word choice."

"I'm going to rip him apart one piece at a time, that's what I'm going to do," Nick said.

"You know this is completely crazy, right? I'm not anything to you. Just some random woman you hooked up with a few months ago."

He tipped his head back and sighed before coming back over to the bed. He crawled in next to me and wrapped his arms around me.

"I'm just going to go ahead and say this, okay? So let me get it all out before you interrupt."

I nodded.

"I've been in a really dark place for a long time now. I'm thirty-four, and I've only ever been in love once. Rachel was so damn sweet and perfect. She meant the world to me, and when I lost her, I lost everything. For twelve years, I've lived with the agony of her loss, feeling like a piece of me was missing, dreaming of her every night, and waking every morning wishing she was here. Then I met you."

Me? What did our one night together have to do with anything?

"I've slept with women since Rachel died, but it's just been a quick fuck to let off some steam, a fast release that never meant anything. I guess I'd thought that it would be the same when we hooked up, but it wasn't. It took me a few minutes, as I stood there alone, and realized that you were different from the others. So I went after you, but it was too late.

"No matter how much I searched for you, not even knowing who you were, it didn't stop me from having vivid dreams about you every fucking night and waking up so damn hard that even my hand wasn't good enough. I have no idea what's between us, Kayla. I'm not going to say I love you because you're right, we barely know each other. But I do know that you're different."

"You dreamed about me?" I asked. No one had ever said something like that to me before. The guys who had wanted in my pants were always off after the next sure thing when I wouldn't put out. But Nick had dreamed of me every night? He'd said more than once that he had looked for me. No one had ever gone to so much trouble for me before.

"Yeah." He smiled a little. "What do you know about life in the club?"

"Nothing. I know Johnny is a Prospect and that means he works his ass off for you in hopes of being patched in, whatever the hell that means. And he's told me about the wild parties that happen in the clubhouse, without any details of course. I know the women who are just with one guy are called old ladies, and I guess that's the biker equivalent of a marriage?"

"Something like that," Nick said. "Some of the guys marry their old ladies, some don't."

"I'm going to assume that not all the club dealings are what one would consider legal."

"Um, no, they aren't. But we don't put drugs in the hands of kids, and we don't deal in women. And we never will." His arms gave me a little squeeze. "I want you to be my old lady, Kayla. We're having a baby together, and I know that's not necessarily a reason to stay together, but I want a family with you. I think we can make this work."

"It doesn't bother you that you're thirty-four and I'm nineteen?" I asked. I honestly didn't care how old he was, but I knew some people would give him grief over our age difference.

"Have you met my President and his old lady? There's like thirty years between them, and they're completely crazy about each other. Age is just a number. As long as you're legal, I don't see a problem with it."

"What exactly does it mean to be an old lady?" I asked, not completely opposed to the idea. Nick had seemed like a great guy that night, even if he'd been in a lot of pain. And I had to admit the idea of waking up next to him every morning wasn't a horrible one.

"You'd be inked as *Property of Preacher*, and you'd get a cut like mine but with a property patch on it. Some of the old ladies are about your age and have kids, so you'd have people to hang out with, and our kid would have an extended family close to his or her age. Sometimes the old ladies put together events for the club or help in other areas, but never anything illegal. And I'd never put you in danger."

"I don't know." I glanced up at him through my lashes. "Maybe the sex wasn't as good as I remember. I'd hate to tie myself to someone permanently who was a dud in the bedroom."

His smile was predatory as he leaned in closer. "Then I guess I'd better give you a reminder."

Chapter Four

Preacher

She hadn't agreed to be mine, but before we left this bedroom she damn sure would. I'd fuck her every way imaginable until she agreed, give her so many orgasms she'd be willing to do anything for me. Our last time had been quick, but now I had all the time in the world. If that had been her first time, I was going to make sure I made it up to her. She should have been worshipped, should have been screaming my name over and over, but I'd fucked all that up. Not this time, though.

I tossed the covers to the foot of the bed and just took in the beauty of her. She reached for me, but I pinned her hands over her head, wrapping my fingers around her wrists. Her lips parted, and I watched as her eyes dilated. It seemed my sweet girl liked it when I got a little forceful. It made me wonder what else she'd like.

I kissed her slow and deep, savoring her the way I should have done before. She moaned a little as I rubbed my beard against her jaw, then placed a kiss there. Her skin was so fair, she'd end up with beard burn if I wasn't careful. Although part of me liked the idea of marking her. She was so fucking responsive, her nipples already hard and poking against me. I released her hands, but when she tried to move them, I growled at her.

Kayla placed her hands back over her head, and I smiled at her. "Good girl. Keep them there."

"Yes, sir," she said softly, and fuck if I didn't get even harder. Where the hell she'd learned that I didn't know, but I'd find out. Later.

I latched onto one of her perfect, pink nipples, sucking and grazing it with my teeth until she was squirming beneath me. Kayla kept lifting her hips, as if silently begging for my cock. And she'd get it, just not right this minute. I took my time, lavishing attention on first one nipple, then the other. Her breasts were pink from my whiskers by the time I started moving lower. When my shoulders pressed her legs farther apart, she let out a little gasp.

"Nick, I... "

I gently blew across her pussy, and her thighs clenched against me. She'd been bare last time we were together, but now there was a fine dusting of hair. I actually found that even sexier. The scent of her arousal teased my nose as I spread her open. Fuck, but she was gorgeous, all pink and soft, and so fucking wet.

I lapped at her folds, gathering her nectar on my tongue. If I'd known she tasted so damn sweet, I'd have done this the first time. It had been a while since I'd bothered to really pleasure a woman, but the soft sounds Kayla was making told me I was on the right track. Maybe making a woman scream wasn't a skill you ever lost. I licked, sucked, and lightly nipped her with my teeth until she was panting and begging me for more.

"Please, Nick," she said. "Please."

"Please what?" I asked.

"Please make me come. I need it, need you."

I sucked on her clit again, getting her right to the edge, then backed off. "Look at me, Kayla."

She looked down her body until her gaze met mine, though she looked so far gone I wasn't sure she was really seeing me.

"I was your first, wasn't I?" I asked.

"Yes."

"Anyone ever make you come before me? Put their hands or their mouth on this pretty little pussy?"

"No one's ever made me come but you."

"That didn't entirely answer my question. Has anyone touched you, Kayla?"

She whimpered. "Yes."

"Did they taste you?"

"N-no."

I stroked the lips of her pussy. "This is mine. Understand? No one touches you, no one tastes you but me. And no one sure as fuck puts their cock in you except me. You're mine."

She bit her lip and slowly nodded.

"Say it, Kayla."

"I'm yours."

Fucking right she was. I went back to pleasuring my woman, not stopping this time until she was thrashing on the bed and screaming out her release. I lapped up all her cream as she shivered from the force of her climax, then I slowly rose over her. My cock was more than ready for what came next.

"Eyes on me, baby."

She tried to focus on me, but she looked a little dazed. My cock slid against her pussy, and then I started sinking into her. If I'd thought she felt good before, being inside her completely bare was goddamn intense. I couldn't remember anything ever feeling this incredible before, and soon I was driving into her, not able to hold back. Her nails bit into my shoulders as the headboard banged into the wall with every stroke.

"Nick! I'm coming!"

I growled and took her harder, faster, as her pussy gripped me tight. I felt the gush of her release and kept thrusting until I came inside her. As my cock twitched and pulsed inside her, I knew that as soon as I recovered, we were doing this again. And again. And again. Kayla was like a drug, and I was completely addicted to her.

"Mine," I said, looking into her eyes and pressing my cock a little deeper.

"Yours," she said softly.

I didn't understand the possessiveness I felt toward Kayla. I'd been married to Rachel, had known her for years, and I'd never felt like this. Sure, I'd loved her. I'd loved her so fucking much I'd thought I'd hurt forever after she died. But with Kayla, I felt as if the broken pieces could possibly be mended, as if I had a second chance, and I didn't want to squander it.

I kissed Kayla, a slow and lazy kiss, that started to turn into something more. Her stomach growled, and I chuckled as I pulled away, slipping free of her body. Her cheeks flushed, and she looked so damn adorable.

"Sorry," she said. "I had some pie when I got to town last night, but I guess it's time for breakfast."

"Come on, honey. We'll go shower, and I'll take you out for breakfast."

She hesitated.

"What's wrong?"

"I just... I've ridden on a motorcycle before, with Johnny, but now that I'm pregnant I don't know that I should."

She was right to be concerned. I was a cautious driver, but the other idiots on the road were what made riding a bike so hazardous. There was an SUV in my garage, a car I'd kept well maintained yet hadn't driven very often. It was old, and I knew it was time to let the damn thing go. But for now, it would get my woman and my baby safely where they needed to go.

"You look like you want to say something but aren't sure if you should," she said.

"I kept Rachel's SUV. It's fifteen years old, and I don't know how you feel about riding around in it until I can get something different, but it runs well."

She cocked her head. "How do *you* feel about me being in Rachel's car?"

I smiled a little. Here I was offering her something that I thought would be awkward for her, and she was more concerned about how it would affect me. Just proved that Kayla was right where she belonged -- here with me.

"I think she'd be okay with it, and so am I. It's time for me to move on. I can't start a life with you and our kid if I'm still holding onto the past. She's gone. Yeah, I loved her, and she loved me. She's the one who died, though, not me."

She got a pinched look on her face and looked down at the bed, then around the room. "Is all this... "

"No. I bought all new furniture when I moved in here. The car is all I kept, other than a small box of photos and some of her favorite things. Her wedding ring is in there too. I used to keep her picture by my bed, but... " I shrugged. "After a week of dreaming of you nonstop, it didn't feel right keeping it out, so I put it up too."

"I don't mind if you want to keep a picture of her out," Kayla said softly. "She was important to you, and I don't want you to feel like you need to keep her hidden away."

God, but she was fucking perfect. I had to bite my damn tongue because I almost blurted out that I loved her. It was entirely too soon to feel something like that. Right? Sure, I'd thought myself in love with Rachel for years before I'd proposed, but even with her

I hadn't felt this instant connection. It was a little frightening, but I was going to trust in fate not to steer me wrong. Kayla had been dropped into my life right when I needed someone most. I'd never met anyone like her before.

"Breakfast," I said. "We can talk about things later."

She nodded and followed me into the bathroom. As I started the shower, I realized she only had the clothes she'd worn last night. I didn't know if her things were still at her apartment, or if she'd brought everything with her last night. Yet another thing we needed to talk about.

* * *

Kayla

The Nick I was seeing today was so different from the broken man I'd met at the clubhouse two months ago. He was attentive and touched me so reverently. It seemed like he was kissing me every few minutes, not that I was complaining. I didn't understand exactly what had happened to make him change, but he seemed to think that I had something to do with it. Over breakfast, we'd discussed a few things, mostly me moving in with him, which wasn't up for negotiation since I was his, as he liked to remind me throughout the day. I didn't mind, though, not really. I've give him a mock glare or two whenever he did that growly thing before kissing me senseless and saying "mine" in that possessive tone of his, but really I was loving every minute of it.

The only disagreement we'd had all day had been over Carter. My brother and a few others had brought Carter back here, and he was stashed somewhere in the compound. Nick was determined to take care of "the little shit" as he referred to him. I didn't want him to get his hands bloody on my account. Not that I cared if Carter lived or died, as horrible as that might sound, but I just didn't want Nick to do something he might regret later.

I'd managed to distract him so far, but I knew time was running out. There was only one thing I could think of that might keep him by my side and not off handing out justice to the guy who'd tried to rape me. We'd been back at the house for an hour now. My clothes, what little I'd owned, were now put away, and he'd promised me a shopping trip in the near future. Which was nice, but not necessary.

I straddled his lap while he sat on the couch and ran my hand down his chest. "Nick, did I tell you that my pregnancy seems to have some side effects?"

"Like morning sickness? Are you feeling okay?"

"I do have morning sickness sometimes, although I seem to be fine today. I was talking about other things." I leaned down and kissed him slowly. "Things that can be a lot more fun."

His lips tipped up on one corner. "Is my naughty minx trying to say she wants to come again?"

"Mmm-hmm." I pressed my lips to his again as my hands started working his belt, then unfastening his jeans. His cock was already hard, and he thrust into my hand.

"Stand up," he said.

I reluctantly pulled away and stood.

"Did you forget something?" he asked.

"What?"

"When we're intimate, and I give you a command, isn't there something you're supposed to say?" he asked.

My cheeks flushed, and I got even wetter. I'd read so many naughty books over the years, some a bit racier than others, that my "yes, sir" had slipped out earlier without thought. But it seemed Nick had liked it, a lot, and expected it of me. Who'd have known I could get so turned-on by something like that?

"Sorry."

"Clothes. Off."

"Yes, sir."

I slowly removed my clothes, hoping that I looked sexy doing it. I'd never really done a striptease for someone before, but there were lots of things I wanted to try with Nick. When the last of my clothes hit the floor, his gaze raked over me from head to toe. He didn't reach for, though, didn't ask me to do anything. I felt exposed, and extremely hot.

"Go get your toys, and get the lube out of the bedside table," he said.

My heart gave a kick as I hurried to obey. When I came back, my vibrator, small anal plug, and the lube in hand, he was staring at me with an eyebrow raised.

"You forgot something again," he said. "Come here, Kayla."

I stepped closer, and he took the items from my hands, placing them next to him, then he reached for me. Before I had time to protest, I was across his legs, and his hand smacked down hard on my ass. I gave a yelp and tried to get up, but his arm pressed against my back and held me down.

"What was it you were supposed to say?" he asked.

"Yes, sir," I said softly as his hand cracked against my ass again.

The first few swats had hurt, but now there was this burn and the beginnings of a delicious ache. His hand smoothed out the sting before he spanked me a few more times. I was trying so damn hard to hold still, but my pussy was starting to throb, and I felt so damn empty.

He stopped, but he didn't let me up. I felt him reach for something next to him, then he held the plug up for me to see.

"If you were a virgin, why did you have this?" he asked. "Maybe instead of asking if anyone had licked your pussy before, I should have asked if you'd had a cock in your ass."

I gasped, and my eyes widened. "N-No, sir. I haven't."

"Then why do you have this, Kayla?"

"I... " My cheeks flamed, I was so embarrassed to admit why I had it.

"I'm waiting, Kayla."

"I like the way it feels inside me when I use my vibrator."

I thought for sure I would die from admitting such a thing, but he set the toy down and didn't comment. Not at first. The hand on my ass slowly slid down, his fingers stroking my pussy. I spread my legs a little, as far as I could considering my position, and he rubbed my clit. A moan slipped past my lips as he teased me. Then, suddenly, his hand was gone.

I heard a click and then the whirring of my vibrator. He lightly rubbed my pussy with it before trailing it upward. As he pressed the toy between the cheeks of my ass, I gasped and froze.

"You said you liked the way the plug felt when you were using your vibrator, but have you tried to put your vibrator somewhere other than your pussy?"

I swallowed hard and slowly nodded. Yeah, I was a dirty girl. I might not have ever let a guy stick his cock anywhere other than my mouth, before Nick anyway, but I'd tried as much as I could on my own, wanting to know how everything felt.

He pressed the toy a little harder, but not enough to penetrate me.

"It's not as big as my cock. Think you could take me?"

I stopped breathing for a moment. "Yes, sir. I think I can take you."

The vibrator was back against my pussy, trailing up and down. Light, teasing strokes that made me want to beg for more. When he rubbed it against my clit, I cried out and nearly came from the shockwave of pleasure. He turned up the vibrations, and soon I was coming. My clit throbbed from the force of my release, and I tried to pull away from the toy, but Nick swatted my ass.

"Be still," he commanded.

"Yes, sir," I said, whimpering.

He made me come twice more before he shut off the vibrator and tossed it aside. I didn't know what to expect next, but I was ready for it. I heard the bottle of lube open and then felt it drip between my ass cheeks. Nick spread my cheeks wide and slowly worked a finger inside me. I tried not to clench, did my best to relax and let him in. It burned as he added a second finger, and eventually a third. When he stopped, I waited in anticipation of what he'd tell me to do next.

"Stand up, Kayla," he said.

"Yes, sir." I scrambled to my feet, and he stood up. Nick pushed his pants a little farther down his hips, then pointed to the couch.

"Bend over the arm."

"Yes, sir," I said as I quickly moved around the edge of the couch and leaned over, my belly pressing against the padded arm.

His hand caressed my ass cheeks, then he nudged my legs farther apart. Nick reached over me and picked up the lube off the couch, and I heard the bottle open again. I moaned as I heard him applying it to his cock in swift strokes. Then he tossed the bottle down and picked up my vibrator again.

"Since you like having this toy in your pussy while you use your plug, we're going to see how you like using it while I fuck your ass with my cock," he said.

His words were almost enough to make me come, and I moaned as he turned the toy on and slid it into my pussy. He stroked it in and out several times, before pulling it out and teasing my clit. Nick alternated between fucking me with it and making me squirm as it buzzed relentlessly against my clit. Again and again. I was so damn close to coming, and yet he wouldn't let me.

He pressed the toy inside me again and gave it a tap. "Let's see if you can hold that inside you."

I braced myself as he spread me open, and I felt the head of his cock press against me. I was nervous as hell, but excited too. He took his time, working his cock into my ass, being careful not to hurt me. There was a pinch of pain as I stretched to accept him, but he didn't stop until he was balls-deep inside me.

"You feel fucking incredible," he murmured. "You ready, baby? Ready for me to fuck this luscious ass?"

"Yes," I said, my voice almost a whine as the vibrator inside me sent pleasure rippling through me.

Nick was gentle at first, but when he realized I could handle more, he began thrusting harder. The intensity of his cock and the vibrator pleasing me at the same time was almost too much, and I came so hard that I nearly cried. One orgasm turned into three, and I was a quivering mess before long. He didn't stop, didn't slow down.

"I love watching your ass take me," he said, pounding me a little harder. "I'm gonna come, baby."

I bit my lip as he kept thrusting, not stopping until he'd filled my ass with his cum. I felt his cock twitch inside me, his hands still gripping my hips. He didn't seem to be in a hurry to pull out, but I didn't mind. His hand slipped between my hips and the couch, and those wicked fingers of his started playing with my clit.

"Come for me one more time, honey. Let me feel that ass squeeze my cock."

I didn't think I could, didn't think I had anything left to give, but it didn't take him long to wring one more orgasm from me. Nick slid free of my body, and turned off the toy, tossing it aside. I was boneless and nearly tumbled to the floor, but he swung me up into his arms and carried me to the bedroom. After tucking me under the covers, he disappeared again, only to return with the toys and lube. He placed the bottle next to the bed, then took the toys into the bathroom. I heard water running, and when he came back, his hands were empty.

"I think it's time for a nap," he said, easing into bed with me.

I pressed my cheek to his chest and draped my arm across his waist, snuggling into his side. "Nick."

"What is it, honey? I wasn't too rough, was I?"

"No." My cheeks warmed. "I liked it. A lot."

"Good." I could hear the smile in his voice. "Then what is it?"

"I think I could love you."

He audibly swallowed, and his voice sounded thick when he responded. "I think I could love you too, sweet girl. Real damn easy."

"Nick?"

"What, baby?"

"Thank you."

"For what?"

"For not turning me away that night. For letting me into your home, into your life. Just... thank you. No one's ever made me feel the way you do, and it scares me a little. But I know you'd never hurt me."

"No, honey. I'd never hurt you." I felt his lips press against the top of my head. "Get some sleep. We can talk more after you've rested."

I smiled softly and slowly succumbed to sleep. But if I'd known what he had planned, I'd have fought harder to stay awake. Sneaky bastard.

Chapter Five

Preacher

I knew Kayla wouldn't be happy when she woke up, but I needed to do this. Carter had dared to touch what was mine, had tried to violate Kayla, and I wasn't going to let that stand. I'd called Torch as soon as she'd fallen asleep, and he'd agreed that I had the right to take care of Carter any way I saw fit. Yes, he'd betrayed our club, but it was my woman he'd hurt.

Rage burned hot in my veins as I stepped into the old barn at the back of the property. It was far enough away, that no one would ever hear the screams, and with all the land we owned, hiding a body wasn't an issue either. The dimly lit interior smelled musty and faintly of piss. As I approached Carter, the piss smell made more sense. His pants were soaked across the crotch.

"What's the matter, boy?" I asked. "Piss your pants like a little bitch?"

"Fuck you," he said, glaring at me defiantly, but I saw the fear lurking there as well. Oh yes, he was scared, and he had every right to be.

"You knew I was searching for Kayla. You knew exactly who she was, and it seems you knew where to find her."

"She's just a hot piece of ass. You've fucked club sluts and not cared if we had a turn," he said.

"She's not a slut." My hand clenched into a fist, and I swung with all my might, knocking his head to the side with the force of the blow. "She's my old lady, you dipshit. The mother of my child. And you fucking tried to rape her."

He paled, and I could tell that he knew he was well and truly fucked.

Johnny stood next to me, looking ready to commit murder, but he held back. He knew it was my job to protect Kayla now, my job to take care of any trash who dared to touch her. Two other Prospects, our President, and two brothers were here as well. All watching and waiting. I knew they wondered if I had it in me to do what needed to be done. At one time, I'd have said no. It was one thing to break the law and another to murder someone. But he'd touched Kayla, and he deserved to die.

I worked him over with my fists, bones crunching as I broke his nose, his jaw, and a few ribs. He cried and begged me to stop, begged for his life. I wondered if Kayla had begged too. Had she pleaded for him to stop? To not rape her? Fury engulfed me as I made him bleed.

A phone rang, but I didn't stop. Carter was barely recognizable, but he was still breathing, and that was a problem for me. A hand landed on my shoulder, and I looked at Torch.

"It's Kayla," he said softly.

"What about Kayla?" I asked.

"She woke up, and you were gone. Tank's there, and he tried to calm her down, but she was freaking the fuck out, talking about how the daddy of her baby was going to be in jail because he was too stupid for his own good." Torch chuckled a little, then sobered. "She got a little too worked up and passed out. I know you want to finish this, but you need to take care of your old lady."

I glanced at Carter.

"I'd be honored to finish the job," Johnny said. "I promise he'll suffer. I'll make it last all night if I have to."

I glanced at the Prospect, the twin of my woman, and nodded. "Do it."

Someone handed me a towel, and I cleaned up as best I could before heading home. When I walked through my front door, Tank was standing next to the couch, staring down at Kayla with a helpless expression on his face. I knew exactly how he felt. I wasn't going to touch her, though, until I was clean. After taking the fastest damn shower, and pulling on fresh clothes, I relieved Tank of guard duty and gently roused Kayla.

"Sweetheart, can you open your eyes for me?"

Her chest rose and fell, but she didn't so much as twitch otherwise. My hand smoothed across her cheek, and I tried several more times. My heart thudded heavily as I worried that the stress had been too much for her. Weren't pregnant women supposed to be coddled or something?

"Baby, please wake up. You're scaring the shit out of me."

Still nothing.

I left her only long enough to get a cold, wet rag, and then I pressed it against her cheeks and forehead. Slowly, she started to come to, her eyes a little unfocused at first.

"What happened?" she asked.

"Tank said you flipped out, and then you passed out."

She blinked a few times, then glared at me. "You left me! You fucked my brains out, then you snuck away to deal with Carter, knowing that I didn't want you to do that."

"Honey, I couldn't let him get away with hurting you. What if you'd lost the baby when he knocked you down? What if Jeremy hadn't come along in time to save you? If he'd gone free, someone else would have suffered."

"He's dead, then?" she asked, her voice eerily quiet.

"I don't know. If he's not yet, he will be."

Her gaze met mine. "Then you didn't kill him?"

"No, sweetheart. I beat the hell out of him, but he was still breathing when I left. Someone else will take care of it." I didn't think she needed to know that someone was her brother. "You know, being part of the club means I'm sometimes going to have to do things you might not like. Are you going to lose it every time I go somewhere?"

"No. I'm sorry. I just... " A tear slipped down her cheek, then another. I gathered her into my arms and stroked her hair. "I don't want to lose you."

I couldn't help but smile a little. "You're not going to. I'm going to be here for a very long time. I'm going to hold your hand as you give birth to our baby, and then I'm going to knock you up a few more times. We'll have to practice a lot."

She giggled and pressed closer to me.

"I'm sorry that you were scared when you woke up."

"I'm sorry I flipped out," she said. "I'll do better next time. I've just never had anyone to worry about before, except Johnny, and he can take care of himself. But now I have this baby, and I have you. I've never had a real family except Johnny, and he walked away. I guess part of me is scared that it's going to disappear."

My heart ached for her. "I'm not going anywhere, honey. We're going to grow old together, okay?"

"Okay," she agreed softly.

"I know I've said that you're mine, and I mean that to the depths of my soul. But it means something else too."

"What's that?" she asked.

"It means that I'm yours."

She smiled a little. "Does that mean you're getting a property tattoo too?"

"Come on. Let's head to the clubhouse for a minute. There's someone I want you to meet."

She nodded, and I walked her out to the SUV. It wasn't a far walk, but after her passing out, I didn't want to take any chances. We drove to the clubhouse, and I noticed Zipper's motorcycle was out front, just like I'd hoped it would be. The man was completely bad-ass, but he was also an incredible artist and did all the ink for the club. He even had a special room set up in the clubhouse for tattooing.

We went inside, and I found Zipper kicked back at a table, nursing a beer.

"How drunk are you?" I asked.

"That's my first one," he said, motioning to the still mostly full mug.

"I need some ink done."

He stood and motioned for us to follow. When we stepped into his makeshift studio, Kayla checked everything out. I let Zipper go through his spiel about the machine he used and how everything worked. Then I sat on the chair, and he looked at me in confusion.

"I thought you wanted a property tattoo for Kayla? Everyone said you'd claimed her last night."

"She does need one, but there's something I need done first." I pulled off my cut and my shirt, then pressed a hand right over my heart. While my arms were inked, and part of my back, I didn't have a single tattoo on my torso. Yet. "Right across my heart I want Kayla written in a script. Something dainty like her."

She snorted. "Not dainty."

"You are to me."

She blinked at me, then smiled a little.

Once Zipper had sketched something out, and I'd approved it, he got to work. Kayla sat on the stool next to me and watched in fascination as Zipper inked her name onto my chest. When he was finished, he swabbed it with A&D ointment, then put some Saran Wrap over it. I stood up, and Kayla immediately sat in the chair.

"Honey, I don't think you need to get inked today. You passed out earlier," I said.

"I was justifiably upset," she said. "You're wearing my name, now I want to wear yours."

Zipper shrugged. "If she starts looking a little pale, we can always stop and pick it up another day. Are we just doing a plain font?"

"No," I said. "But I'm not going to ask for butterflies or flowers, or anything else girly like the others did. Kayla's right. She might be dainty to me, but she's also incredibly brave and strong. She's got the heart of a Dixie Reaper through and through. Kayla has the heart of a lioness, and I think she's going to be just as protective of her family. All of us."

Zipper quirked an eyebrow. "So what am I inking?"

"Have you ever seen a Celtic symbol for family that looks like a tree with knotwork?" I asked.

Zipper pulled out his phone and tapped and swiped a few minutes before showing me an image. "Like this?"

The tips of the branches were Celtic knots, as were the roots. "Yes, just like that."

"It's beautiful," Kayla said.

"You need a break at any time, you just say so," Zipper told her. "Any color preferences?"

Kayla told him her favorite colors were purple and teal, so Zipper pulled those out as well as black for the lettering. The trunk and branches of the tree were purple and he made the knotwork teal. Across the top it said *Property of* in a black script, and under the roots it said *Preacher* in a more classic font. Kayla didn't cry once, and as Zipper tended to the tattoo and gave her instructions for how to care for it, she smiled brightly at me.

I pulled her into my arms and kissed her hard. "Now you're never getting away."

"Good," she whispered before pressing her lips to mine again. "Because I'm right where I want to be."

* * *

Kayla
One Month Later

I rubbed a hand over my belly, which was starting to show a little already, and watched in amusement as Nick tried to put the crib together. He'd been at it for an hour, and so far, he hadn't done much except spew a ton of cuss words. I'd tried really hard not to laugh, but it was getting harder and harder. For a man who claimed to do all the work on his bike and the SUV, he sure was having a rough time with one piece of baby furniture. The parts were scattered around him in complete chaos. It was almost like the box had exploded and the pieces just went everywhere.

"Nick, I have something being delivered for the baby's room," I said.

He gave me a pained look. "Does it have to be put together?"

"Yep."

He groaned and closed his eyes, probably praying for patience. I'd actually seen him praying a few times over the past month, something he'd told me he hadn't done since Rachel died. He'd never be a true minister again, even if he was still ordained, but I think having me and the baby in his life had brought a little of his faith back. He definitely smiled more and seemed lighter overall. He'd even taken me to Rachel's grave and introduced us, which might seem weird to some people, but I think it gave him a sense of peace.

In all our talks, he'd never once said *how* she had died, and I'd always been a little curious. That day, the entire story came out. It seemed their life together hadn't been quite as perfect as he'd said. Rachel had been spending time with another man, and while it might have been innocent, it had driven a wedge between Nick and her. The day she'd died, she'd been out with the other guy, and the car they were in had been broadsided by a guy who ran a stop sign. It just happened to hit on Rachel's side. Nick said she'd lingered a few days, but she'd never woken up.

He'd confided that even knowing she'd been out with someone else, he'd still loved her, had still wanted their marriage to work. And maybe that's what he'd truly been mourning all this time. Not only the relationship they'd once had, but the one he'd wanted them to have. The kind he and I shared.

There was a knock at the front door, and I went to answer it, letting in my brother and Ivan, who carried a large cardboard box. Johnny winked at me as they went upstairs and carried the box into the baby's room.

"Another fucking bed?" Nick yelled as I neared the doorway. "Christ, woman! How many beds does the kid need?"

"Remember that appointment you couldn't make two days ago?" I asked as I stepped into the room. "The one where I got to hear the baby's heartbeat?"

He nodded.

"Well, unless you want your babies to share a crib, we're going to need two."

Nick stared at me. "Two?"

I nodded. "Yep. There were two heartbeats. It seems we're having twins."

He flopped onto his back and stared up at the ceiling a moment, then sprang to his feet and held me tight. "Twins. We're having fucking twins," he murmured against my hair.

"You just better hope they're nothing like their mother," Johnny said. "Kayla got into all kinds of shit when she was little. I always got blamed, but nope, she was the instigator."

I stuck my tongue out at my brother.

"I love you," Nick said as he held me tight. "I don't fucking care that it's too soon to say something like that. It's how I feel."

I breathed in his scent and closed my eyes. "I love you too. I think I have from the moment I saw you sitting all alone at the bar in the clubhouse. You looked so damn lost and broken, and I wanted to fix you."

"You did," he said. "You healed me, Kayla. You've given the life I always wanted. The family I always wanted."

Johnny cleared his throat. "If you two are going to get mushy or get naked, I think there's somewhere else I need to be."

Ivan snorted. "Yeah, like anywhere but here."

I turned in Nick's arms and smacked my brother on the back of the head, then whacked Ivan too.

"Just you wait. Both of you. One day, some woman is going to walk into your lives and knock you on your asses. And I hope like hell I'm there to see it. You know what I'm going to do when it happens?"

"What?" Johnny asked, looking a little worried.

"I'm going to laugh my ass off."

Nick chuckled. "I think she just cursed you. Maybe you should stay away from the ladies for a while. Just to be safe."

I grumbled under my breath, but my irritation was quickly forgotten as Nick swept me up into his arms.

"You two know the way out," he called out over his shoulder as he carried me down to our bedroom.

He slowly undressed me, then knelt at my feet, pressing his hands to my slightly rounded belly. "Twins," he muttered.

"Yep. Twins."

He pressed a kiss to my stomach, then murmured softly, "I love you, both of you, so damn much."

I ran my fingers through his hair and wondered how I'd ever gotten so damn lucky. Me, the girl who had never known what a family truly was, who had never known love. Somehow, I'd ended up with a wickedly sexy, honorable man who worshiped the ground I walked on. And I loved him more than anything. Life was about as perfect as it could get, and I had to wonder if maybe wishes really did come true... because Nick was everything I'd ever wanted. And so much more.

Ryker (Roosters 2)

Harley Wylde

Ryker: After 20 years in the military, I find myself doing my dad's dirty work. But as the "prince" of the Hades Abyss MC, it's expected of me. Doing a little recon in a small Alabama town should have been boring as shit, until the hot little minx I met at a bar turned my life upside down. Women always fall at my feet, but this one was different. If I'd known she was a virgin, I might have backed away, but now that I've had a taste I just want to keep coming back for more. Little did I realize that I'd just fucked the sister of a Dixie Reaper, and my life was about to become all kinds of complicated. I had to wonder... had she fucked me because she wanted me? Or was it all some kind of setup?

Laken: My big brother Flicker is always ruining my fun, keeping the guys away from me, so when I finally get a chance for a hot guy to get rid of my V-card, I'm all for it. Ryker's hot and has that alpha vibe, and the fact he's ex-military just made me wetter. It never occurred to me that he was a biker, or that I might have just screwed up a big deal for the Dixie Reapers. It seems my sexy Ryker isn't just some hot military guy. No, he's the son of the President of the Hades Abyss MC. So I hide like big brother asks me to. Just one problem... Ryker doesn't leave, and now I'm late. How am I supposed to tell Ryker that I'm carrying his child? When life fucks me over, it does it royally.

Chapter One

Ryker

I threw back another shot of whiskey, and slammed the glass down on the bar top. It was my tenth. Or was it twelfth? I'd lost count somewhere along the way, but I wasn't even remotely drunk. There was a slight warmth spreading through me, but I was one hundred percent in charge of my actions. So when I slid my hand up the back of the thigh of the hottie standing next to me, yeah, that was all me. What can I say? That sweet, curvy ass of hers was calling to me.

She slowly turned her head to look at me over her shoulder as my hand slipped up farther, sliding under the hem of her too short dress. Mmm. No panties. I gave her ass cheek a squeeze and watched as heat flared in her eyes. Whatever schmuck she'd been talking to was forgotten as she turned to face me. Oh yeah. The front matched the back. Nice, luscious breasts that were barely contained by the stretchy top of her dress, and damn if her nipples weren't poking through.

"Normally a guy buys me a drink before he grabs my ass," she said.

"Guess I'm not a normal guy."

She reached out and fingered the dog tags that I still wore, despite the fact I'd been out of the service for a month. "No, soldier, you certainly aren't."

"Marine," I said.

She bit her lip and moved in a little closer. "Guess that makes you something of a badass, doesn't it?"

I smirked and squeezed her ass again. "Something like that."

She reached out and rubbed a hand down my chest, her fingers trailing across my abs and stopping at my belt buckle. I could tell she liked what she saw, and I damn sure liked the way she filled out her dress. It would look even better bunched around her waist while I fucked her.

"You're so big and strong," she said with a purr.

"Oh, baby. You have no idea."

I slid my fingers farther down the curve of her ass until they teased her pussy. She was already wet and so damn slick, and she looked like just the type of girl who would let me fuck her in the bathroom. I knew the type, and those hard nipples and wet little pussy told me that she wanted me bad enough to let me do whatever I wanted. Women tended to fall at my feet, always had, and this one wasn't going to be an exception. Kneeling was a good place for them, easier access for sucking my cock.

"Bigger doesn't mean better," she said. "It's all in how you use it."

"I know how to use it. I can make you scream my name all night long."

She shrugged. "Maybe you can and maybe you can't."

Oh, I could. It was a proven fact. Women always screamed in ecstasy whenever I was pounding into their pussies, or anywhere else I pleased. They begged me for it.

"What's your name, sugar?"

"Laken."

"I'm Ryker. What do you say we get to know one another a little better?" I stroked her pussy again, letting my fingers dip inside. She bit her lip, and a flush started creeping up her chest. I'd be willing to bet I could get her off right here and now.

"Maybe I'm not that kind of girl," she said, her voice dropping as I stroked her some more.

"Honey, my fingers are coated in your cream, right here in front of everyone. I bet I could get you so turned-on, you'd let me fuck you anywhere I pleased. Just bend you over the bar and take what I wanted." I smirked. "In any hole I wanted."

She gasped, but her eyes dilated, and I knew she'd liked the idea. Naughty girl.

I rubbed her a little more, getting her even wetter. Yeah, this sexy woman was a wild one. I knew the type. A tremor raked her body, and I knew she was close to coming. I thrust a finger inside her and nearly groaned at how damn tight she was. Fuck, but she'd squeeze my cock so damn good. I played with her pussy until she was a quivering mess, barely hanging on. Then I slipped my hand free from her dress, wrapped my fingers around hers, and dragged her off to the nearest bathroom. If the stickiness on my fingers bothered her, she didn't complain.

I pushed open the bathroom door, hauled her in behind me, then snapped the lock into place. She gave me a coy smile as she leaned back against the counter. I prowled closer, thinking of all the filthy things I wanted to do to her. Our options were limited in this bathroom, though. Maybe I'd take her back to the motel with me. She looked like a screamer, and I'd love her my name on her lips all fucking night and into the morning. When I was done with her, she'd be feeling me for a week.

I traced the top of her dress, my finger lightly trailing along the curve of her breasts. She licked her lips, and I knew she was going to give me what I wanted. They always did. I eased the straps of her dress down her arms and pulled the top half down under her breasts. So damn perky! They were a little more than a handful, but the minx had gone without a bra. Her nipples were hard and the prettiest pink I'd ever seen.

Leaning forward, I traced my tongue around first one then the other before sucking one into my mouth. Her fingers slid into my hair, holding me to her as I lavished attention on her luscious tits. My cock was hard as a fucking steel post, and the cute little sounds she was making just made me even harder. I couldn't wait to get balls-deep inside her. Something told me once wouldn't be enough.

I pulled away and turned her to face the mirror.

"Hands on the counter, baby, and stick that gorgeous ass out for me."

She leaned over and wiggled her ass at me. I gave her a playful slap, then pulled up the hem of her dress until the material bunched around her waist. A tattoo caught my attention, a delicate feather that curled around her hip. It wouldn't be all that remarkable, but the ink looked almost metallic. My finger stroked over it before my cock demanded attention.

I used my foot to kick her feet farther apart, admiring the way her pussy parted, as if it were begging to be fucked. I didn't waste any time and started unbuckling my belt, then undoing my pants. I pulled my cock out, giving it a few strokes as I stared at the sexy woman in front of me. Our gazes locked in the mirror, hers pleading for me to touch her, to fuck her.

I pulled out my wallet, going for the condom I always kept there, but her voice stopped me.

"I'm clean," she said. "You don't have to use that. Unless…"

"Unless?" I prompted.

"Unless you're not clean," she said, her cheeks flushing.

"Honey, I never go in unwrapped. Not since I was fifteen and fucking my first girl. But, yes. I'm clean." No way I was getting trapped by some slut who wanted a baby daddy to pay all her bills. I'd seen too many of my Marine buddies get stuck in that trap, and I'd sworn it would never happen to me.

"You could pull out," she said.

I knew that wasn't foolproof, but that pretty pussy of hers was awfully tempting. All wet and slick, the dewy lips a nice pink. I'd bet it would feel like wet silk wrapped around my cock. I could feel my resolve wavering, even though I knew better. A little voice in my head whispered that there was always the morning-after pill. That pretty much decided it for me. Sometime tonight we'd have that talk, or I'd go pick it up for her myself in the morning.

I stuffed my wallet back into my pocket and rubbed my cock along her slit. Fuck but she felt incredible! She moaned and thrust back. Yeah, she was an eager one. I smacked her ass, leaving a handprint, but it only seemed to turn her on more, so I slapped the other side too.

"So good," she murmured.

Damn. She might just be fucking perfect.

"You like that, baby? Want me to spank that ass?"

"Please," she begged. "I've been such a bad girl."

I chuckled and swatted her ass again, three times on each cheek. She had to be feeling the burn as her ass turned red, but fuck if she didn't get even wetter. I couldn't wait any longer. I gripped her hips and thrust deep and hard. When Laken tensed and cried out, I looked in the mirror to see a sheen of tears in her eyes. What the hell? I eased out of her, thinking maybe she didn't really want this, but the pink tinge along my shaft froze me in place.

"You're a fucking virgin?" I asked. Shock hit me for a moment. I hadn't ever had a virgin before, but I'd heard they bled the first time.

"Don't stop," she said. "Please. I want this. I want you."

I was torn. Part of me wanted to fuck her until neither of us could stand anymore; some caveman part of me thrilled over the fact that I was the first to get inside her. The other part wanted to run for the damn hills. I'd always heard that virgins spelled trouble, which is why I'd steered clear of them for so long. And now here I was, fucking one in the bathroom of a bar, her tits and ass on display. She was good, I'd give her that. I hadn't had a clue that she wasn't experienced. She'd come off as being a siren, some sex kitten who picked up men in bars all the time.

My cock twitched, begging me to fuck her. I wanted to, even though she'd lied by omission. I didn't know why she'd done it, and my dick didn't care. The primitive side of me wanted to pound that tight virgin pussy, claim her as mine.

"Ryker. Please," she said in a soft voice, her eyes pleading with me.

"Why do you want this?" I asked.

"Because no one will touch me. I don't care if it hurts. I want you to fuck me, and don't stop. You can take me however you want."

Maybe it made me an asshole, but what guy could ever walk away from an offer like that? This sexy little virgin was begging for my cock, telling me to do whatever I wanted to her. Yeah, I was likely going to hell, but I was going to have fun on the way there.

"Hold on tight, sugar," I said.

I gripped her hips again and began thrusting into her. I watched as her breasts bounced with every stroke, and soon the pinched look on her face turned to pleasure. Her pussy opened up even more, welcoming me in. I fucked her hard and deep, wanting to own every inch of her. She felt really damn good. Too good. My belt buckle jangled as I pounded her pussy, and soon she was crying out, begging me for more. I knew what she needed, what she wanted.

My cock swelled, and I knew I was going to come at any minute. Reaching around her, I pressed my fingers against her clit and started rubbing in fast little circles until she was bucking against me, her release coating my dick. With a growl, I thrust faster until my balls drew up, and I shot load after load of cum into her tight little pussy. *Fuck!* Too late, I remembered I was supposed to pull out, but fuck if I really wanted to. I hadn't come inside a girl bare since that first time, and it felt like fucking heaven.

I plunged deep once last time, and held still as both of us panted for breath. She looked beautiful as I stared at her in the mirror, her breasts heaving and her nipples even harder than before. Her cheeks were flushed, and her eyes were bright. My cock throbbed inside her, still just as hard as it was before we'd started. Yeah, one time wasn't going to be enough with this one. No fucking way.

I pulled out and watched as my cum slid down her thighs. Some of it coated her pussy, and I had this urge to shove it back inside her. Knowing I'd been her first, I felt like I wanted to brand her, mark her with my scent and let everyone asshole out there know I'd been here first, that she was mine. She started to straighten, but I pushed her down again. Her startled gaze met mine as I thrust into her again. The bathroom might not be the best place for this, but we weren't leaving just yet.

"One more time," I said. "Then you're coming with me because I'm nowhere near done with you, sugar. We're going to the motel, and then I'm going to fuck this gorgeous ass, come down your throat, and fuck your pussy again. All night long."

She moaned, and her eyes slid halfway closed. "If it all feels this good, you can do whatever you want to me."

"Oh, baby, it gets even better. Just wait and see."

I fucked her hard and deep, not stopping until we'd both come again. Then I helped her straighten her dress, and I led her out to the parking lot. She came to a halt when she saw my Harley Davidson and looked uncertain for a moment. There was something in her eyes, something I couldn't figure out. Did the bike scare her?

"I swear it's completely safe," I told her. "Come on, kitten. I'll protect you."

Something shifted in her gaze, and a soft smile curved her lips. Within seconds, she was climbing onto the back of my bike, wrapping her arms around my waist, and we were off, the wind blowing our hair. I had no doubt I'd have cum on my seat from her pussy, but it would be so worth it. Yeah, that pussy was mine. For tonight at least. And I was going to make sure she enjoyed every second of it.

Chapter Two

Laken

Sunlight nearly blinded me as I squinted at the room around me. The shower was going in the connecting bathroom, and I wondered if I should sneak out while Ryker was busy. I remembered everything we'd done the night before, and well into the morning. My body ached in the best of ways. Staying wasn't an option, though. If I wasn't home soon, my big brother would send out a search party. I was twenty-one, but he acted like I was twelve. I quickly pulled my dress over my head, ran my fingers through my hair, and slipped on my shoes. Then I crept out of the motel room as quietly as I could, not ready to face Ryker. We'd had fun, but I'd known going in that was all it would be. He wasn't looking for forever, and I didn't want to deal with the awkward morning after stuff I'd heard about from my friends.

When I'd seen he rode a bike, I'd frozen, wondering if it was some sort of trap. He hadn't been wearing colors, but that hadn't meant anything. Everyone around here knew my brother was an officer with the Dixie Reapers, and several had tried to use me to get to him over the years, or as an in to the club. But Ryker had been too damn tempting to pass up. I'd been wanting a guy to fuck me since I'd turned seventeen and accidentally walked in on my best friend at a party going at it with two guys. Flicker had made sure I was untouchable, though, and I'd reached the age of twenty-one with my virginity intact.

I smiled. Not anymore. Ryker had thoroughly deflowered me last night. My thighs were still sticky from all the fun we'd had. If I hadn't had my Depo-Provera shot two months ago, I might have worried about pregnancy. When I'd first started thinking about having sex, I'd gotten on the shot. But then Flicker had made certain no guy would ever touch me. Asshole. I'd watched him whore his way through the club pussy, and yet I wasn't allowed to have any fun. Not that Flicker condoned me being in the clubhouse except on family days, but I don't always listen to my brother.

Well, the double standard was at an end because now I'd lost my V-card. Now that I knew just how incredible sex was, there was no way I was going back to being celibate. I'd just have to find ways around big brother. The closer I got to the compound, the more I started to feel a little antsy. Had I been wrong for walking out on Ryker like that? We hadn't shared more than first names with each other, and I doubted he'd stick around for long. Guys like him usually didn't.

The Prospect manning the gate gave me the once over before letting me inside. He shook his head, and I had to wonder what the hell that was supposed to mean. I'd taken all of four steps into the compound when Flicker appeared on the steps of the clubhouse, his arms folded and his gaze disapproving. He met me halfway across the parking lot, his hand gripping my upper arm as he looked me over.

"Jesus, Laken. You look like you've been fucked three ways to Sunday."

I smirked. "Probably because I have."

Flicker scowled, and I could hear his teeth grinding together. "Who the fuck touched you?"

"No one you know. Just some guy passing through town. Guess you don't tell quite everyone what to do around here."

"It was for your own good, Laken. Did you even use a fucking condom? What if he gave you something?"

I squeezed my thighs together. No, we hadn't used condoms, and that had been my choice. I'd wanted to feel everything, and not have any barriers between us. But when Flicker put it that way, maybe I'd been a little too hasty to tell Ryker to put the condom away. I'd just have to make sure I got tested, just to be safe. And until then, I'd avoid men. It wasn't like they didn't give me a wide berth anyway, thanks to big brother here.

"I'm fine, Flicker. I just want to go home and shower."

"Christ, are you telling me that you're walking around with his cum still all over you?" Flicker's scowl deepened. "You want to know why I treat you like a child? It's because you do stupid shit like this, Laken."

His words hurt, but I'd never let him know that. Flicker was all I had left in the world, and his opinion mattered to me. For the most part. His obsession with keeping me chaste had gotten out of control, though. I'd been waiting to find out that he was going to trade me to some biker to sweeten a deal or something, not that the Dixie Reapers had ever done something like that, but I'd heard rumors of other clubs doing similar crazy shit.

"Go home," Flicker said with a bit of a growl to his voice. "We have some new blood coming in today, some big shot who wants to make a deal, and I want you to make yourself scarce. From what I've heard, the guy's a real ladies' man, and if he sets his sights on you, he might not take no for an answer."

"Fine."

I brushed past my brother and continued down the road that wound through the compound, until I reached the house I'd been sharing with him. My mom had died when I was sixteen, and Flicker, being a lot older, had taken me in. No one had any idea what had happened to our dad, and while we had different moms, he'd never looked at me differently. To him, I was just his baby sister, Laken.

Flicker never locked the house so the door swung open when I turned the knob. When it shut, I leaned against it a moment and closed my eyes. I had this sinking suspicion that instead of gaining my freedom by losing my virginity, I'd just locked my cage up even tighter. Now he'd be even more vigilant, and I had only myself to blame. I kicked off my shoes, leaving them by the door, and made my way to my bedroom. I didn't have my own bathroom like Flicker did, but I knew he wouldn't be home anytime soon. After pulling my dress over my head and letting it fall to the floor, I walked across the hall to the bathroom and started the shower.

The hot water felt good, easing my aches. Not that I regretted what I'd done. Ryker had been amazing, and despite the hint of caveman I saw in him, he'd been surprisingly tender at times. It was almost a shame I wouldn't see him again. I certainly wouldn't have minded spending more time with him, especially in bed. I smiled as I washed my hair and thought about how incredible it had been. There hadn't been much I hadn't let him do to me, and I'd loved every minute of it. In some ways, giving complete control over to him had been freeing, which was funny since Flicker tried to control my every move and I just felt stifled when he did it.

I finished my shower and pulled on a tank top and shorts before heading to the kitchen to find something to eat. I'd skipped dinner last night, wanting to sneak out when Flicker wasn't looking, and I hadn't had breakfast today. My stomach was ready to stage a revolt if I didn't eat something soon. It looked like one of us would have to make a trip to the store soon, as the cupboards were almost bare, and the fridge contained bottled water, beer, expired milk, and some juice that I didn't even remember buying. I wrinkled my nose at the offering.

I settled for dry cereal and toast with some water, then carried everything to the kitchen table. Flicker's house was pretty awesome all things considered. There was a large bay window in the kitchen that overlooked the backyard. He'd let me plant some rose bushes outside the window, and I always enjoyed looking at them while I ate. Truthfully, he'd tried to make this place a home for me, had never made me feel like I wasn't welcome. I knew that having his kid sister here had to be a bit trying at times, especially when I'd been younger. It was no secret that any hook-ups he'd had, he'd kept to the clubhouse, but now the Pres had moved the Prospects into the rooms in the clubhouse to free up the duplexes for patched members. I didn't know where Flicker was going now for a good time, and I wasn't going to ask. He still came home smelling of cheap perfume and sex, so I knew he wasn't abstaining, but there were just some things I didn't need to know about my brother.

I finished my meal and decided to see what was on TV. I wasn't up to socializing at the clubhouse, and Flicker had said to stay away. Not that I could care less about some guy who wanted to set up some sort of deal with my brother's club. All the guys were nice to me, but they could be real assholes when they wanted to be, and I was sure the new guy would be no exception. Just what I needed. More testosterone in my life. Having Flicker watching my every move was bad enough, but add in all the Dixie Reapers? Yeah, my life could be hell sometimes. It was like having an infinite number of big brothers. Even the Prospects felt like they needed to keep an eye on me, and I was older than some of them.

Why did men always think having a dick made them superior to women? I'd never understand it. We were the ones who carried a human around inside us then gave birth to something the size of a watermelon, but being able to pee standing up gave them some sort of superpowers? I snorted. Yeah right. They were delusional, every last one of them.

I was just closing my eyes, my long night having caught up with me, when the front door slammed open, and Flicker roared out my name. I sighed, wondering what the hell I'd done now. Prying myself off the couch, I padded to the front entry and stared at him, trying to figure out why he looked both furious and ready to sneak me out of the country. What the hell was going on? Big brother looked almost panicked.

"You slept with fucking Ryker Storme?" Flicker said.

"We didn't exactly exchange last names," I said, flipping my hair over my shoulder. "But yeah, the guy I spent the night with was named Ryker. How did you even find out? More of your crew spying on me?"

"He's here," Flicker said, his voice dropping. "And had he not been talking about the hot piece of ass with a swan feather on her hip in metallic ink, I'd have never known it was you. But no one else in this fucking town has that tattoo. Hell, Zipper is the only one within a hundred miles who will mess with those inks."

"I'll bite. Who is Ryker Storme? Must be someone important for you to damn near have a coronary because I spent the night in his bed."

"Ever heard of Trent Storme?" Flicker asked.

I shrugged. The name was familiar. I thought about it a minute before the name clicked into place. "The President of the Hades Abyss MC?"

"Yeah. Ryker Storme is Trent's son. You just fucked the prince of the Hades Abyss MC. Do you know how much shit this could bring to our door?" Flicker asked. "Every guy in that meeting knew exactly who Ryker was talking about. It's no secret that you have that silver feather on your hip. Who the hell else but you would get something like that around here? Zipper inks more butterflies and panthers than anything. Not to mention I really didn't need to hear about how tight my sister's pussy is."

I winced and commiserated with him. Yeah, just like I didn't like hearing about how big his dick was when the club sluts started talking.

"It's a little late to change things now. I don't have a time machine," I said. I honestly didn't know what he wanted me to do about it. Even if I could change things, I wouldn't. Being with Ryker had been beyond amazing.

"He's only here for a week, checking things out. Torch wants to reach an agreement with Trent Storme. We can always use more allies. The club talked things over after Ryker left, and we want you to lay low until Ryker leaves. Maybe you should stay somewhere else."

I rolled my eyes. Yeah, because I had so many options. If I'd ever had somewhere to go, did he honestly think I'd have moved in with him indefinitely? He wouldn't let me work, so I had no income for my own place, and the only friends I had were here at the compound. I'd ditched my high school friends when it became apparent they were only hanging out with me to drool over the bikers in my life.

"I'll just stick close to home. But you're going to have to restock the kitchen if you don't want me leaving the house. I'd starve to death before morning."

"Fine," Flicker said. "I'm hoping no one opens their damn mouth about who you really are. With some luck, Ryker will lose himself in alcohol and club pussy. Maybe he won't even remember you in a few days."

That hurt. A lot. And for some reason, I didn't like the thought of him spending time with the club sluts. I had no claim on him, and I knew it, but I'd felt special when I was with him last night. Then again, if he was bragging about me to my brother and the other Dixie Reapers, I was likely just another piece of ass to him. That's probably all I'd ever be to anyone. Who would want to settle down with Flicker's sister? He was the treasurer for the Dixie Reapers, and if anything ever happened to me, he'd wreak havoc and start kicking ass. Most of the time when a guy paid attention to me, I had to wonder if he was trying to find an in with Flicker and the club. It's why Ryker had been perfect. I'd figured a complete stranger was a safe bet for some no strings fun.

"I'll stay here," I promised my brother. "He'll never know I'm here."

"See that it stays that way."

Flicker shook his head and disappeared out the front door.

It suddenly felt like the weight of the world had settled on my shoulders. I had the most incredible night of my life and still managed to fuck things up. Sometimes I wondered if Flicker would be better off if I did take off, just vanished one day for parts unknown. He was always bailing me out of trouble, usually brought on by too much drinking. I'd been detained more than once for drunk and disorderly, and there was the time I spray-painted the high school, or the time I TP'd the principal's house my senior year. Yeah, I hadn't been an angel. There were times I wondered why he even let me stay here.

Feeling sorry for myself, I went back to the living room and flopped onto the couch. So much for going to the doctor. I figured something like this would be time sensitive, not that I've ever had to research STDs before. I'd just wait out Ryker and hope he hadn't given me anything that couldn't be easily cured. On the plus side, I could make a dent in my to-be-read pile. I probably had over two hundred books on my Kindle I hadn't had a chance to read yet.

See, silver lining. I'd just find me an awesome book boyfriend, and then I'd be like, *Ryker who*?

Chapter Three

Ryker

The gorgeous girl I'd taken back to my motel about a week before still haunted me. The Dixie Reapers had been more than welcoming, and I'd had more club pussy shoved at me than I knew what to do with, but they just didn't interest me. I couldn't bring myself to fuck someone so thoroughly used after having my very own virgin for an entire night. Not to mention they all looked worn around the edges and wore so much makeup it looked like a mask. I wondered where my little ex-virgin was and what she was doing now.

Hell, I wondered who she was doing now. Someone that sensual, that sexy, wouldn't exactly be lounging around her house on a Friday night. I might have been her first, but now that I'd popped that cherry, I had no doubt she'd be looking for her next hook-up. Maybe I should have made sure she had my number before she ran off. I didn't know how long I would be in town, but we could have had some fun. And maybe I could have talked her into going home with me, if I ever went back home.

Being the son of the President of a club just wasn't all it was cracked up to be. Everyone had assumed I'd follow in Dad's footsteps and take over one day. And hell, maybe I would. I never wore my cut, but I had one. I was wearing it now just because I was hanging with another MC, but it generally stayed buried in my bag when I was on the road. There was a sense of freedom in just being an average guy and not Trent Storme's kid. I'd joined the Marines and served twenty years in an attempt to distance myself from that life, but the minute my dad had heard I was coming home, he'd enlisted my help.

I could have been an asshole and turned him away, but he'd seldom asked me for anything. So I'd agreed to check out the Dixie Reapers and see if they were the kind of club Dad might be interested in. So far, everything seemed fine. There didn't seem to be any drugs in the clubhouse, and even though they did have club sluts like every other MC I'd seen over the years, they weren't into selling women. From what Torch and his VP had told me, they made a good bit of their money off arms deals, and while I'd speculated that they might be running drugs, the members seemed clean. I'd found that clubs who dealt in drugs had a tendency to sample the product, and that wasn't happening here. Couldn't fault them for the arms deals, though. There was good money in guns. A lot of clubs were into a lot worse.

I sipped my beer and winced when I realized it had gotten warm. Pushing it away, I decided to step out for some fresh air. A few guys were smoking on the porch so I kept walking. The Dixie Reapers were welcoming enough, but I preferred spending my nights with a woman in my bed, not running my mouth with a bunch of bikers. If I went back home, I'd have to get used to it. No way my dad wouldn't demand my presence at the clubhouse on a regular basis. I'd avoided his life for so long, but I didn't know how much longer I could keep running.

It was nearly pitch-black outside, the moon and stars hiding behind the clouds that had rolled in over the last hour. I was so busy staring up at the sky, I didn't see the other person slinking along in the dark, until soft curves plowed into me. Instinctively, my arms went around her and held her against my chest.

Had to be a woman with those perky breasts and rounded hips. Maybe my night was looking up. I didn't think a club slut would be prowling around out here, but the luscious body pressed against me was mighty damn tempting.

"Sorry," she said, trying to free herself from me.

Wait. I knew that voice. My arms tightened, not wanting to let her go. "Laken?"

Startled eyes met mine. "Ryker."

I didn't know what she was doing in the compound, or why she was sneaking around, and I didn't much care. I was going to consider it a miracle that I'd found her again. And she felt damn good in my arms. The white tank, booty shorts, and flip-flops were a contrast to what she'd been wearing the last time I'd seen her, but she was still sexy as fuck. If anything, I think I liked this look on her even better. Not that either compared to having her naked in my bed.

"I shouldn't be here," she murmured, pushing against my chest.

I refused to let go, though. No way was she slipping through my fingers again.

"I think you're right where you're supposed to be."

"I can't be caught here," she said, trying to twist away from me again.

I didn't understand why she couldn't be here. Had she snuck into the compound? And if so, who had she been looking for? If she wanted to get down and dirty with a biker, I was more than happy to oblige. The way she'd screamed my name last time I didn't think she'd have any objections to another round. It wasn't unheard of for a woman to come back begging for more. My fellow Marines had called me the pied piper of pussy, and for good reason. Once the ladies knew what I was packing, they followed me around just waiting for another taste. Sometimes I was nice enough to indulge them, especially the ones with talented tongues.

My cock was already hard and pressing against my zipper, just thinking about getting inside her again. From the way her nipples were poking against me, it was safe to say the attraction wasn't one-sided. But I didn't have a place on the compound where I could take her. They'd offered me a room inside the clubhouse, but I didn't want to parade her through there, especially if she wasn't supposed to be here. I could put her on the back of my bike and go back to the motel, but the Prospect at the gate would still see her. For whatever reason, she wanted to hide.

"Come on," I said, taking her hand and leading her around the back of the clubhouse. It was even darker back there, and I found a spot where no one would be able to see us. The music was pulsing inside, and we could hear the sounds of everyone partying. And then some. From the pounding and cries of pleasure on the other side of the wall, it sounded like someone else was getting their dick wet.

I pressed her back against the building and before she could utter a protest, I claimed her lips in a kiss that was sure to melt her panties. Or better yet, make them come off. Assuming she was wearing any. I slid my hand down and cupped her ass, giving it a squeeze. Nope. No panty lines. It seemed my sexy ex-virgin had something against undergarments, and I fucking loved it. Just gave me easier access whenever I wanted to fuck her. Maybe we could make this a regular thing for however long I was here, even if it meant meeting in the dark away from prying eyes.

I eased her shorts over her hips, and she gasped as they fell down around her ankles. Pulling up her tank top, I leaned down to lick and tease her pretty nipples, until she was fisting my hair and begging for more. I felt her tremble and knew she wanted me. She might be inexperienced, but Laken was a wildcat when it came to sex. Like she was made for fucking.

I unfastened my belt and pants, eager to get inside her again.

"Step out of your shorts," I told her.

She did as I commanded, her blue gaze fastened on mine, shining even in the darkness with complete trust in her eyes. I wasn't sure I'd earned that trust, or deserved it, but it did something to me. I reached for her, gripping her thighs and lifting her. I urged her legs around my waist, wanting inside her so damn bad. That sweet pussy of hers opened, and I couldn't wait another moment. I sank into her, groaning at how perfect she felt. I cupped her ass with my hands as I thrust into her, each stroke going deeper and harder. Her nails bit into my shoulders as I fucked her, not holding back even a little. I knew she could take it, could take me. Her pussy welcomed my cock, getting wetter by the minute.

"Fucking missed this," I murmured, kissing the side of her neck.

"Ryker," she said, my name a sigh on her lips.

"You been with anyone else?" I asked, stopping for a moment. Maybe I should have wrapped my dick, but this was Laken. And after taking her bare the first time, I didn't want to have her any other way. We hadn't discussed the morning-after pill before, but I'd be sure to say something this time.

"No. Just you."

I kissed her, our tongues tangling. "Good."

"Wh-what about you?" she asked, looking uncertain.

"No one but you, sugar."

She smiled, and the happiness shining in her eyes told me I was fucked, but it was too late now. I started thrusting again, and I didn't stop until she'd come twice, her juices soaking the both of us. My dick was still hard, and my balls were full, but I was wishing we had a bed. There were things I wanted to do to her, things I couldn't make happen out here in the open, pressed up against a building. I'd fucked her ass twice the other night, and I wanted to do it again. Her pussy was tight, but fuck! Her ass was even tighter, and I'd damn near come the second I'd gotten inside her.

"Don't stop," she pleaded.

I drove into her until I finally let loose, my cum filling her. My cock twitched inside her, and as her pussy squeezed me, I knew that once again I would need her more than the one time. I didn't know what it was about Laken, but she bewitched me. Whenever my cock got anywhere near her, I just wanted to fuck her until we both passed out.

My time here was coming to a close, but I didn't like the thought of leaving her behind. What would she think if I asked her to go with me? I needed to report back to my dad, but then we could go anywhere we wanted. We could stay with the Hades Abyss, or we could move on. Make our home anywhere in the world. I had connections in several states here, and a few in other countries.

My heart hammered in my chest. Was I seriously thinking of keeping her? Sure, I liked to get my dick wet, but I hadn't had a girlfriend since high school. Was that what I wanted from Laken? Or was she just a really good fuck that I wasn't ready to let go of just yet?

"I need to go," she said. "You can't tell anyone you saw me here."

"Laken, I…"

She squirmed until I pulled out of her and set her back down on her feet. She jerked her shorts up and straightened her top before running off into the night. I didn't know what the fuck to think and ran a hand through my hair. It only took a moment before I decided to follow her. Just to make sure she was all right, or so I told myself. Truth was, I needed to know why she was here. Had she come looking for me? Did she somehow know who I was? Fuck! I'd forgotten again to tell her to take the morning-after pill. I was so fucked if she didn't take one without any prodding. Or was that her game plan?

Maybe it had been a play to get into bed with me. Had I fallen into her hands? I'd tried to keep it quiet, that I was Trent Storme's son, but there were club sluts everywhere and groupies outside of the club who just wanted to get it on with a biker. I didn't think in the darkness she'd been able to read my cut, and even if she had, she likely wouldn't have recognized my road name. I hadn't pegged Laken as being a club slut, but what if I was wrong? I paused and decided to let her go. No, I wasn't going to play into her hands. If she came back, if she found me again, then I'd question her.

And maybe I would stick around a while longer. If for no other reason than to find out what her endgame was. Would just any biker do, or did she want me specifically? Fuck, women could be so damn complicated. And they were damn sneaky and conniving too. I'd thought Laken was different, but what if she wasn't?

I'd had enough for the night. Walking back to my bike, I climbed on and decided to just ride until my mind cleared. Nothing was better for the soul than a ride at night, the wind blowing in my hair, the thrum of my bike between my legs. And if that didn't sort me out, then I was well and truly fucked.

Chapter Four

Laken

It had been more than three weeks since my first encounter with Ryker, three miserable weeks. And almost two weeks since I'd run into him here on Dixie Reapers' territory. Knowing he was here, so close, and yet I couldn't touch him? It was pure torture. The only thing that made me feel better was Flicker's confusion over why Ryker wasn't fucking every female who wandered by. It seemed he was abstaining from club pussy, and my stupid heart hoped it was because of me. Was he thinking about me as much as I'd thought about him? Did he stroke his cock at night as often as I played with my pussy, wishing it was him getting me off?

I'd wanted to sneak out again, see if I could find Ryker without anyone being the wiser, but Flicker had almost caught me last time, and I hadn't wanted to chance it. If he thought for one minute that I'd been with Ryker again, he might kick me out. I'd defied a direct order, and they might even see it as a betrayal. So I'd confined myself to the house, but as I stared at the calendar on my phone, I realized that I couldn't hide anymore.

And I couldn't talk to Flicker.

Pulling up my contacts, I rang Isabella, hoping she'd be sympathetic. She was the President's wife, but I didn't think she'd tell Torch my secret. At least, I hoped she wouldn't. I had a feeling this entire thing was about to blow up in my face, and I didn't know how to stop it.

"Everything all right, Laken?" Isabella asked as she answered.

"I need a ride to the doctor, and you know the Prospects won't let me leave. Everyone is afraid Ryker will see me."

"Why do you need a doctor?" Isabella asked.

"Just... please, Isabella. I need to see Dr. Myron."

Isabella was quiet, and I knew she was probably putting two and two together, but finally she agreed. While I waited for her, I changed my clothes and brushed my hair and teeth, then I went onto the front porch to sit. I didn't think it was likely Ryker would wander this far. Her SUV pulled up a few minutes later, and I ran down the steps and climbed inside, hoping no one had seen me and knew I was escaping my prison. If anyone told Flicker I was getting into Isabella's car, someone would stop us. And I really needed to see Dr. Myron. I didn't have an appointment, but I hoped that wouldn't matter.

Thankfully, Isabella's windows were tinted enough that the Prospect at the gate could only tell two people were in her car, and since everyone knew what Isabella drove, they didn't even stop her. The gates opened, and she pulled through. As the Dixie Reapers compound got smaller and smaller behind us, I began to breathe a little easier. We'd made it! Of course, I still had to sneak back in, and hope Flicker hadn't noticed I was missing. This hiding out thing was getting to be a pain in my ass. And boring as hell.

"Are you going to tell me what's going on?" Isabella asked.

"I'm late."

"You couldn't reschedule your appointment?" Isabella asked.

"No. I'm *late*."

Her eyes widened, and she stared at me a moment before jerking her gaze back to the road.

Okay, so maybe she hadn't figured out why I'd wanted to see the doctor. She didn't say anything for a few minutes, and I wasn't sure if it was because of shock, or if she was just trying to find a way to tactfully ask me whatever was on her mind. When she pulled into Dr. Myron's and still hadn't said anything, I began to worry that she would call Torch and tell him where I was. Even worse, that she'd tell my brother.

"What are you going to do?" Isabella asked softly. "If you're pregnant, and it's Ryker's..."

"It can't be anyone else's. He's the only one I've been with."

"You were a virgin?" she asked.

I nodded, my cheeks flaming.

"This isn't good, Laken. Ryker's been in a bad mood the last few weeks, and the way he's been avoiding the club sluts, your brother has been concerned that it has something to do with you. Are you sure you didn't say something to him when you were together?"

"He didn't know who I was. Still doesn't. But he did see me at the compound a few weeks ago."

Isabella mumbled under her breath.

"I didn't plan it!" I said. "I was tired of being stuck in the house. It was so dark I didn't think anyone would see me. And Ryker probably wouldn't have, except I hadn't seen him either, and I literally ran into him." I conveniently left out what happened after that. I didn't think it would help my case any.

"Come on," Isabella said. "Let's get this over with. Maybe you just missed your period from all the stress of Ryker being here."

I nodded, part of me hoping she was right. But the other part? I couldn't lie. The thought of having a part of Ryker with me always was rather appealing. I had no doubt he wouldn't want anything to do with me, or the baby. He didn't seem like the daddy type. I didn't know how all this would play out, and I was a little scared to find out. But sitting in the car all day wasn't going to help anything.

I got out, and when we got inside, my stomach started knotting. The receptionist smiled but looked a little confused.

"I don't have an appointment for either of you," Janie said.

"I really need to see Dr. Myron," I said. "I don't know when I can make it back here, so it has to be now."

Janie winced. "Dr. Myron is at the hospital delivering a baby. He had someone call and tell me there were complications, so all we have on staff right now is a Nurse Practitioner. Dr. Myron likely won't be back until tomorrow."

My cheeks flushed. "I need to take a pregnancy test."

Janie's eyebrows shot up. "I see. Have a seat, and I'll let Nurse Owens know that you're here."

I sat and Isabella claimed the seat next to me. My hands were shaking, and I felt like I might throw up at any moment. I didn't think it was because I was pregnant, though. I figured it was more nerves than anything else. I was terrified about the results of the pregnancy test, and even more scared to tell my brother. Oh, God. I'd have to tell Torch and the other Dixie Reapers! This really wasn't going to go well.

Nurse Owens popped her head out into the waiting room. "Laken, why don't you come on back?"

I stood and took a deep breath before I followed her down the hall. She handed me a plastic cup and nodded to the bathroom. I knew the drill after having a series of UTIs last year, and filled the cup, then stepped back into the hall where she was waiting. Nurse Owens led me to an exam room, and I climbed onto the table, the paper crinkling underneath me.

"Now, why do you think you might be pregnant?" Nurse Owens asked.

"Well, my period is late by four days. And I'm never late. If anything, it comes a day or two early every month."

Nurse Owens nodded. "I checked your file, and the last time you were here, you told Dr. Myron that you're a virgin. I take it that has changed."

Did she think it was an immaculate conception? How else would I think I was pregnant?

"Yeah. I had sex for the first time about three weeks ago, and then again about a week later."

"You're on the Depo-Provera shot, but it's not one hundred percent foolproof. You'd actually be surprised how many women get pregnant while they're on the shot. We'll see what your urine shows, but we may do a blood test too, just to be sure. It sounds like you aren't very far along if you are pregnant, so blood would be more accurate."

"Can we go ahead and do that?" I asked.

"I'll send someone in to draw your blood. Once I have the results from both tests, I'll come back and let you know what we've found."

"Thank you," I murmured as she stepped out of the room.

It didn't take long for someone to draw my blood, then I was stuck waiting. My phone vibrated in my pocket and I pulled it out, wincing when I saw Flicker's face. I swiped the screen, ignoring the call, and knew he'd just keep calling until I answered. But I didn't want to talk to him, not yet anyway. Hell, maybe not ever depending on what the test results revealed. I didn't know how I could go home if I was pregnant. Flicker would be pissed, and likely all of the Dixie Reapers would be too. And I could only imagine how Ryker would react.

When Nurse Owens stepped back into the room, the expression on her face said it all. My shoulders slumped as she came closer and patted my hand.

"You're pregnant, honey, but it's not the end of the world. I'm going to give you a prescription for prenatal vitamins, and I'll have Janie set up an appointment with Dr. Myron in a few weeks. But if you have any questions in the meantime, you just call us night or day. You still use the pharmacy on Main Street?"

"Yes, ma'am. Thank you, Nurse Owens."

The older woman smiled and opened the door, waiting for me to get off the table and walk out. When we reached the front, Nurse Owens asked Janie to set up my next appointment, and then I walked out with a silent Isabella by my side. She unlocked her SUV, but I just stood on the sidewalk staring at it. I couldn't go back to the compound, not right now anyway. I needed some time to think. I knew I couldn't keep this a secret, but I didn't know how to tell everyone either.

I got into Isabella's SUV and asked her to take me to the pharmacy.

"Are you pregnant?" she asked.

"Yeah. But don't tell anyone. Not yet, please. I just need some time to figure everything out."

"If they called in prenatal vitamins, they likely aren't ready yet. I love our pharmacist, but he's kind of slow. Why don't we go get something to eat, and then we'll stop by there, okay?"

"Sure, but I'm running low on money. Flicker usually gives me some every week, but since I've been housebound, he hasn't given me any."

"My treat," Isabella said.

"Great. It can be my last meal, like the ones they give people on death row."

She snorted. "You're pregnant, not dying."

"Same difference. Have you met my brother?"

"Torch won't let Flicker do anything stupid," Isabella said.

I was glad she had that much faith in her man, but I didn't think anyone would keep Flicker from murdering me when he found out. And the compound had lots of land where he could hide my body. I suppose it could have been worse. At least we didn't raise pigs. Maybe he'd at least break a sweat digging a six-foot-deep hole to bury me in.

Isabella stopped at a little café down the street from the pharmacy. We decided to sit on the patio since it was nice outside. The way my stomach was flipping around, I didn't know how I was going to manage to eat anything. But if I was pregnant, then I needed to make sure the baby got the nourishment it needed. Oh God. I was going to be a mom! I broke out in a sweat, and my hands started shaking again. Could I do this? Raise a kid? Where would we live? I didn't even have a job, much less a way to afford diapers and shit.

"Take a breath," Isabella said softly. "Everything will be fine, Laken."

I nodded and looked over the menu. We ordered our food and drinks, then Isabella did her best to take my mind off things. By the time we'd finished our lunch, Isabella thought my prenatal vitamins might be ready. The pharmacy was close enough that I walked while Isabella waited in the car.

The pharmacist had it ready for me, and agreed to add the fee to my brother's tab. Flicker was going to love that, I was sure, once he found out what I'd picked up. When I stepped out onto the sidewalk, I walked into a hard body and nearly fell on my ass. Strong hands gripped me and as I looked up, my heart nearly stopped.

Ryker smirked at me. "You seem to like running into me. If you want my attention, there are other ways to do it."

"Sorry," I said, my cheeks flushing.

His gaze dropped and he saw the bag with my prescription, and he quickly frowned. Maybe I should have asked for a regular sack to hide the small paper bag.

"Are you sick?" he asked.

"N-no. These are just vitamins." Not a total lie.

"Vitamins don't come in a prescription sack," Ryker said. "What the hell is going on, Laken? Why are you lying to me?"

"It's nothing, Ryker," I said, twisting out of his grasp.

"I haven't seen you lately. I kind of thought maybe we'd spend some more time together before I leave," he said. "I'd hoped you'd come find me again."

"Ryker, my life is complicated, and my brother is overprotective. Seeing you isn't a great idea."

"I see." He took a step back. "Guess you got what you wanted then."

Seriously? He was going to play that card? The guy was a man-whore from what my brother said, and I'd had no doubt I was just easy pussy for him. So what did Ryker care if I wanted to spend more time with him? It wasn't like he'd fallen in love with me. And now that I was carrying his child… he couldn't find out. He'd think I was trying to trap him, and that's the last thing I wanted.

"Ryker, I…"

"Laken, are you coming?" Isabella yelled through the window she'd rolled down.

Ryker glanced at Isabella, then back at Laken, his gaze questioning. "You know Torch's wife? Are you two friends or something?"

"Something like that," I said.

"So have you been blowing me off for personal reasons or because of the Dixie Reapers?"

"They asked me to stay away from you," I said, and then wished I'd kept my mouth shut. Now he would pry and likely find out who I was. Not what I needed!

"They asked you to stay away from me?" he asked, his voice low and far too calm. I had a feeling I'd just made a huge mistake.

"It's fine, Ryker. I mean, you're leaving soon anyway, right? We had fun, but it was never going to be more than that. I knew that the first time we were together. I never expected more from you."

"Laken, I --"

His words were cut off as a motorcycle rumbled down the street. When I saw my brother heading our way, I wished I could hide, but it was too late. I clutched my prescription sack tighter and sent a panicked look toward Isabella, but she lifted her hands, and I knew I was on my own. Flicker came to a stop in a parking spot just a few feet from me, and he slid his sunglasses down his nose. His blue eyes were icy as he glared from me to Ryker, then back to me.

"Laken, get on the bike," Flicker said.

I took a step in his direction, but Ryker reached out and gripped my arm.

"Just let me go, Ryker," I said softly. "Please."

"No. What the fuck is he to you?"

"Ryker, I..."

"Laken," Flicker said, his voice a deep growl. "Get. On. The. Fucking. Bike."

My heart hammered in my chest as Ryker tightened his grip on me, and I knew things were about to get really bad. I had no idea how to defuse the situation. I frantically looked at Isabella again, and saw that she was on her phone, no doubt calling her husband. Peachy. And I'd thought things were complicated now? Once Torch got here, I was beyond fucked. I'd been told to stay home, and here was I was parading around town. Even worse, I'd run into Ryker. Again.

"She's not going anywhere with you, asshole," Ryker said. "I don't know what you think you have going on with her, but Laken is staying here with me."

I closed my eyes and mentally groaned. That so wasn't going to go over well.

I heard Flicker's bike turn off, and I opened my eyes in time to see him swing his leg over the seat and head toward us. Ryker pulled me back and stepped in front of me. I thought it was a little sweet, and really stupid. He had no idea who Flicker was to me, but he'd just waved a red flag in front of a bull. I needed to de-escalate the situation, and fast.

I tried to step around Ryker, but he wouldn't let me.

"Flicker, it's not what you think."

Ryker growled and glared at me. "It's exactly what he fucking thinks. You're mine until I say otherwise, Laken. I claimed your virginity, and that makes your pussy mine. Got it?"

I narrowed my eyes. That macho bullshit wasn't going to work. "Um, no. Last time I checked, it was attached to *my* body, and therefore it belongs to me. I just let you borrow it for a night."

He arched a brow.

"All right. Two nights." My cheeks flushed.

"Laken, what the fuck is going on?" Flicker asked. "I told you to keep your ass at home. If I'd thought you were going to run off, I'd have left a Prospect guarding the damn door."

"She lives with you?" Ryker asked.

"She's my sister, asshole. Of course she fucking lives with me," Flicker said.

Ryker tensed. He turned to face me, and his eyes had turned ice cold. I'd never seen such a hard look on his face before, and I wasn't certain if I was facing the Marine or the biker. But he definitely wasn't *my* Ryker in that moment.

"You knew who I was that night, didn't you? Did you deliberately stick your ass in my face, hoping I'd take the bait?" he demanded, his tone harsh and unforgiving.

"What?" My eyes went wide. He thought I'd what? Set out to trap him?

"So what was your endgame, Laken? You wanted to be Hades Abyss royalty and thought you'd lure me in? Or were you trying to sweeten the deal I had with your brother's club? Because they threw enough club sluts my way that you weren't really necessary. Or was I supposed to be captivated by your virgin pussy?" His eyes narrowed. "Please tell me you took a fucking morning-after pill."

My heart was hammering so hard I could hear it, and I was certain everyone else did too. I took a step back, the sack in my hand crinkling as I tightened my grip. Ryker reached for it, but I gasped and took off running. No way was I telling him about the baby now. Not if that's what he thought of me. Tears blurred my vision as I ran, and a sob caught in my throat. I'd had no delusions of a happy ever after with him, but it hurt to know he thought I was capable of such a thing. If I'd had any idea who he was that night, I'd had avoided him like the damn plague. The last thing I needed in my life was another asshole biker.

I heard someone calling my name, but I didn't stop. I ran until my lungs burned, and as I turned to look over my shoulder, I took a misstep and fell off the curb. The wind was knocked out of me as I crashed onto the street, and I heard the screech of tires and a horn honking. I tried to stand, tried to get out of the way, but all I did was give the driver a larger target. The car slammed into my side and sent me flying. My head cracked against the pavement when I landed, and everything fucking hurt.

"Laken!" I heard my brother roar my name, and then he was kneeling over me. "Laken, Jesus. Please tell me you're okay."

"Hurts," I managed to croak.

My prescription sack had fallen to the pavement. "She dropped this," a stranger said.

I heard sirens in the background and knew that things must be even worse than I thought. There was warmth seeping into my clothes and I didn't understand where it was coming from. Before I could figure anything out, everything went black.

Chapter Five

Ryker

I was in a foul mood when I got back to the Dixie Reapers compound. As Laken had stormed off, I'd gotten on my bike and taken off. The last thing I'd wanted was to stick around. My bike roared to a stop outside the clubhouse, as I decided what the hell I was going to do. I didn't know if Laken had acted on her own or if someone had put her up to it, but I was damn sure going to find out. I slammed into the clubhouse and came to a halt, when I saw the devastated looks on the faces at the bar.

"Who the fuck died?" I asked.

One guy winced, and the VP shot me a glare. "You'd better fucking hope no one dies."

What the hell? How was this shit my fault?

A small hand gripped my arm, and I looked down at the VP's wife. I couldn't remember her name, but I'd met her briefly shortly after I got here. She'd seemed nice, and not quite who I would have pictured paired with the older man. Then again, I'd noticed all of the old ladies seemed to be quite bit younger than the bikers they were paired with.

"It's Laken," she said.

"What about that lying bitch?" I asked, my anger flaring all over again.

Tears gathered in the woman's eyes and she bit her trembling lip. "There's been an accident. Laken was…"

Laken was what? What kind of accident?

The VP came over and wrapped his arms around his wife. He spoke to me over the top of her head, his look unforgiving and accusing.

"Laken was hit by a car when she ran from you. She's at the hospital, and that's all we know right now. Flicker called and said there was blood everywhere."

My breath froze in my lungs. Laken was hurt? Yeah, I'd lashed out at her, and I was pissed that she'd used me. But part of me still wanted her, still cared on some level. I'd thought she was special, might even be someone I wanted around for a while. I didn't like the idea of her in a hospital bed. And blood everywhere? Just how fucking badly had she been hurt? There was this squeezing sensation in my chest, and it hurt to breathe for a minute. Had I caused this? If I hadn't lashed out at her...

The VP's wife whispered something in his ear, and he shook his head.

"He needs to know," the woman said.

"No, Ridley. That's not for us to decide. We should have never ordered Laken to keep away from Ryker. It was her decision to make, and so is this. When she wakes up..."

"If," Ridley said.

"No, *when* she wakes up, if she wants to tell him, then that's up to her," Venom said. "If we hadn't tried to keep her away, then maybe none of this would have happened. It's our fault he didn't know who she was."

I had a feeling I was missing something huge, and I wasn't going to get answers by sitting around here. There was only one hospital in town that I knew of, at least only one that I had seen, so I went back out to my bike and decided I'd go see Laken. Maybe I'd been too harsh, and I should have let her explain. I was used to women trying to use me to get my dad's club, they'd done it since I turned sixteen and bulked up. Yeah, I'd been mostly gone the last twenty years, but every time I was home the same shit happened. But if

I'd been wrong... If it really was my fault that she'd been hurt, I'd never forgive myself. I'd killed people, beat the shit out of them, even killed females in Afghanistan who posed a threat to my team, but I'd never been responsible for hurting an innocent woman before. And that it was Laken made my gut churn.

At the hospital, there was a line of bikes near the ER. I parked alongside them and went in to check things out. Flicker, Torch, Bull, and several others were in the waiting area. All of them looked like they'd been beaten, and I figured that meant the news wasn't good. There was a heaviness in my chest as I tried not to think about what would happen if Laken died. Was it that serious? Could I lose her before I ever really had her?

I approached Flicker, and he surged out of his seat, his hands clenched at his sides. If this really was my fault, then I wouldn't stop him from beating the hell out of me, if that's what he wanted to do. He'd have every right.

"You don't deserve to be here," Flicker said.

"Just tell me she's all right."

He looked away and refused to talk to me. Bull pulled him down into a chair again, and I found an empty spot to sit and wait. The minutes ticked by, and then an hour had passed. The longer we waited, the more the tension grew in the small room. By the time a harried-looking doctor appeared, I'd lost track of time and was starting to get really damn worried. The doctor pulled a mask down under his chin and looked around the room.

"Laken Beaumont's family?" the doctor asked.

"That's us," Flicker said, standing along with the other Dixie Reapers. I got to my feet and stood on the outer edge, wanting to hear that the man had to say, and yet feeling like I was an outsider. I guess I really was, even though I knew a part of Laken they didn't.

"We were able to stop the bleeding. She has two cracked ribs, and there was some internal damage from the impact. She has a gash on her head that took twelve staples to close, and some bruising on her side from where the car hit her. We had to induce a coma in hopes the swelling in her brain will go down, but the baby is fine," the doctor said.

At the word "baby" the Dixie Reapers turned to glare at me, and I felt like the world was beginning to tilt. Laken was pregnant? So, she hadn't taken the morning-after pill. Had that been her plan all along, or was it just an accident? I didn't hear anything else the doctor had to say, but as he walked off, Flicker approached me.

"You got my sister pregnant, dickhead. And you nearly got her killed."

"I didn't mean for her to get hurt. And I'd thought she'd take the morning-after pill so she wouldn't get pregnant. I should have made sure she took it." Not that she would have if her goal had been getting pregnant from the beginning. She'd not seemed to pay me any attention in that bar until I'd run my hand up her leg, but what if she'd been baiting me. Wouldn't be the first time. But it was the first time anyone had actually caught me. I'd always been super cautious and wrapped my dick… until Laken.

"Laken was on the Depo-Provera shot," a soft voice said behind me. I turned and saw Isabella, the President's wife. "She probably didn't think she could get pregnant. I went with her when she had it done, and I don't think she was scheduled to go back for another one until next week or week after."

"She was on birth control?" I asked.

"You mean you fucked her and didn't even ask?" Flicker asked. "What the fuck, man?"

"She told me to just pull out, but then..." I closed my mouth. No way I was going to tell her brother that her pussy had felt so damn good I'd lost my head. I'd already said too much before, not knowing she was related to a Dixie Reaper. Fuck, the way I'd gone on about her, I'm surprised Flicker hadn't strung me up by my balls that first day. No guy wanted to hear about some guy fucking his sister.

"I'm going to go see my sister. And you," Flicker said, pointing at me, "had better not fucking be here when I get back."

"I'm not leaving," I told him. "I need to talk to Laken."

"No one's talking to her thanks to you. Didn't you hear the doctor? She's in a coma." Flicker turned on his booted heel and stormed off.

Isabella patted my arm. "Let him cool down, and he'll eventually come around. Laken means a lot to him, and not just because she's his sister. She came to live with him when she was a teenager because her mom died. Flicker took her in, and she's lived with him ever since. No one's allowed to touch her, she's not allowed to work... I don't think she's been on a date since she came to stay with him. He's a little obsessed with keeping her safe."

Torch studied me with his arms folded over his chest. "You need to decide how you're going to handle this. You have something of a reputation with the ladies, and it's not a good one. When Flicker found out you'd slept with his sister, he nearly came unglued. I thought he was going to pound your ass into the pavement."

"Why didn't he?" I asked.

"Because I told him to get his shit together and cool the fuck off. Laken's a grown-ass woman, but Flicker's never going to see her that way. He's twenty-one years older than Laken, and I sometimes think she's more like a daughter to him than a sister. Not because of the age difference but because he raised her the last five years," Torch said. "Other than the Dixie Reapers, she's also the only family he has. They have a dad out there somewhere, and possibly more half-siblings, but no one has heard their old man in a long-ass time."

"She's carrying my kid," I said.

Torch shrugged. "Is that all that matters to you? Because the kid will be taken care of. He or she is a Dixie Reaper, and Laken will have all the help she could ever need. We take care of our own. Any man in my club would lay down their lives for her and that kid."

Was that all that mattered to me? No. I'd come here to check on her before I knew about the baby. Hell, before I'd thought she'd been screwing me over, I'd wanted to take her with me when I left this place. But I didn't know if anyone here would listen or would care. I needed to see Laken, to talk to her and make her understand. If she really hadn't set out to trap me... yeah, I was feeling like an asshole right now. Maybe the women I'd known had made me a little jaded, possibly a lot jaded. A lot of my military buddies had been screwed over by girlfriends, or women wanting to be their girlfriends. I'd seen too many trapped over the years. Or maybe if I hadn't fucked Laken before I got to really know her, then all of this could have been avoided. Not that I'd planned on more than one night with her, not at first. That's all I'd ever wanted from anyone... until now. Until her.

"I need to see her," I said. "I won't leave until that happens."

Torch shrugged. "Suit yourself. I doubt they'll let anyone but family see her until she's awake. And father of her baby or not, you're not family. If Flicker has anything to say about it, you never will be."

I might not be family to Laken, but I was family to the baby in her belly. That might not mean shit to the men glaring at me right now, and maybe it didn't mean shit to Laken either, but I'd be damned if anyone was going to keep me from seeing her. Flicker glared at me as I approached the nurse's station, obviously not having any luck in getting back to see Laken, but I did my best to ignore him. The nurse looked up at me, her eyes lighting up as I gave her the smile guaranteed to drop panties. I leaned in a little closer and prepared to give her the sexy growl that made panties wet every damn time.

"May I help you?" she asked, a little breathless, and the pulse in her neck fluttering. Oh yeah, I had her.

"My pregnant girlfriend just came out of surgery. I was wondering when I might be able to see her," I said, lying a teensy bit. Pregnant, yes. Girlfriend? Eh, it was a gray area. I hadn't asked her to be mine, but now that I knew we were having a kid together, no way in hell I was walking away without her.

"Oh." The nurse blinked up at me, some of her excitement fading. Maybe I shouldn't have called Laken my girlfriend? "Name?"

"Her name's Laken Beaumont," I said. "The doctor was just out here, but I didn't get a chance to ask when I could see her."

The nurse tapped on her keyboard, then frowned. "She's in a coma according to the doctor's notes. I'm not sure when she'll be awake."

"But I can check on her? Maybe she can hear me, and I can at least let her know she isn't alone," I said. I turned my smile up a notch and leaned in a little closer. My muscles flexed, drawing her attention to my biceps. When she licked her lips, I knew she'd give me whatever I wanted, even a little consoling in the nearest bathroom if that was my wish.

"I'm sure a short visit can be arranged. She's in recovery right now, but they'll be placing her in ICU once a bed is available. The elevators are around the corner and at the end of the hall. Go to the fourth floor and follow the signs to ICU. They'll have visiting hours posted."

"Thank you," I said, giving her a little wink that had her sighing.

I pushed away from the counter and made my way to the elevator. The stomp of boots behind me told me I wasn't alone, and it was likely Flicker. I had no doubt he'd want to keep an eye on me, but fuck if I was leaving this place until I'd seen Laken. Even if she couldn't talk to me, I needed to see that she was okay.

The elevator opened, and Flicker stepped inside with me. The glare he was giving me would have made a weaker man cower, but I just lifted my eyebrows and stared back. I was Trent Storme's son. He didn't really think I was going to crumble, did he? Even if I hadn't had Storme blood in my veins, I was a motherfucking Marine. I'd faced insurgents, been tortured, had more bullet holes put in me than I'd like to admit... one pissy biker wasn't going to keep me away from Laken, even if he was her brother.

We got off on the fourth floor, and I followed the signs to ICU. The hours were posted just like the nurse had said, and it looked like we had a while until they'd let us see her. If she even made it into a room by then. I knew hospitals could move really fucking slow unless someone was literally dying. And even then I didn't have the utmost faith in them. Anyone who worked as many hours as medical staff, usually without much of a break or sleep, was bound to make a mistake here and there. It was just part of being human. We needed rest, and doctors and nurses didn't seem to get a lot of it.

I claimed a seat in the ICU waiting area and watched the TV mounted in the corner of the room. Flicker sat beside me, his presence dark and menacing. Or at least, it was to anyone else in the room. My lips twitched in a smile as two people got up and moved quite a ways off from us. The leather cuts would have been enough to do it, but Flicker's current scowl was sure to make people run. He looked rather ferocious, and I could almost picture him scaring off any men who had looked Laken's way. No wonder she'd still been a damn virgin. I was grateful, though. It meant she was mine and mine alone.

Fuck. I ran a hand through my hair. Yeah, I was seriously thinking about keeping her. Even if there wasn't a baby, I'd still want her. There was just something about her, something different. She was a wildcat in the bedroom, but there was an innocence to her, and a sweetness that I didn't often experience.

"What the fuck are you doing?" Flicker asked.

"Waiting to see Laken."

"What do you care? It's your fault she's here to begin with. The way you turned on her, accused her of using you? That was fucked-up."

I winced. Yeah, it hadn't been one of my finer moments. "In my experience women fall into two categories. Easy, fun pussy. Or manipulative bitches. She wouldn't have been the first woman to try to sleep her way into a high-ranking spot with my dad's club. Women have been trying it since I turned sixteen."

"How could you have spent any time with Laken and have thought she'd be like that? She was sweet, innocent… until you got your filthy hands on her. Laken is the kindest person I've ever known." Flicker narrowed his eyes at me. "You should be damn thankful she even gave you the time of day. Instead of bitching about how she tried to trap you, you should have been kissing the ground she fucking walks on."

I rubbed the back of my neck. "Look, I know I didn't handle things well, and I'm sorry. But what would you think if you were in my position? If some woman you'd hooked up with a few times, one who had insisted you not use a condom, had said she was pregnant, wouldn't you wonder if she'd done it on purpose? Not to mention she never, not once, mentioned that she was connected to the Dixie Reapers. I'd have backed the fuck off if she'd said something." Well, maybe. She'd been so fucking hot, I might not have been able to resist even knowing her brother was an officer in the club I was checking out.

I could see some of the tension ease from Flicker and he sighed as he looked away. When his gaze swung back toward me, I could see that he understood exactly what I'd been thinking and feeling.

"Yeah, I guess I might have wondered," Flicker said. "She really did that?"

"I shouldn't have listened to her, but…" I shrugged.

I wasn't going to tell him I couldn't walk away from the temptation of his sister's wet pussy. That wouldn't go over well. He'd heard enough from my first day at the clubhouse, and now that I knew I'd been running my mouth not only about his sister, but the mother of my baby... I felt really damn small. Talking shit about women had never been a problem before, but this one wasn't just some random fuck. Not that I'd realized that at the time. I should have, though. From the very beginning, Laken had been different from the others. Well, maybe not the very beginning, but once I realized I was her first... That had changed things. Maybe it had even changed me a little.

"Are you going to take my sister away?" Flicker asked.

Was I? I'd thought about taking her with me, but what if she didn't want to go? She had family here. Not just Flicker, but all of the Dixie Reapers. Could I ask her to walk away from that? I didn't owe my dad shit, so it wasn't like I had to return to the Hades Abyss. Yeah, I'd done him this favor, but only because he'd seldom asked for one. I was patched in, but I hadn't spent much time there over the last twenty years. Going Nomad wouldn't really be an issue, not for me anyway. I didn't think it would really matter if I ever returned. It wasn't like my dad didn't have a VP who could take over if the unstoppable Trent Storme ever decided to step down. Not fucking likely unless a bullet stopped him, but stranger things had happened. Like me being a fucking dad. I was still wrapping my head around that one.

"I don't know," I answered honestly. "I'd thought about it, but I don't know what she wants."

Flicker smiled a little. "As long as you're thinking about her and not you, then we aren't going to have any problems. I have to admit, you taking her back to Hades Abyss sucks, though. She's been part of my life for so long now. I don't want her to go anywhere."

"I kind of figured that part out when she told me that her big brother chased everyone off."

Flicker chuckled. "Yeah, I'd have kept her a virgin until she was thirty if I had my way. Guess I wasn't ready for her to grow up. And my baby sister is having a baby. Not sure how I feel about that yet."

I snorted. "You'll be Uncle Flicker. If we stay here, I hope you plan to babysit at least once a week."

"You treat my sister right, and I'll make sure you have time to romance her. She deserves all that shit, you know? Flowers, nice dinners, all that crap women seem to like in the movies."

"I can do that." At least, I thought I could. I'd honestly never tried to romance a woman before. But Flicker was right. Laken deserved all that shit, and more.

"I won't stop you from seeing my sister," Flicker said. "But when visiting hours are over, maybe you need to go figure out a few things. She'll want answers you may not have. I don't want her stressed out more than she needs to be."

He wasn't wrong. I did need to figure some shit out. First, I'd check on Laken. Then I'd call my old man and see what he thought about all this. I had a feeling he was going to be thrilled about being a grandpa. The man turned into a teddy bear whenever a kid was nearby, and he'd probably figured I'd never claim a woman for more than a night. I had no doubt I'd first get a safe sex lecture, because even at thirty-eight there were times my dad thought I was some smartass teen, and then he'd grill me about Laken.

That wasn't a call I was looking forward to. At all.

Chapter Six

Laken
Two weeks later

My eyes felt like they were weighed down by sandbags. I struggled to open them and wondered how long I'd been asleep. My fingers twitched, but the rest of my body wouldn't respond. Everything ached, especially my head and my ribs. I tried to shift and wanted to scream at the agony that shot through me, but what came out sounded more like a moan.

"Laken?"

That voice. I knew that voice. Didn't I? I struggled harder, trying to wake up, to move. Things slowly came to me. Like the scent of antiseptic and the hard bed underneath me. My fingers twitched again, and I fought harder to open my eyes. To do something. Anything. Why wouldn't my body listen to me? Had something happened? Was I paralyzed? Panic filled me.

"Laken, sugar. Can you open your eyes for me?"

Sugar? I calmed a little. Only one person had ever called me that. I tried to smile and failed. *Ryker*.

"Come on, babe. Show me those pretty eyes."

I felt his rough hand take mine, his thumb brushing over my fingers. As if I needed more encouragement to open my eyes than just knowing he was here. A warmth filled me, just hearing his voice, but there was something that didn't feel right. A voice in the back of my mind was pushing me, trying to get me to remember something. But what? And where the hell was I?

It took more energy than I had to finally open my eyes, and I quickly closed them again as the bright light pierced them. Wherever I was, that had been as painful as looking at the sun.

"Shit," Ryker muttered. He released my hand and I heard him walk across the room, then I heard the flick of a switch. "Try again, sugar. I turned off the lights for you."

I struggled but managed to open my eyes once more. It took me a minute to focus, then I realized I was in the hospital. Why was I here? And why did I hurt so much? My head throbbed as I fought to remember what had happened to me, my brain almost feeling like it had spikes being driven into it. How could I remember Ryker, but not remember why I was here? What the hell was wrong with me?

"Easy, baby," he murmured, taking my hand once more. "You've been in a coma for the last two weeks. Take your time and don't force yourself to do too much too soon."

I licked my lips, my mouth dry as cotton, and he picked up a cup from a nearby table. He held a piece of ice up to my lips and I gratefully took it. It soothed my throat, and I moaned a little at how good it felt. When it had melted, I opened my mouth for another. After I'd had three, Ryker set the cup back down.

"Not too much, sugar," he said. "I need to let someone know you're awake."

He pushed the call button on my bed, and a few minutes later a nurse bustled into the room. She smiled widely when she saw I was awake and came closer.

"It's good to see you up," the nurse said. "This guy has been so worried about you, and so has that hunky brother of yours."

The way her eyes lit up when she mentioned my brother, I could tell she was smitten with Flicker, but then, most women were. He'd been compared to a

Viking more times than I could count, and every female he spoke to nearly fell at his feet, just hoping he'd take her home. It had always amused me to watch them make fools of themselves over Flicker. Maybe if they knew he left the seat up, had dirty clothes piled all over his room, and barely knew how to boil water, they might not be so impressed. Not that I'd rat him out.

"She hasn't spoken yet," Ryker said, sounding a little worried.

"She will," the nurse said. "Just give her a little time. I'm going to check your vital signs, Laken, and then I'll page your doctor to let him know you're awake."

I barely paid any attention to the nurse as she did her thing, my gaze focused on Ryker. He was tense and watched the nurse like a hawk. How long had he been here? He'd said I'd been in a coma for two weeks, but why? I still didn't remember anything that had led up to me being here, and it worried me. Was there something wrong with my brain? Was that why I'd been in a coma? What if it wasn't reversible? Would I always have pieces missing of my memories? What if I couldn't speak because of some sort of brain damage?

The nurse squeezed my hand. "Your blood pressure is a little high. Try to calm down, sweetie. You're in good hands here, and I'll let your doctor explain everything to you."

I took a deep breath and tried to do as she said. When she left the room, Ryker sat in the chair by my bed again, and took my hand once more. His touch comforted me, and I slowly started to calm down again. I tried to squeeze his hand, but I felt so damn weak.

"You have a lot of people scared and worried about you," he said. "They tried to kick me out, but I refused to leave. Security came, took one look at me, and turned right back around."

I smiled a little at that. I could imagine that happening. Ryker was well over six feet of pure muscle, and I doubted any security guards were going to scare him into leaving. I wasn't even sure the police could get him to budge unless a small army of them came in and took him by force.

"Were you going to tell me?" he asked softly. "About the baby?"

My vision darkened for a minute as my brain throbbed. The word baby triggered something, something I wasn't sure I wanted to remember. Pain, sharp and unrelenting, hit me, and had I been standing, I'd have collapsed. It was suddenly like a dam broke, and I was flooded with memories, ones that I didn't want. Ryker yelling at me, accusing me of getting pregnant on purpose, then me running. I gasped as I remembered the car hitting me, and then everything going dark as Flicker leaned over me.

I stared at him, not sure how I felt. He was here, and that had to mean something, but he'd been so angry, so accusatory. My hand trembled in his, and I felt my eyes tear up. He hadn't wanted me, hadn't even let me explain anything. He'd been furious, had lashed out at me. That he'd thought for one moment I'd gotten close to him for any reason other than I had found him attractive proved that he knew nothing about me, and had likely never cared at me at all. I'd figured I was just a one-night stand to him, with an encore, but the way he'd spoken to me only proved that was true. No one who cared about me could have said those things, could have thought for one minute I was underhanded and sneaky enough to try something like that.

"Hey," he said, his voice softening. "It's okay, Laken. You're okay."

"Baby," I said, my voice scratchy and sounding like it hadn't been used in forever.

"Yeah, we're going to have a baby. I'm so sorry, Laken. I'm sorry I yelled at you, that I didn't let you explain. I know you're different from anyone I've ever met before, but in that moment, all I could think about were the women who wanted to trap me, those who just wanted to be connected to someone of consequence with Hades Abyss, or had wanted a military husband. I should have never compared you to them, but I did. When I realized you were part of the Dixie Reapers, even lived there with them, I guess something inside me snapped."

I didn't know what to think of what he was saying. He looked contrite, like he meant the words he was saying now, but could I believe him? My heart ached as I remember the look in his eyes as he'd spoken to me on the sidewalk, the look he'd had when he realized Flicker was my brother, that I was related to a Dixie Reaper. He'd looked betrayed, and I never would have done that to him. Even though we hadn't spent much time together, I'd given him a piece of my heart during those encounters, and I'd wanted more from him.

"Laken, I didn't mean any of those things," he said. "That day, on the sidewalk... I wasn't thinking clearly, and I can never say I'm sorry enough times. Before any of that happened, I'd thought of taking you with me when I leave. I wanted you. Still want you. And I want this baby."

Pain spiked in my head, and I whimpered as my eyes slid shut. The pain went on and on, and I heard the machines start going nuts. There was shouting, but I couldn't focus on any of it. Agony rolled over me in waves, making it hard to breathe. I gasped, and my body jerked as I fought against everything I was feeling. The voices grew louder and after a few minutes, the pain began to dull, and I felt sleep pulling me under again. I succumbed to the darkness, welcoming it and the relief it brought to me. The next time I opened my eyes, it was darker outside my window, and it wasn't Ryker sitting with me but my brother.

Flicker smiled, looking tired and haggard.

"Hey, baby girl."

"Ryker," I croaked.

"They asked him to leave. Said it wasn't good for you or the baby if he was going to upset you." He bit his lip. "Actually, they kind of threw him out. It took three security guys and some off-duty cops who were here visiting someone to manhandle him out of her room and escort him from the hospital. He's no longer allowed in the ICU, not even the waiting room."

Was that what had happened? I must have looked confused because Flicker moved a little closer.

"They said that Ryker was pushing you too much too soon. Your body and your mind couldn't handle it. They gave you something to make you sleep and to numb the pain in your head. You suffered a brain trauma, and you're not going to be one hundred percent for a little while. The doctor came by and said you may experience headaches off and on for a while, and that pushing yourself too hard can trigger intense pain. Once you're released, if you black out, I'm supposed to call an ambulance."

"Home?" I asked, wanting to leave the hospital as soon as possible.

"They want to keep you here a little while longer. Make sure everything is okay. When they're convinced you can stand, walk, and take care of yourself, they'll release you. They also want to run some more tests, make sure everything looks okay. But I'm going to be with you every step of the way. Torch said he won't call me in for anything except emergencies until you're back on your feet, and the Prospects are all ready to help any way they can."

"Ryker," I said again, wondering where he was. He'd left the hospital, but had he left town too?

"We'll talk about Ryker when you're feeling better. Right now, you focus on getting better. I don't think talking about him is going to help your brain any right now. He's obviously a trigger for you, and the more upset you get, the longer you'll likely have to stay here. And I know how much you hate hospitals."

Flicker brushed a kiss against my forehead. I could see the care and concern in his eyes, and I hated that I'd worried him. He'd always been there for me, ever since I landed on his doorstep, homeless and without family. He hadn't so much as hesitated to take me into his home, into his life, and I would be forever grateful to him for that. I loved him, and I was so glad he was here with me.

"When you're better, the others will come see you," Flicker said. "Isabella and Ridley have asked nonstop how you're doing. Everyone at the compound misses you."

"Miss them," I said. And I did. The Dixie Reapers had become my family, and I knew they would always be there for me. It was like having a bunch of big brothers, and while that drove me nuts when it came to dating, I knew I could count on every single one of them.

"Get some rest, Laken. I'm not going anywhere. Anything you need, I'll get it. Just get better, because I hate seeing you in this hospital bed with all these wires attached to you. Love you, baby sis."

"Love you," I murmured as my eyes started to close again.

I briefly wondered if I was going to spend the next few weeks sleeping nonstop, or if I'd ever stay awake for any length of time ever again. I hated being here, hated that I'd been injured. And it was even worse that everyone was worried about me.

My brother was right. I needed to focus on getting better, and getting out of this place. I didn't like being here any more than he liked it. I'd do whatever they told me to, and soon enough I could deal with Ryker. Just as soon as I figured out what exactly he meant to me, or if I meant anything at all to him. Other than being an incubator for his offspring, a baby he hadn't even wanted.

But I could think about all of that later. Right now I needed to sleep, to heal. And to take care of the little one growing inside me.

I was no longer only responsible for myself. All of my actions, and the consequences, would now impact a little baby. A son or daughter who would rely on me for everything. Someone I could love, who would love me in return.

I placed a hand over my belly, vowing to do everything I could to give them a happy and healthy life.

Even if that meant it was a life without Ryker.

* * *

One Month Later

I glared at my brother as he handed me a plate with apple slices and cheese, then set a glass of milk on the table next to me. He'd thrown out all my favorite junk foods and soda before I'd gotten home from the hospital, and had given everyone strict instructions that I was to have healthy foods and drinks only. I knew he meant well, but he was killing me.

"You know cookies aren't good for the baby," he said, urging me to take a bite of the snack he'd provided.

I angrily bit into a chunk of apple and chewed, my gaze casting daggers at him the entire time. He didn't even look a little bit remorseful. He was mothering and smothering me. I'd only been home from the hospital for a few weeks, after they'd made sure all the swelling was gone in my brain and had checked me over thoroughly. My ribs were no longer sore, but I still got headaches periodically. They weren't as bad as they were when I first came home, though, so that was an improvement. I'd honestly take any small victory I could at this point.

I hadn't seen Ryker since the first time I'd woken at the hospital. At first, I figured he was keeping away because the hospital had banned him from ICU. Then I'd moved to a regular room, and he still hadn't come to see me. When I came home the following week, I'd looked for him, and waited. A day had passed. Then two. Then three. When Ryker still didn't show up, I'd asked him about him, and been informed that he was no longer here.

It hurt. So damn much. I shouldn't have been surprised, though. He probably had time to think about the daddy thing and decided it wasn't for him. It wasn't like he'd loved me. He didn't seem like the type who would ever fall in love and settle down, but that didn't stop my heart from aching at the thought of never seeing him again. One day, my baby would ask about their daddy, and I wasn't yet certain what I'd say. The truth, or some degree of it, but only enough that it wouldn't hurt my son or daughter until they were old enough to better understand what had happened. The last thing I wanted was for my baby to think their daddy didn't want them.

"Are you sure you want me to go with you to your appointment?" Flicker asked.

I set the plate down and twisted to face him. "Do you not want to go? You can always stay in the waiting room."

"It's not that. I just thought you might prefer having a woman back there with you, like Isabella or Ridley."

"You're my family, Danny," I said, using his real name, or the version of it I liked to use. His real name was Daniel, which he hated. "There's no one I'd rather have hold my hand through all this than you."

He smiled softly. "Love you, Laken."

"Love you too."

"I know living with me hasn't always been easy. I know you've felt like I'm too controlling, and maybe I have been, but I've only wanted to keep you safe. I can't help but think if I'd done something differently, then none of this would have happened."

"Danny, I know things didn't work out with Ryker, but I can't regret being with him. This baby may not have been planned, but I'm going to be an awesome mom, and I'm going to love him or her with all my heart. I could never wish my baby away, even to avoid the heartache Ryker caused."

Flicker sighed. "You've grown up so much. I'm proud of you, Laken. Really damn proud."

"I'm a little scared, though. I don't have a job, and it's not right to ask you to pay for everything. Babies are expensive."

Flicker waved a hand. "Don't worry about any of that. I checked with our health insurance, and they're going to cover your pregnancy. It seems when you turned eighteen, Torch had a maternity rider added to your policy just in case. Guess he saw this coming sooner or later, and it's a really damn good thing he signed the club up for a health plan back when you came to live with me."

"It's not right, though. You're going to end up paying for everything. Diapers. A baby bed. Clothes."

"And I will gladly pay every penny for the things my niece or nephew needs. Stop worrying, Laken. It's not good for you or the baby. We'll just take things one day at a time, okay?"

"All right."

"Go take your shower and get dressed. Your appointment is in an hour."

I stood up and kissed his check before hurrying to my room to get ready. Coming to live with Flicker was one of the best things to ever happen to me. He'd been an amazing big brother, and I knew he'd be an even better uncle. But my heart still ached for the one person I couldn't have. Ryker.

Maybe one day it wouldn't hurt so much. But that day wasn't today.

Chapter Seven

Ryker

"Son, what the hell are you doing?" my dad asked as he leaned against the bar in the Hades Abyss clubhouse. "Anyone with working eyes can tell you don't want to be here."

I could have played dumb and acted like I didn't know what he was talking about, but we both knew better. I was physically here, but that was it. Laken still consumed my every thought, and I missed her so fucking much. It had taken me leaving to realize just how much she meant to me. Once I'd heard we were having a baby, I'd known I'd make a life with her. But now... now I knew I didn't just want a life with her. I wanted her heart, because she'd sure as fuck taken mine.

"I'm no good for Laken," I said, taking another swallow of my beer. "She's better off without me."

"Are you sure about that? You know, I've never taken you for a coward. I know the Marines sent you into some hellish situations, and since you've been home, you've taken on club tasks I never would have asked you to do. I used to think you had balls of steel, but the way you're hiding from a woman, I'm starting to think they're more like marbles."

I scowled at him.

Bear, the sergeant-at-arms, snickered. "More like shriveled peas. No, no... Wait. What's smaller than a pea? I know! Mouse balls. He has a really tiny mouse balls."

I growled at him, wanting to put my fist through his face.

"Don't go insulting mice," Marauder said as he walked up and joined the conversation. "Those bastards are bold as fuck."

Bear fingered the patch on my cut. *Diablo*. I'd hated that fucking name ever since they'd given it to me, which is why I never used it unless I was around the club. Everywhere else I was just Ryker. I'd done some fucked up shit in my lifetime, and I might have earned the name on my cut, but it didn't mean I was necessarily proud of everything I'd done.

"Maybe we need to change this out. I'm thinking Princess would be a better name for him these days," Bear said.

"Nah," Marauder said. "A princess has to be tough. He's more like... Fuck. I got nothing."

"Chickenshit," Bear said. "That would be a good one."

"Are you assholes done?" I asked, glaring at them. "I'm not a fucking chicken. You didn't see what happened when I was at the hospital. I could have fucking killed her."

My dad patted my shoulder. "But you didn't. And now she's home, she's doing fine, and I'm betting that she misses you."

"Do you have a crystal ball now?" I asked.

"No, he asked me," said a voice behind me.

I turned and saw Torch, the President of the Dixie Reapers MC, standing behind me. No one had said a word about him coming here, and I wondered if they'd planned it that way. If I'd known he would be there, that anyone tied to Laken would be here, I'd have made myself scarce. I didn't need a reminder that I was here and she was there, not when I was pretty fucking certain I'd left my heart back there with her.

"And in case you're wondering, she's asked about you. When she found out you'd left and hadn't even said goodbye, I watched as her heart shattered into pieces. She's putting up a good front, acting like nothing's wrong, but we all know different," Torch said. "And from what I hear, you aren't doing so great either."

"He doesn't even look at the club sluts," Marauder said with disdain. "Who the fuck gives up free pussy? I think your girl broke him."

Bear smirked. "Or maybe her pussy's just..."

Bear didn't get to finish his sentence before I stood and put my fist through his face, just liked I'd been dying to do. Blood trickled from his mouth and covered his teeth as he grinned at me. Asshole. He'd baited me on purpose, and I'd fallen for it. He wiggled his teeth and spat some blood onto the floor.

"You're lucky you didn't knock any out," Bear said.

I snorted. "Yeah, because all those are really yours."

"Boy, do I have to take you back home the hard way or are you going to come easy?" Torch asked. "Because I didn't come here on vacation. One of mine is hurting, and you're the cause. So you're going to man up and fix it."

"You're here for me?" I asked, then glanced at my dad who suddenly seemed very interested in the wall across the room. Yeah, the fucker had set me up. I should be pissed, but part of me was glad he cared enough to interfere. We might not have the typical father/son relationship, but he was there for me when I needed him, and he'd understood when I'd left and joined the Marines.

Torch scratched his beard. "The club and I have talked, and as much as we don't like the way you handled things with Laken, the truth is that she wants you there. It's obvious to any of us that she misses you, and I think she's a little scared having to face this pregnancy alone."

"Alone?" I asked. "She has all the Dixie Reapers there with her."

"Yeah, but none of us is the daddy to her baby. You're the one she wants," Torch said. "Flicker would be content if you never showed your face again, but even he agreed that something isn't quite right with Laken. She's healed up just fine. Still gets headaches here and there, but the doctor said everything looks good. Baby is doing good too."

"Then it sounds like she's just perfect without me," I said.

"Then why does she look so fucking sad when she thinks no one is watching her?" Torch asked. "I've seen her get this melancholy look on her face and put her hand over her belly, and I know she's not sad about the baby. She's excited even though she's worried about her brother having to pay for everything."

Wait. Flicker was buying my kid the things they needed? That was my job. If anyone should be providing for my son or daughter, it was me.

"He's been good about taking Laken to her appointments, asking the doctor questions to make sure he takes care of her properly," Torch said.

There was a look in his eyes that I couldn't quite decipher, but I knew he was telling me all this for a reason. Maybe he knew I wouldn't like the idea of someone else taking care of my kid, taking care of my woman. And fuck, but that's what Laken was. Mine. I think I'd known it as soon as that first night. I should have tied her ass to the bed so she couldn't leave. Maybe things would have turned out differently if she hadn't snuck out that next morning, or if I'd asked more questions the second time I saw her.

"What's it going to be?" Torch asked. "You coming willingly, or do I have to do this the hard way?"

"And what's the hard way?" I asked.

My dad cleared his throat. "That would be me, as your President, ordering your ass to go with Torch. As of this moment, you're the liaison between the clubs. We reached an agreement, but he's sending one man here, and I'm sending you to the Dixie Reapers. You'll still be Hades Abyss, but you'll follow Torch's rules while you're there."

"And if I don't want to go?" I asked.

"Didn't realize I was asking," my dad said.

I could read between the lines. Either I did as I was told, or I was out of the club. The Hades Abyss had never meant much to me, not after I was old enough to leave and start my own life, but being back here... I'd realized that maybe they meant more to me than I'd ever admitted to myself. They were family, and you didn't turn your back on family.

"If Laken wants to move here with you," Torch said. "None of us would stop her, or you, from leaving. Your dad would just send someone else to our club. But Laken is family to us, and we're hoping the two of you decide to stick around."

"Looks like my future is all decided for me. And here I got out of the Marines so I'd be allowed to think for myself."

My dad snorted. "Son, you were born into this club. You've never been allowed to think for yourself, so don't go acting like that's anything new. You've either followed my rules or the government's, and I think between the two, you'd prefer mine."

He wasn't wrong. I sipped my beer and studied the two men over my mug. Assholes. They both looked like they knew I was going with Torch whether I wanted to or not, and really, they hadn't given me any choice. I wasn't about to give them the satisfaction of thinking I actually wanted to go, though. The thought of seeing Laken again both thrilled me and terrified me. I didn't know what kind of reaction I'd get when she saw me. But fuck if I didn't want to hold her again, to breathe in her scent, and run my hands through that silky blonde hair that hung nearly down to her ass.

"Fine. When do we leave?" I asked.

"Now," Torch said.

"Your stuff is already boxed and ready to go," my dad said. "Had it done while you were down here moping in your beer. A Prospect will drive the truck down with your shit. As a courtesy to me, and in hopes you decide to stay there with Laken, Torch is letting you use a house on the compound. Mostly furnished."

"If I'm not here to work, how the hell am I going to earn money to take care of my family?" I asked.

"You're working, just not doing what you normally would. Torch needs help on any jobs, he'll let you know and pay you accordingly. But I'll have funds transferred to your account every month, for as long as you're there. Don't think being a liaison is going to mean you sit around on your ass all day. We're going to work you. Hard," my dad said.

I shrugged and finished my beer. I'd never been afraid of hard work. As long as I didn't bring shit home to Laken and my kid, I'd do what I was told without question. But the second that shit came to my door, then everyone would remember why I was called Diablo.

"Guess we'd better hit the road, then," I said.

"I'm only stopping for gas," Torch said. "So if you need to piss, do it now."

"Just how long have you been here?" I asked. I'd thought I'd have a night or two while he hashed things out with my dad. No way he drove straight here and was ready to turn around and go right back. That was a long-ass haul, and no offense to Torch, but he wasn't exactly young.

Torch smirked. "Two days. Ironed everything out with your old man, and now I want to get home to my wife and daughter. So move your ass."

I pulled my keys from my pocket and followed him out to the parking lot. He walked around the corner of the building while I went to my bike, and a moment later, I heard his engine rumble from the backside of the clubhouse. No wonder I hadn't known the fucker was here. They'd made sure I wouldn't see him. Fuckers. If this came back to bite me in the ass, if Laken didn't want me, I was going to be fucking pissed.

Torch pulled through the gates and stopped at the street, waiting for me most likely. I started my bike and looked at the Hades Abyss clubhouse, wondering if it would be for the last time. Yeah, my dad might have said I was a liaison, but I knew he was really just trying to get me back together with Laken, and likely didn't think I'd ever return. I had mixed feelings about it. I'd always thought that I could put this place in my rearview and never look back. Now I wasn't so certain. I'd made a home here the last month, or as much of a home as I could have without Laken.

What the fuck would I do if she didn't want me? What if she was pissed when she saw me? She had every right to be. I'd taken off without so much as saying goodbye, even if I had thought I was doing the right thing at the time. But what if Torch was right? What if she did miss me? Had I made a huge mistake by leaving her behind? I didn't know if she would forgive me, wasn't certain I deserved forgiveness, but it looked like I would find out soon enough.

True to his word, Torch only made stops to refill his tank, and we drove straight through to Alabama. By the time we pulled into the Dixie Reapers compound, I was more than ready to get off my damn bike. My ass hurt, among other places. He bypassed the clubhouse, and I stayed with him, not sure where we were going. When he pulled to a stop in the driveway of a small home, I figured this was the place I was supposed to claim as my own. For now anyway.

Torch didn't even shut off his bike, just tossed me a set of keys, then pulled back onto the road that wove through the compound. The Prospect from Hades Abyss, who was driving a truck of my things, pulled in a minute later, with two Dixie Reapers Prospects right behind him. I leaned against the porch rail while they unloaded everything into the house, not giving a shit where they put things, and once they were gone, I decided to check the place out. They'd dumped my boxes in the middle of the living room, not that I had a ton of shit anyway. Being in the military for so long, I'd never accumulated much.

The house was bigger inside than I'd thought it would be. Three bedrooms, two bathrooms, a large kitchen, and decent living room. There was even a screened-in porch on the back of the house that was probably a nice place to sit in the cooler months. There was a brown leather couch and a coffee table in the living room, with a modest size flat-screen TV on a three-shelf stand in the living room. The kitchen had a round table with four chairs in a little breakfast nook that looked out over the front yard. The appliances seemed to function, as I twisted the knobs on the stove and opened the fridge to check things out. No coffeemaker or microwave, but I could fix that easily enough.

It wasn't much, but I could work with it. It wasn't like my bank account was hurting. I probably had more saved than most people made in several years. Some of it was from the military, and the rest was my share of profits from Hades Abyss. When I stayed at Hades Abyss, I had a room over the clubhouse that had the basics. The rest of the time, I lived out of cheap motels. Not because I couldn't afford better but because after being in the middle of the fucking desert, eating sand and sleeping with one eye open, even a cheap-ass mattress in a pit of a motel was a step up.

I hauled my box of clothes into the master bedroom, the only one that actually had furniture in it, and threw my stuff into the dresser drawers. The bedroom actually had the most furniture in it. A queen-size bed, dresser, two nightstands with drawers, and a tall five-drawer chest. I didn't have enough shit to use all of it, but if I convinced Laken to live with me, I'd be grateful for the extra storage. I'd always heard that women had a lot of shit that came with them when they moved in.

The furniture was in decent shape and would more than suit my needs. I'd lived a pretty simple life so far, only splurging when it came to my bike and electronics. Honestly, this stuff was better than anything I'd had before. I'd mostly been raised by my dad and his club, and no one there gave a shit about furniture or matching dishes. Hell, I hadn't even checked to see if there were dishes. I'd have to look and make a list of things I'd need.

As much as I wanted to see Laken, I knew now wasn't the right time. My head was all over the place, even though I'd done nothing but think on the way here. I needed to sort things out before I went to see her. I knew she'd likely have questions for me, and I wasn't entirely sure I had all the answers. I knew that if she'd give me a chance, I wanted to try to make things work with her. And I definitely wanted a place in my son's or daughter's life.

Despite my exhaustion, I found a place for all my shit and finished unpacking, then I showered and planted face-first onto the bed. I didn't even bother to cover my naked ass with a blanket before I closed my eyes. Not that I thought I'd fall asleep anytime soon, not until I'd seen Laken. I rolled onto my back and stared up at the ceiling.

I'd spent a lot of sleepless nights wondering what she was doing, wondering if she was glad I'd left. If what Torch said was true, maybe she'd been missing me as much as I missed her. Then again, she could take one look at me, slap my face, and tell me to get the fuck out of the compound. After the way things had ended between us, I wouldn't blame her. Anyone with as much passion as Laken had, probably had a volatile temper when she was angered. I hadn't seen that side of her yet, but it didn't mean she didn't have one. Everyone had a temper, it was just a matter of pushing the right buttons. And I was excellent at pushing buttons.

Any other woman, I'd have walked away and never given her a second thought. Women had only ever been good for one thing. Fucking. And once I was done, I moved on to the next one. I'd fucked my way across the US and several other countries, always having my choice of pussy everywhere I went. I'd thought it would be the same here, but then I'd grabbed Laken's ass and my world had changed, even if I hadn't realized it right then. In some ways, I owed her brother big-time. If he hadn't kept her on such a tight leash, she might not have even looked at me twice. But she'd been so desperate to lose her virginity that a stranger had seemed like the perfect choice.

I couldn't blame her. She'd just wanted to experience the same pleasure everyone else was getting. And I'd been more than happy to help her scratch that itch. Hell, after one taste, I'd been addicted to her. I'd spent my entire time here hoping I'd see her again, just waiting for a chance to fuck her. Even now, my dick was hard as a steel post just thinking about her.

I opened the bedside table and pulled out the bottle of lube I'd stashed there when I unpacked. Squirting some on my hand, I wrapped my fingers around my cock and stroked it. It was nowhere near as good as Laken's pussy, but it was all I had for now. I closed my eyes and remembered the sight of her bent over the bathroom sink that first night, her dress shoved around her waist, and pussy on display. She'd been so fucking wet, and so damn tight. It had felt like heaven being inside her. The only thing tighter had been her ass when I'd claimed it in the motel room a few hours later.

Oh yeah, my Laken had been a wild one, letting me do whatever I wanted to her. She'd begged me so sweetly, asked me to fuck her ass, and I'd been helpless to say no. I'd spread those cheeks wide, gotten her nice and slick, then worked my way inside. My balls drew up just thinking about coming inside that tight ass of hers. I'd ridden her hard and deep, not stopping until I'd filled her with my cum. I'd fucked her all night, in several different ways.

I grunted as cum shot up onto my abdomen and coated my hand, my cock twitching as I came. I looked up at the ceiling again, cursing that I was lying here alone. After I cleaned myself up, I pulled on some boxer briefs and was about to figure out what the hell I was going to eat when my phone rang. I didn't recognize the number, but answered it anyway.

"How'd you get this number?" I asked, my voice more of a growl.

"You're invited to dinner, asshole. Get your ass here in the next fifteen minutes."

The line went dead, and I stared at the phone. Flicker was inviting me to dinner? Or had someone told Laken I was here and she'd invited me? Either way, I wasn't going to pass up the opportunity to see her. I pulled on some clothes, put my boots back on, and rushed outside to my bike. He'd said fifteen minutes, and I sure as fuck wasn't going to be late. Not when Laken was waiting for me.

I got to the end of my driveway before I realized I had no fucking clue which house was theirs. I pulled my phone back out and called Flicker.

"What?" he said in a biting tone.

"I don't know where your house is, dickhead."

He snarled at me, then told me how to get there before ending the call. I had no doubt that had he been using a landline with an older phone, he'd have slammed the fucker down. Pushing "End Call" just didn't pack the same punch. I smirked as I pulled onto the road that wound through the compound and went in search of his house. It wasn't as hard to find as I'd thought it would be. I could see little touches here and there that screamed a female lived here. The flowers along the front were likely not Flicker's doing, nor were the little gnomes.

I shut off my bike and went up to the door. Before I could knock, it was flung open, and Flicker glared at me. He didn't say anything, just stepped back and let me cross the threshold, but before I got farther than the front entry he stopped me.

"You hurt her again, and I will fucking end you. I don't give a shit who you are or who you're connected to," Flicker said. "She's all I got, and I'm tired of hearing her cry herself to sleep every fucking night."

That made my heart ache, knowing that I'd done that to Laken. I nodded and moved farther into the house. He shut the door and motioned for me to follow him into the kitchen. A square table was in the center of the room with three place settings, and a ton of food in the center. The kitchen was a lot larger than the one in my new home. Their entire house was bigger for that matter, but I had what I needed. The question was whether or not Laken would be content moving into someplace smaller.

"Flicker, dinner's done," Laken said, her back to us. When she turned, she dropped the spatula she had in her hand and turned deathly pale. "Ryker."

"Hi, Laken."

"You're here," she said softly.

"Yeah. Thought I'd join you for dinner, if that's okay?" I asked. If she didn't want me here, I wouldn't stay. As much as it would kill me to walk away, that's what I'd do.

Her gaze shot over to Flicker, then back to me. "You can stay."

I smiled a little and took a seat. Flicker took the spot across from me, leaving Laken between us. She finished what she was doing, then joined us. She cast nervous glances my way as she fixed our plates, loading mine with meatloaf, mashed potatoes, carrots, and rolls. There was a pitcher of lemonade in the middle of the table, and she filled all our glasses. I didn't like her waiting on me, but she seemed to be doing it out of habit so I left her alone. If she ever came home with me, that shit would stop, though. I was quite capable of fixing my own plate and getting my own drink. She'd cooked the damn meal, so I didn't understand why she had to serve everyone too. Had Flicker asked her to do that shit or was it something she'd just always done on her own? If she tried to wash the dishes when we were finished, I was going to put my foot down. This wasn't 1950, and I was a little pissed that Flicker just sat there while she did all this work.

When Flicker dug into his food, I took a bite. And damn near had my eyes roll into the back of my head. It. Was. Awesome. I couldn't remember ever tasting anything so wonderful before. The flavors just burst on my tongue, and I'd eaten three bites before I even remembered to breathe.

"This is really good, Laken. Like beyond amazing," I told her before shoveling more food into my mouth.

Her cheeks flushed, and she smiled at me. "Thank you."

"You cook like this all the time?" I asked.

I'd never really been around a woman who cooked. My mom, not that she'd been with us long, had never mastered anything beyond boxed meals, and this shit tasted like it was made from scratch. Even some of the nicer restaurants I'd been to couldn't compare. If she moved in and cooked on a regular basis, I'd turn into a butterball if I didn't work out every damn day.

She shrugged. "I know how to make a few things, but I bought a cookbook the other day. I figured now that I'm going to be a mom, I should learn to cook more things. I want my son or daughter to have nice dinners, at a table with the family. I never had that growing up."

"Neither did I," I said. "Mom tried for a while, and then she just didn't care anymore. I think being with Dad kind of broke her."

Flicker watched us but didn't say anything. I wished that I could talk to Laken alone, but it seemed her guard dog wasn't going anywhere. I couldn't really blame him. I didn't have a stellar record when it came to Laken. First I took her virginity in a bathroom and knocked her up, then I yelled at her and she was hit by a car, then I abandoned her when she was in the hospital. Yeah, I was a fuck-up, but I wanted to make things work with her. If that's what she wanted.

I'd give her anything. All she had to was ask.

The woman already had my heart.

Chapter Eight

Laken

He was here. Ryker was really here, sitting next to me, eating a meal that I had cooked. Part of me was panicking, and the other half was just thrilled to see him again. But why had he returned? I still didn't know for certain why he'd left. Had he been called back to Hades Abyss? Or had he left because of me? I had so many questions, and I wasn't sure I was brave enough to ask. Mostly because I didn't know if I wanted to hear the answers. If I was the reason he'd left, my heart would likely break a little more, and I wasn't certain there was much left of it. When I'd found out he was gone, had left without saying goodbye, I'd felt completely shattered.

The way Flicker was watching us didn't help matters any. I wanted some alone time with Ryker. I needed answers, and I didn't think Ryker would be very forthcoming with Flicker hovering. I didn't think big brother was going to let that happen, though. He'd made it no secret that he didn't care for Ryker, and I doubted that had changed in the past month. If anything, he probably hated him even more, with the way Ryker had taken off and left me.

"I guess we don't know much about each other," Ryker said. "You're a good cook. I'm going to assume the flowers and gnomes out front were your doing. Do you enjoy gardening?"

"I do," I said, smiling. "I like mixing different colors of flowers and finding cute things to accent the garden and yard. Makes the place feel more like a home and not just a house."

"Maybe you can do something with my place," Ryker said.

I set my fork down and stared at him. "Your place?"

He nodded. "A little house down the road a bit from here. Torch is letting me use it. I'm now the liaison between Hades Abyss and the Dixie Reapers."

My mouth dropped open a little. Did that mean he was here to stay? Torch wouldn't have given him a house if this wasn't a long-term thing, right? But the question was whether or not Ryker had been forced to come, or was he here for me and the baby? Did he actually want us in his life?

"You have a house here?" I asked, not sure I'd heard him correctly.

He nodded. "It's a three-bedroom, two-bath. Not as big as this place, but I think it has potential. I'm shit when it comes to decorating and gardening, though. Think you might want to come check the place out? Give me some pointers?"

"You want me to decorate your house?" I asked softly.

"I want you to make it a home," he said. "Maybe a home you'd like to live in one day."

I swallowed hard, and my hand shook as I reached for my fork. I couldn't look at him, not without giving away all of my feelings. I wanted that, so very much. But I was afraid that if I reached for that dream, he'd change his mind. I didn't just want a father for my baby, I wanted Ryker. No one had ever made me feel the way he did, and yeah, we might not know a lot about each other, but there was a spark between us.

Maybe that was enough.

"The last time you were alone with my sister, you nearly killed her," Flicker said. "Why would I let her go to your house?"

I glared at my brother.

"I never meant to hurt Laken," Ryker said. "That's the last thing I want to do. If she'll give me a chance, I'd like for us to start over. Get to know each other, spend some time together. When it comes to Laken, I don't just want sex. I want to have something more with her."

I melted a little at his words, but Flicker didn't look pleased, if the tic in his jaw was any indication. I wasn't certain that Ryker would ever be able to win over my big brother, but as far as I was concerned, he was saying everything right. Something bothered me, though. Ryker wouldn't have just invited himself over. At least, I didn't think he would have. So who had asked him to come to dinner?

"Danny," I said softly, drawing his attention my way. He lost a little of the hard glint in his eyes as he looked at me. "Don't chase him off. Please."

"He's not good enough for you, Laken. He goes through a different woman every night, sometimes more than one a night," Flicker said.

"Not anymore," Ryker said. "That's the old me. Since my first night with Laken, I haven't been with anyone else."

"Really?" I asked, looking his way.

"I don't want anyone but you," Ryker said. "Whether you believe that or not, it's the truth. All it took was one taste, and I was hooked on you. But it's more than that. I don't just want another night in bed. I want all of you, Laken. The good and the bad."

Flicker shoved his plate away and stood up. "I can't stand to listen to this shit. He's going to hurt you, Laken, just like he did last time. I won't keep the two of you apart, but I don't like him being on Dixie Reapers' territory. And I sure as fuck don't like him being with you."

"Danny, please try to get along with Ryker. He's the father of your niece of nephew. Doesn't that mean anything to you?" I asked.

Flicker shrugged. "I'll be home late. Don't wait up."

He stomped out of the room, and I heard the front door slam a moment later. I winced, hating that I'd chased him out of his own home. Ryker reached over and took my hand, giving it a squeeze, and I smiled at him. My brother was always an ass, so I didn't know why it should be any different now, but my hospital stay was still a bit of a blur. If anything had happened between them to make things worse, I didn't remember it. Had Ryker and Flicker gotten into it?

I'd lost my appetite and stood up, gathering my plate and Flicker's before heading over to the sink. I heard Ryker's chair scrape as he stood. I'd expected him to leave his plate, then take off, much like my brother did most nights. But he didn't. He hip-checked me to scoot me over, and he took my place washing dishes. I'd never seen a man wash a dish before, and if anyone had ever asked, I'd have said it was a myth that such a thing ever happened. But there was Ryker, scraping and scrubbing the dirty dishes, then handing them to me to place in the drying rack.

"You don't have to do this," I said.

"You cooked dinner, then you served everyone. You shouldn't have to do the cleanup too," Ryker said.

I was a little surprised. Danny had never thought to wash the dishes for me, and I didn't think it was something he'd ever think to do. It made me wonder if Venom or Torch ever did the dishes for Ridley and Isabella. Did men do housework too? Maybe I should have trained Flicker better. I felt sorry for whatever woman ended up with him. He was a complete slob. My brother had a heart of gold, at least when it counted, but he definitely had a lot of rough edges.

We finished the dishes, and then Ryker took me by the hand and led me into the living room. Now that Flicker was gone, I felt a little more at ease around Ryker. As I sat down, he claimed the spot next to me, but he didn't release my hand. It felt right, sitting here like this with him. But Ryker wasn't the same as before. He'd always been a little arrogant, and dare I say smug, but I didn't see that when I looked at him now.

"You seem different," I said.

"I missed you. I never meant for things to end up the way they did, and I'm sorry I left without saying bye."

"Why did you?" I asked.

"I thought I was doing the right thing. I never wanted to hurt you, and I was worried that if I stayed, something bad would happen. Flicker told me to leave the hospital and not come back. I guess I just figured it would be better if I left town altogether."

"I didn't want you to leave."

He squeezed my hand. "I'm sorry, Laken. And I'm really damn sorry for the way I reacted before your accident."

"The accident wasn't your fault," I told him. "It was no one's fault. It's why they call it an accident."

"If you'd died... if you'd lost the baby..."

"But I didn't. I'm fine, Ryker. I have headaches sometimes, but even those will go away."

He slowly reached over and placed his hand on my belly. "You're sure the baby is okay?"

"They used a special monitor at the hospital to check on the baby. Everything is fine."

"Can I go to your next appointment with you?" he asked.

"I'd really like that."

"I should go, and let you get some rest." Ryker stood, but I clung to his hand.

"Take me with you," I said. "Flicker will be gone for hours, maybe even all night. I don't want to be alone, Ryker. And... I just got you back."

He pulled me to my feet and placed his hands on my waist. "I'm not going anywhere, Laken. Not as long you want me here. But I don't want to take things too fast either. We did that already, and I made a mess of things."

"Ryker, please. Take me home with you. I'm a big girl, and I know what I need and what I want."

He smiled a little. "All right, but I brought the bike. I'm not sure you should be riding on one while you're pregnant, especially after a head injury."

"You'll be careful, and you can go really slow," I said. "It's not like I've never been on a motorcycle before."

His eyes narrowed a little. "You better have only ridden with Flicker."

I bit my lip. Maybe the caveman side of him wasn't completely gone after all. Was it wrong that I got a little thrill that he was a bit possessive of me? Maybe he really did care about me. I could hope anyway. He seemed sincere and like he'd changed. The Ryker I'd met at the bar had been a total playboy, but the man standing with me now? He was different, and in a good way.

"Come on," he said, tugging on my hand. "I'll take you to my place, but don't expect much. I haven't even checked the kitchen to see if it's stocked with food and drinks."

"We could take one of the trucks and pick up a few things," I said. "Anyone can use them. You'd just have to take me to the clubhouse on your bike. They keep the keys behind the bar."

"Any place around here that sells furniture, towels, and food?" Ryker asked.

"There's a twenty-four hour store not too far from here. They have everything. Well, except live animals, but they have a gardening section, furniture, kitchenware, food, movies, clothes."

"Sounds like the perfect place." Ryker smiled. "All right. But if you get tired or start getting a headache, you let me know, and we'll come back."

He led me out to his bike, and I swear there were snails passing us he was driving so damn slow. It touched me, though, that he was trying to be careful with me. When we reached the clubhouse, he left me in the parking lot with a promise to wait for him. I wasn't sure if I should be amused or upset. It wasn't like I didn't have a clue what went on inside the clubhouse, but honestly, part of me was glad I didn't have to deal with the club sluts. It was sickening, watching them hang all over the bikers I considered family.

Ryker returned a few minutes later, keys in hand, a smudge of lipstick on his neck. My eyes narrowed as I stared at those lip prints. The color was rather distinct too, so I knew just who had left it there. I brushed past Ryker and stormed up the steps and into the clubhouse. After scanning the room, I found just who I was looking for. Bambi. I still didn't think that was her real name, but it's what everyone called her.

I shoved my way through the crowd and walked up to her. She looked me over, then dismissed me, but that was a huge mistake on her part.

"Hey, bitch!" I snapped at her. "Keep your nasty ass lips off my man."

She smirked at me. "*Your* man?"

I felt a hand at my waist and a hard abdomen pressed against my back.

"She means me," Ryker said over my head. "And I'd have to second what she said. Stay the fuck away from me."

"Oh please, honey. Like that mousy little girl can give you what you need," Bambi said. "When you're ready for a real woman, you know where to find me. And I promise, I will do anything you want."

I lashed out at her, my hand cracking across her cheek, and making the room go dead silent. The footsteps of half a dozen bikers drew closer.

"What the fuck is going on?" Zipper asked.

"This slut insulted my woman, so Laken decided to teach her a lesson," Ryker said.

"Your woman, huh?" Zipper asked, smiling a little. "That means I'll be doing some ink soon?"

"Ink?" Ryker asked.

"Dixie Reapers ink their women," Zipper said. "Hades Abyss doesn't do that?"

I felt Ryker shrug behind me. "Never had a woman before, and my dad never really claimed my mom. I have no fucking clue what Hades Abyss does for their old ladies. I was gone more than I was there. There are some brothers with old ladies, but I was never around when those women were claimed."

"Come see me when you're ready to make it official," Zipper said. "I'm the resident ink slinger."

"I want her gone," I said.

"You can't throw me out, you whore," Bambi said, practically spitting at me.

"I'm the whore?" I asked. "You're the one who fucks anyone who crooks a finger at you. I've been with one man. And he still wants me. I wasn't a fuck and dump like you are."

Bambi screeched and lunged at me, but Ryker spun me out of the way. Before he could retaliate, I heard Bambi slinging curses at everyone as the Dixie Reapers dragged her out of the clubhouse. Zipper patted me on the shoulder.

"You okay, darlin'?" he asked.

"I'm fine. Thank you for taking out the trash, though."

He chuckled. "No problem."

"Come on, sugar. Let's run to the store, then I'll show you my new home. You can figure out how you want to decorate it." Ryker kissed my cheek. "That was pretty fucking hot, seeing you go all savage on her."

I smiled and let him take me back out to the parking lot, then we got into the truck and went shopping. And shopping with Ryker was way more fun than I'd ever had before.

Chapter Nine

Ryker

Laken had put a dent in my checking account, but it was well worth it. She'd helped me pick out some more furniture for the living room, had picked out kitchen stuff that I'd likely seldom use, and then she'd selected everything I could possibly need or want in my bathroom. When I'd showered earlier, I'd found two towels with the tags still on them, but I'd needed more than that.

I hauled everything into the house, and while I was putting the furniture together and setting up the electronics, Laken busied herself in the kitchen and bathroom. It took us about two hours to get everything set up, but the house looked a lot better when we were finished. It almost felt like a home. Although, I didn't know how much of that was because of things we'd bought, and how much of it was due to Laken being with me. Maybe she was the one who made it feel like home.

I pulled a bottle of water out of the fridge and carried it to the bedroom. She was curled up on the bed, half asleep, and looking far too tempting. I set the bottle on the nightstand and smoothed her hair back from her face.

"I should take you home," I said.

"I am home." She smiled. "Let me stay here with you tonight."

"You didn't bring anything with you, or buy anything at the store."

"I can sleep in one of your shirts," she said. "Then I can go back to Flicker's tomorrow to change."

"All right, sugar. I'm not going to fight you, not when I really want you here."

She gave me a sleepy smile, and I went over to the dresser to pull out a T-shirt. I helped her off the bed, and slowly removed her clothes. It felt like it had been forever since I'd seen her this way. And one of those times had been rushed. One of these days, I was going to love her all night long, like I'd done at the motel, and I was going to take my time doing it.

Even though I knew my son or daughter was growing inside her, her belly was still just as flat as before. Once I had her stripped bare, I knelt in front of her and pressed a kiss there, right where our baby was. Something wet hit my cheek, and I looked up to find Laken crying. My heart squeezed at the sight, and I stood up, pulling her into my arms.

"What's wrong?" I asked.

"Nothing, I just…"

"Talk to me, Laken."

"When we first met, I never imagined this side of you existed. The guy I met that night was…"

"An asshole," I finished for her.

"Not quite how I would have put it." She smiled. "I like this side of you, Ryker. It just surprised me is all."

"This is the man I want to be, for you and for our baby. The two of you deserve the best of everything, and while I don't think that's me, I don't want to walk away. I'll do it if that's what you ask me to do, but I won't like it."

"I'd never send you away," she said. She ran her fingers through my hair. "Make love to me, Ryker. It's been so long, and I've missed you so damn much."

"I've missed you too, sugar, but I don't think we should…"

She placed her fingers over my lips. "Hush. I'm perfectly fine, Ryker. Remind me that I'm yours. Show me how much you've missed me."

I kissed her. Slow and deep, holding her tight against me. Laken melted against me, one hand curling behind my neck, and the other on my shoulder. I loved the way she felt in my arms, so damn sweet and perfect. I pulled away long enough to remove my clothes, then wrapped my arms around her once more. Feeling her, skin to skin, was like heaven on earth.

"Promise me this is the beginning," Laken said. "Promise me that you won't send me away in the morning."

"Sugar, your brother isn't going to be happy if you move in here the second I come back to town."

"I don't care what Flicker wants. I know that I owe him a lot, but this is my life, and I belong here with you, Ryker. Or do you not want me?"

I pressed my cock against her, the damn thing so fucking hard I could probably drive nails with it. "What do you think?"

She smiled softly. "I think it's been too long since I felt you inside me."

"Then I guess we'd better fix that," I murmured, then took her down to the bed.

Her nipples were hard and looked so damn pretty and pink. I took my time, exploring her with my lips and hands, wanting to memorize every inch of her. She was so soft, so curvy, and so mine. Now that I had her in my bed, in my home, I didn't want her to leave. I might not deserve her, but I wanted her. Needed her. Fuck, I think I even loved her.

I parted her thighs and teased her pussy with my fingers, feeling how hot and wet she was. All for me. She whimpered as I teased her clit, circling the little bud until her body flushed with pleasure. Her body tensed, and I knew she was getting close. My cock ached to be inside her, but this wasn't about me. I wanted her screaming my name, but only because it meant she'd found her release. I lightly pinched her clit, then rubbed it slowly again.

"So good," she said in a near whisper. "Please don't stop. So much better when you do it."

That damn near froze me. "Better when I do it? Who's been touching you, sugar?"

"Me," she said. "But it didn't feel as good."

Oh, God. That was so fucking hot. "And did you think of me while you played with this sweet pussy?"

"Yesssss," she said, dragging the word out.

"Did you imagine my cock filling you? Fucking you?"

"God, yes."

"And when you came, was it my name you said?" I asked.

"Yes. Ryker, please. I need to come."

I eased two fingers inside her, feeling how tight she was, as my thumb pressed down on her clit. I couldn't fucking wait to feel her wrapped around my cock. I fucked her with my fingers while I teased her clit, not stopping until she was arching off the bed and screaming out her release. My fingers were coated with her cream as I eased them out of her.

Laken lay panting on the bed, her legs still spread, and it was the prettiest sight I'd ever seen. I gripped her thighs and spread them a little more as I settled between them. My cock pressed against her, and I slowly entered her. It felt like fucking heaven to be inside her again. So damn tight and wet. So fucking hot. I ground my teeth together to keep from fucking her hard and deep.

"Ryker," she cried out as I slid in a little more, not stopping until I was balls-deep.

"Mine. Say it, Laken."

"Yours. Only yours," she said. "I've always been yours."

Just hearing those words nearly made me snap. I growled low as I thrust slowly, wanting to drag the moment out longer. I tried to hold back, to make it good for her, but she felt too fucking incredible. When she wrapped her legs around my waist, taking me even deeper, I couldn't hold on anymore. I fucked her like I was possessed, driving into her as if I were trying to brand her. And maybe I was. She cried out again, her pussy clamping down on my cock. My balls drew up, and then I was coming, so damn hard. I didn't stop, our hips slapping together, until every drop had been drained from me.

If I hadn't worried about crushing her, I'd have stayed inside her a while longer. But I pulled out and sat back, watching as my cum spilled out of her. Her pussy was all pink and pretty. I reached between her legs and used my fingers to shove my cum back inside her, thrusting them in and out a few times.

"Keep that in there," I said.

She giggled at me and closed her thighs around my hand, trapping me. Not that I was complaining.

"Maybe you can think of some other places to put it," she said.

My cock went hard as a steel post just thinking about fucking that ass of hers. But I wasn't about to do that tonight. She was carrying our child inside her, and while part of me wanted to fuck her in every way imaginable, I wasn't sure how I felt about getting all wild and crazy with a pregnant woman. My pregnant woman.

"Let's get cleaned up and get some rest. This isn't a one-time thing."

Her gaze went all soft and dreamy. "You really want me, don't you? Not just for tonight but for longer?"

"I want you for forever," I told her.

And I meant every damn word.

"Come on, sugar. Shower, then bed," I said.

I helped her up and got the water running in the bathroom. When it was warm, but not too hot, I helped her over the edge of the tub and pulled the curtain closed behind us. I couldn't help but explore her body as I washed her from head to toe. It almost felt like a miracle that she was here with me, that I'd been given a second chance. And I wasn't going to fuck it up this time.

Once we were both clean, I helped her dry off. She wandered back into the bedroom while I finished up, and I found her curled on her side, already asleep when I joined her a few minutes later. Guess I took more out of her than I'd realized. I shut off the light and curled around her, holding her close and just breathing her in. I almost felt at peace, getting to hold her like this. After so many sleepless nights, wishing she was with me, I finally had what I wanted. I just hoped I could hold onto her this time.

I didn't sleep, even though I was exhausted. I spent the night watching over her, and as the sun began to rise, there was a knock at the front door. I had a feeling I was about to be put to work, so I pulled on some boxer briefs and went to see who the hell was bothering me so damn early. And I hoped like hell they didn't wake up Laken.

I threw open the door and stopped and stared at Flicker.

"What?" I asked, my voice harsher than I'd intended.

"I'm going to assume my sister is here with you."

"Yeah. She asked to stay."

He nodded. "Look, you know I don't like you. I haven't made a great secret of it. Be good to her, though, or I'll beat the shit out of you. And I'll just be at the head of a long line of Dixie Reapers anxious for a pound of your flesh."

"I never wanted to hurt her. She means everything to me," I said, hating to admit that to Flicker.

"Good. Then I'll make sure Zipper is ready for the two of you after Laken wakes up. You claim her, and you ink her. If you're serious about staying, about making her yours, then you're going to do this the right way."

I nodded. "All right."

He stared at me another moment before walking off. I shut the door and went back to Laken, holding her another few hours while she slept. When she woke up, I fixed her one of the only things I knew how to cook. Eggs and toast. Then we got ready and headed over to the clubhouse. I wasn't entirely certain about having her inked, but if that's the way this club worked, I'd fall in line. Laken didn't seem worried about it, so maybe she'd expected something like this to happen at some point in her life.

The clubhouse was mostly empty when we got there, except for Zipper and a few others. He was nursing a beer at the bar, even though it was still morning. Too early for alcohol for me, but hey... to each his own.

"What am I inking?" Zipper asked.

"I've never seen a property tattoo before so I have no idea what to ask for," I said. "Far as I know, Hades Abyss doesn't ink their women."

He nodded. "Each old lady has a distinctive tattoo that is unique to them. If you want, we can just do a basic script that says *Property of Diablo*."

"Diablo?" Laken asked. "They call you the devil?"

"Misspent youth," I said. She didn't look like she believed me, but she didn't press for more information. I'd take what I could get. The last thing I wanted to do was admit to my sins. There were too damn many of them. "Guess that makes you the angel who tamed me."

She smiled at that.

"I don't need anything elaborate," Laken said. "Just the text is fine."

That didn't seem right to me, though. Laken was special, and she deserved to have a unique mark. Something that was perfect for her. The problem was that we were still learning about each other.

"What if we did something that's a little bit of each of you?" Zipper asked. "You called her an angel, and your name is Diablo. What about a pitchfork with a halo hanging off it? Then we could do the text around it?"

"Perfect," Laken said, smiling widely.

"Come on back. Let's get this done. He'll have to order your property cut from Hades Abyss," Zipper said.

Fuck. I hadn't even thought of that. Something else I'd have to take care of.

We followed Zipper into his studio at the back of the clubhouse, and Laken gripped my hand tight while Zipper went over everything. The ink didn't take all that long since it was pretty basic, and Laken didn't cry once. She was so damn brave, even though I could see the pain in her eyes. When it was over, I kissed her softly.

"So proud of you, sugar."

"I'm really yours now," she said.

"You always were, ever since the moment I grabbed your ass."

She giggled at me, and Zipper snorted.

"Get out of here with that shit," he said.

"Wait. If she's mine, then I'm hers. Can you do one more tattoo?" I asked.

Zipper's eyebrows went up. "Sure."

I pulled off my shirt and took the seat Laken had just vacated. I placed a hand over my heart, and a bare patch of skin. "I want *Property of Laken* right here."

Zipper grinned and started getting everything set up. My tattoo took less time than hers, and I noticed she had tears in her eyes as she watched her name being inked into my skin. A permanent reminder that we belonged to each other.

When Zipper was finished, I pulled her into my arms and kissed her. "I love you, Laken. So damn much."

"I love you too," she said, tears in her eyes and her voice a little shaky.

"Awww. Ain't that sweet?" Zipper said. "Now get the fuck out of here."

I pulled my shirt back on and took Laken home.

I didn't know what the future held for us, but I knew we'd be together. And that was all that mattered. As long as I had Laken, then I had everything I could possibly need or want.

Epilogue

Laken
Six Months Later

"Are you sure you want to know?" Ryker asked.

I bit my lip to keep from laughing. He looked ready to jump out of his skin he was so damn excited. "I'm sure."

The technician moved the little wand over my belly. This was our third ultrasound. I'd had a few complications along the way, but so far we'd decided to wait and be surprised with the gender of our baby. But I knew Ryker really wanted to know, and he was hoping for a boy. I would be happy either way. As long as my baby arrived healthy, that was all I cared about.

"Let's see if Baby Storme will cooperate," the technician said.

My hand tightened on Ryker's, my wedding band likely cutting into him. He'd bought me an outrageous diamond a month after we got our property tattoos, and we were married the following week. He'd decided he wanted to do things the "right" way, and wanted me to have his name.

"Ah!" The technician smiled broadly. "See that there? Looks like Baby Storme is very well endowed."

Ryker chuckled and I smacked him with my free hand. Just like a man.

"I hope you have some boy names picked out," the technician said as she wiped the goo off my stomach.

We did. But there was one I knew was perfect.

"Gabriel Storme," I said.

"The boy has a little devil and a little angel in him," Ryker said. "Maybe if he's named after an angel, he won't make the mistakes his daddy made."

"I'm sure baby Gabriel will live up to his name and be a complete little angel for you," the technician said. "Congratulations, Mommy and Daddy. Dr. Myron will see you at your next scheduled appointment. And as always, call if you have any questions."

"Thank you," I said as I sat up.

After the technician left, Ryker helped me get dressed. I was so round that I felt like a flipped over turtle every time I lay down. It was impossible to get up on my own. Not that Ryker complained about all the extra weight. He seemed to be fascinated with my baby bump, and was always rubbing his hands over my belly, or pressing a kiss there. God, but I loved him.

"I don't know if it was fate or what that put us together that night," I told him. "But I'm so glad you grabbed my ass."

Ryker laughed. "Well, it was a pretty irresistible ass. Still is," he said, giving my ass a smack.

"Careful. You know my hormones are all over the place. You grab my ass right now, I might bend over and beg for more."

He growled and moved in closer. "Don't even fucking tempt me, Laken. Truck. Now."

"And then what?" I asked.

"Then I'm taking you home, and I'm going to make you come until you pass out."

I waddled a little faster to the truck parked at the curb, and Ryker followed behind me. I looked over my shoulder and saw his gaze was glued to my ass, and he had that sexy, arrogant smirk in place. The one I fell for that first night we were together. Whenever he wore that look, I could see a hint of the devil he'd been named after. A randy rooster. But he was *my* Diablo now.

Oh, he was still Hades Abyss, and likely always would be.

But he was my husband, my everything.

And now that I had him, I was never letting go.

Badger (Roosters 5)

Paige Warren & Harley Wylde

Badger -- I went to prison for ten years after beating a man to death. He deserved it, and then some. I only wish he'd suffered more. Now I'm free, but things aren't the same as when I left. The little girl I once saved is now a tempting young woman with curves in all the right places. I should stay away, far away, but I'm drawn to her like a moth to a flame. Griz, the pres of my club, adopted her, so she's definitely a no-fly zone, but damn if I don't want her with every breath I take. A little sample wouldn't hurt anyone, right? As long as Griz doesn't find out, I'll keep breathing. Sneaking around should be easy enough. I never counted on falling for her, or finding out she was carrying my kid. Now what the hell am I supposed to do? I'm a longtime repeat offender. I can't walk the straight and narrow. Can I?

Adalia -- I've worshiped Badger ever since the night he saved me. But what started as a young girl's infatuation has grown into something more. I know he'll never see me that way, or at least I thought he wouldn't. When we're together, it's like we just can't keep our hands off each other. It's probably against his parole for us to be together, but he doesn't seem to care. The heat between us is undeniable. He didn't promise me forever, just right now. But neither of us counted on me getting pregnant, something that wasn't supposed to happen too easily, and I have no freakin' clue what to do. I'm scared Badger will run for the hills. He never asked for this, but then neither did I. One thing is for certain. If he doesn't man up and my daddy finds out, there will be hell to pay. No one can hide from the president of the Devil's Fury MC.

Chapter One

Badger

I cracked my neck and felt my muscles flex as I breathed in freedom for the first time in ten years. I probably could have gotten out sooner, for good behavior, but let's face it, I've never been good, and there was no point in starting now. Being part of the Devil's Fury MC came with certain expectations. One of those was handling any problems on the inside if you were ever sent to prison, and since I'd been the only one in my crew who got sentenced and sent to this particular lockup, it was all on my shoulders. Plenty of guys had tried to kick my ass inside, but I hadn't gotten the name Badger for being nice. I'd fucked up anyone who dared to breathe wrong in my vicinity.

As I exited the gates of Mooreston Prison, I clutched my cut in my hand. The black tee and jeans I'd been wearing when I'd been picked up ten years ago didn't fit me quite right anymore, but they were fine for now. The jeans were a little loose, and the shirt a little tight. When I wasn't kicking ass, I'd spent my time working out. The ladies seemed to love it, or at least the female guards did. For the last ten years, those ladies were the only people of the female persuasion I'd seen. There were plenty of places in Mooreston that had blind spots, and I'd enjoyed every one of them. It never failed to surprise me when even the women in uniform wanted a taste of me.

A large black truck rolled up and stopped. The window slid down and Demon grinned at me. I'd known someone from the club would pick me up, but I hadn't expected it to be an officer. Or maybe they'd sent the Sergeant-at-Arms in case I started a fight on my way out. Like I wanted to turn around and go right back inside. I might be something of a hothead, but I wasn't dumb enough to fuck things up the second I was released. I didn't delude myself into thinking I'd make it through my lengthy parole without going back, but I'd enjoy freedom while I could.

I opened the passenger door, threw my cut onto the seat, and climbed in. The icy air hit me in the face and felt fucking fantastic, but I was still tempted to roll down the window. An hour in the yard didn't compare to feeling the wind in my hair as we sped down the highway. There was a lot I'd missed while being locked up, and fresh air was one of them. A nice cold beer would be appreciated too.

"Good to see you," Demon said. "Had no doubt you'd survive that hell in one piece."

I shrugged. It wasn't my first brush with the law, and it likely wouldn't be the last. If it hadn't been for overcrowding, my ass would still be behind bars. Well, that and the club lawyer had done a lot of sweet-talking. Having to get up at the butt crack of dawn and live my life on a schedule had been a pain in the ass, but it wasn't like I was hurting in there. I had food, a place to sleep, air and heat... and out of all the men inside, I'd been the only one getting any pussy, if those female guards could be believed. Could have been worse.

In exchange for getting my dick wet, I'd made sure no one fucked with the female guards. There were a lot of things you could barter for inside, but I'd been the only one smart enough to trade protection for some pussy. You'd think a prison guard would have a stick up their ass, but the two women I'd gotten to know rather intimately hadn't been so bad. I hadn't even made the first move; they'd come after me. Not that having women throw themselves at me was anything new.

"I know you probably just want to chill, but Griz is throwing a party for you. I told him you wouldn't want that shit the second you set foot outside those gates, but you know how the Pres is." Demon smirked. "At least there will be lots of pussy there. I'm sure all the ladies will be eager to ease the loneliness you must have felt the last ten years."

I snorted. "Yeah, because I wasn't getting laid in there or anything."

His eyes widened.

"Female guards, asshole. Apparently, my charm even works on women wearing a uniform." Not that I'd ever had any doubt about my prowess with the female population. I walked into a room, and panties seemed to just fall off. Hell, I'd fucked a woman in a booth at a club before. Yeah, it had mostly been dark, but anyone nearby would have known what we were doing. I probably could have told her to strip in front of everyone and bend over, and she'd likely have done it. Pussy had come easy to me ever since I was fifteen, and that hadn't changed even behind bars.

I was a god when it came to the fairer sex. I didn't have to ask for pussy; the women just offered themselves up to me. Even the married ones. Fuck, I'd even taken a widow before, on the day of her husband's funeral. Fucked her in the bathroom right before the service. Some called me an asshole, and maybe I was, but it wasn't my fault the ladies all wanted a piece of me. Or at least they all wanted to feel my cock, fucking them deep and hard. Most didn't even mind which hole I used, just as long as I gave it to them good and hard.

Demon snickered. "Should have known you'd find a way to get you some, even while serving time."

"What can I say? The ladies can't resist the Badger. Maybe if your dick was as big as mine, you'd have the same problem."

Demon flipped me off, then put the truck into gear and pulled away from the prison. I'd like to say I'd never see the place again, but really, the odds weren't in my favor. I was nearly forty and had spent half my youth in detention centers, and half my adult years behind bars. I was a fuckup, in society's eyes, but I was loyal to a fault. I'd do anything for my club, even if it meant living life behind bars. I'd been charged with manslaughter during my latest stint and sentenced to twenty years, thanks to my record. I hadn't been on club business that time, though.

The trip back to Blackwood Falls took too fucking long, and I was feeling anxious. It had been a long damn time since I'd been in a vehicle, and I'd much rather have spent the hour-long ride on my Harley. Soon enough, I'd take it out on the open road, and just let the tension melt away. The only thing sweeter than a ride on my bike was being between a woman's thighs.

As Demon stopped outside the clubhouse, he tensed and turned to face me. I had no idea what was going to come out of his mouth, but something told me it wasn't anything I wanted to hear.

"There's something you need to know," Demon said.

"Anyone die while I was gone?"

"No. It's about Adalia."

My breath froze in my lungs as I pictured her wide blue eyes as they'd stared at me in terror. I'd found her in an alley, her clothes torn, and some asshole raping her. I'd seen her around town, knew she was only thirteen, just a kid. Something inside me had snapped, and I'd beat the fuck out of that asshole. Beat him to death. I didn't regret what I'd done, only wished I'd gotten there sooner. Adalia had watched as I killed that man, and she hadn't uttered a word the entire time. Not even when I took her to the hospital to be checked out. I'd known it wouldn't end well for me, but my first priority had been the girl. Anyone else might have gotten off with a lighter sentence, seeing as how I'd been protecting her. But a guy like me with priors? I hadn't had a prayer. Ten years to give her the peace of mind that the asshole who had touched her was six feet under? Yeah, it was a trade I'd been willing to make. I'd made it then, and even knowing I'd get time, I'd do it again in a second.

I might be an asshole biker with a rap sheet, but there were some things that even I wouldn't tolerate. Rape was one of them. Anyone harming a kid was another, and that dickweed had done both. As far as I was concerned, the world was a better place without him in it.

"What about her?" I asked.

She'd be twenty-three now. Probably had a steady job, a nice boyfriend. At least, I hoped that's how her life had turned out. But the way Demon had said her name... had something happened to her while I was gone? Had some other asshole tried to hurt her, and I hadn't been around to save her this time? My gut clenched just thinking anything bad had happened to her. She'd been such a sweetheart the few times I'd been around her, always a little on the quiet side.

"She's here," Demon said quietly.

My heart started pounding, and I flung open the truck door, then reached for my cut and shrugged it on. I slammed the door shut and stomped up the clubhouse steps before going inside. There were balloons and shit everywhere, and the roar of welcome as I stepped inside was near deafening. But as I scanned the crowd, it wasn't my brothers I was taking in... No, I was looking for *her*. I didn't know what she looked like anymore, only remembered her as a teenage girl. She'd been terrified the last time I'd seen her. I didn't know why she was here, but I had to see her, to know that she was okay. I'd thought about her every fucking day that I was inside, hoping she'd been able to get past what happened to her, had gone on to live a good life. I'd thought about writing her once, just to check on her, but had decided it was best if I kept away. She didn't need any reminders from me about what had happened to her.

My brothers hugged me, slapped me on the back, and slowly they all parted. At the back of the room stood a pixie of a woman, long blonde hair curling over her shoulders, and a body made for sinning. It was her eyes that nailed my feet to the floor. Blue. And achingly familiar. My gaze traced her features, trying to find the little girl I'd tried to save. I didn't see even a hint of the terrified teen I'd carried out of that alley. Her features were delicate, much like the rest of her. She had curves in all the right places, and would likely be more than a handful for some men, but I'd be willing to bet she wouldn't even reach my shoulder. Tiny. Almost like a little fairy. Slowly, Adalia walked toward me, her hips swaying with every step. Yeah, she'd grown up while I was gone, and I'd be willing to bet men fell to their knees to worship at her feet. She looked like one of those plus-sized models, but in a shorter package.

She didn't even hesitate when she reached me, just put her arms around my neck and hugged me tight. My arms closed around her, pulling her curves against me, and I breathed in her honeysuckle scent. Closing my eyes, I just drank in the moment. She was here. She was safe. And she felt a little too damn good pressed against me. The way my jeans tightened made me want to put some distance between us. I tried like hell to keep the image of her as a thirteen-year-old girl in my mind, hoping my body would stop reacting to the woman she'd grown into, but no such luck. The breasts pressing against me were more than a handful and far too fucking tempting, as was the rest of her.

"I'm glad you're home," she said, her voice soft and husky.

"It's good to see you, pretty girl. Not a day went by that I didn't think about you."

"I tried to come see you a few times, but they always said you weren't allowed visitors."

I pulled away and smiled down at her. "I had a tendency to get into trouble inside. But now I'm glad you didn't get any farther than the gates. Prison is no place for an angel like you."

Her cheeks flushed and she smiled a little. "Welcome home, Badger."

"There's something you need to know," Demon said from behind me. "Adalia is one of us now."

I took another step back, trying to put more space between us. If she was someone's old lady, the last thing I wanted to do was start a fight with a brother. My gut clenched at the thought of one of my brothers laying claim to her, but it wasn't like I had any say in the matter. I'd been doing time while everyone else lived their lives and moved forward. She sure as hell deserved someone better than any of the fuckups in this club, though.

"Grizzly and May adopted me," Adalia said. "After what happened, my foster family didn't want me. Said I was tainted. So Griz and May stepped up."

I didn't want to analyze the relief I felt at knowing she didn't belong to a brother, at least not as an old lady. I had no doubt the Pres and his old lady had taken good care of her. They'd always wanted kids and had never been able to have any. May had mothered all of us, even those who were too damn old for such nonsense.

My gaze scanned the crowd, looking for the momma bear who would kick my ass if she knew I'd gotten hard while hugging her daughter. "Where's May?"

Adalia's eyes teared up. "Gone. She got cancer three years ago. It was so advanced when we found out that she didn't last more than three months. But she was an awesome mom, best I could have ever asked for."

I found myself hugging her again, wanting to comfort the gorgeous woman who'd been a frightened little girl the last time I'd seen her. I found Griz across the room and hoped he'd see my gratitude for him stepping in the way he had. He gave me a smile and a nod, even though I saw the sadness in his eyes and knew he was missing May. The two had been together since they were just kids, and it hurt to think of the sweet woman being gone. Where Griz was rough and could be as mean as his namesake, May had been all light and laughter.

"Daddy made me promise to only stay until the cake was cut," Adalia said. "He doesn't like me hanging out at the clubhouse once the… other women get here."

I bit my lip. "Is that your polite way of saying the club pussy will be arriving after cake?"

Her cheeks burned a bright red, and she ducked her head. Fuck, but that was adorable. I chuckled and hugged her again before blending into the crowd. If I'd stayed around her much longer, I might not have been able to pry myself away. There was something about this new, older version of Adalia that was far too tempting. I had no doubt Griz would hand my ass to me if I laid a finger on her, and that's how it should be. That sweet girl needed someone to watch out for her, and while I'd kill any fucker who touched her, she didn't need the kind of trouble I'd bring with me. Hell, I was on parole for the next ten years. If I took one step out of line, I'd be going right back to prison.

I tried really damn hard not to watch her, but I seemed to always know exactly where she was in the room. And after the cake had been cut and devoured, I knew the moment she'd left the clubhouse. The club sluts had arrived a short time later, and now the party was in full swing, but I couldn't seem to find much enthusiasm for the overly made-up women. Their perfume was so heavy it made my head hurt, and their faces had such thick makeup, I wondered what they were hiding. Before I went away, I might have taken them up on their offers. But every time I even thought of pulling one of them closer, the scent of honeysuckle would stop me, and blue eyes that seemed to look right through me. I'd have to get over whatever infatuation I seemed to have for the older version of Adalia, before it got me into more trouble than I could handle. The last thing I wanted to do was piss off Griz, or anyone else around here.

Cobra eased up next to me at the bar. "Figured you'd be balls-deep in two or three women by now. You know we brought them here for you."

"Got a headache," I said and took another sip of my beer. I'd missed a good bottle of beer more than I'd missed women, probably because I'd had plenty of pussy in jail and hadn't had a bottle of beer in ten years. Drugs were easy enough to smuggle inside, but beer not so much. Not that I'd touched the hard stuff while I was there. Prison hooch and cocaine smuggled in by someone swallowing it or worse? Yeah, I'd pass. Besides, I'd wanted to keep my head clear, never knowing when someone might come after me. Being vulnerable in prison wasn't the best idea, especially for someone like me, someone who had enemies.

"She lives here on the compound," Cobra said. "In case you were wondering. Griz set her up in the small cottage about two miles down the road. She lived with him and May until she turned twenty, then he decided she needed her own space. I think it had more to do with May, though. I don't think Griz wanted her to watch May suffer, not that Adalia wasn't there every chance she got."

I didn't even play stupid. I knew he was telling me so I could go after Adalia. Not that I had any business being anywhere near her. Even if my dick hadn't gotten hard with all the club sluts hanging off me tonight, I didn't trust myself around the angel who had hugged me earlier. That sweet honeysuckle scent had been too fucking tempting. Hell, *she'd* been too fucking tempting. I'd gotten harder from just a simple hug from Adalia than I had over the bare breasts being thrust into my face tonight.

"No one would think anything of you going to say hi," Cobra said. "You just lost ten years of your life for her. Even Griz wouldn't be pissed."

"So, what? You think I'm going to ask her to repay me by spreading her legs? I'm an asshole, but I'm not that much of one."

Cobra shrugged. "I don't think she'd fight you. Everyone knows she has a case of hero worship. God help anyone who says something bad about you. She'd try to castrate them."

I snorted. Yeah, a hero. *Right.*

"Just go talk to her," Cobra said.

Talking wouldn't hurt anything, right? I wanted to know about her life since I'd been put away. Wanted to make sure she had everything she needed. That was perfectly reasonable.

I might not have talked myself into going to see Adalia if I'd known she'd answer the door wearing my old shirt. And nothing else.

Chapter Two

Adalia

The old flannel shirt I preferred to sleep in was nearly threadbare now. When Griz and May had brought me home, I'd had a really hard time sleeping at night. I hadn't felt safe, even behind the gates of the Devil's Fury compound. After talking to May one night, she'd come back a short while later with this shirt in her hand. I hadn't understood why she would think an old flannel shirt would help any, until she'd told me it belonged to Badger, the man who had saved me.

It fell nearly to my knees and hung on me. I always rolled up the sleeves, but just feeling the soft material against my body, and knowing it had been *his* was enough to make me sleep like a baby. Or it had until I hit about fifteen. My hormones had been out of control by my fifteenth birthday. I hadn't wanted anything to do with boys at school, though. I'd spent every night dreaming of Badger, and as I'd snuggled in my bed with his shirt wrapped around me, I'd imagined it was his arms holding me. Not that he'd have wanted anything to do with a kid like me. He'd been in his late twenties when he'd been sent to prison and had only seen me as a child. I couldn't blame him. Didn't stop me from daydreaming or fantasizing about him, though.

Hell, he probably saw me as a kid now. He had to be at least fifteen years older than me. I sighed and sipped at the hot tea I'd brewed when I'd gotten home. I hadn't even stopped to think before throwing my arms around him. He'd walked through the door, and it was like every nerve in my body came alive. Just knowing he was that close was more than I could handle. I'd made myself wait, to hold still and not throw myself at him. And then he'd seen me, and I hadn't been able to hold myself back.

He'd been polite, and pulled away as soon as he'd been able. I felt like an idiot. Everyone in the club knew about my crush on Badger, and I didn't doubt that someone would tell him before the night was over. I didn't know if I could ever look him in the eye again. In the last ten years, I hadn't gone on a single date. Not a real one. One of the Devil's Fury had taken me to prom and other school events, only because May had insisted I go even when I'd refused. Twister wasn't much older than me and had been nice enough to take me, both as protection and insurance I'd actually go. He was like a brother to me. All of the Devil's Fury felt like family, either brothers or uncles. Except Badger.

There was a knock on my door, and I wasn't sure if it was Dad, here to tell me that I'd made a fool of myself, or someone else checking to see if my heart was broken. I don't know what I'd expected. The man had been away in prison for ten years, hadn't seen me since that night. It was stupid to think he'd take one look at me and fall in love. That shit only happened in the romances I liked to read. I set my cup of tea down and answered the door, but as it swung open, I froze, my eyes going wide and my jaw dropping a little.

Badger. He was on my doorstep, looking all kinds of sexy. His gaze dropped down to the shirt I was wearing, and I hoped like hell he didn't recognize it. I'd be beyond embarrassed if he knew I'd been sleeping in his shirt every night for ten years. What kind of psycho did that? Slept in a stranger's shirt, and pictured her wedding to said stranger every time she closed her eyes. Me, apparently.

"Damn," he said, his voice low and gruff.

"I thought you'd be partying all night."

"Wasn't in the mood."

I bit my lip and stepped back, opening the door wider. "You could come in, if you want."

"Not sure that's a good idea, pretty girl. Seeing you in my shirt is fucking with my head."

I dropped my gaze, and my breath caught when I saw just how tight his jeans had gotten. Holy hell! I'd dreamed of Badger being the one to claim me, but my imagination hadn't done him justice if that bulge was all him.

"Fuck." He groaned. "Don't look at me like that. I'm barely holding on, Adalia. Griz would kick my ass if I did even half the things I'm thinking of right now."

My heart started pounding, and I squeezed my thighs together. If he was trying to scare me off, it wasn't working. If anything, I wanted to jerk him into my home, slam the door, and throw all the bolts. I couldn't think of anything I wanted more than for Badger to step over the threshold. Having him here was like a dream come true, and I was worried he'd come to his senses at any moment and run.

"Come inside," I said, moving back even farther.

He hung his head a moment, then entered my small home. I closed and locked the door before taking his hand and leading him into the living room. He sprawled on the couch, and I fidgeted, not knowing what to do now that I had him here.

"Do you want some coffee or something? I could make some tea."

He winced.

"Okay, no tea." I smiled. "Coffee? I have one of those Keurig machines, and I have three different flavors of coffee. Hazelnut, vanilla, and just regular, which is what Daddy prefers. Tastes nasty to me, but he calls my flavored drinks girly shit."

"Let's not bring up Griz while I'm here. I'm trying not to think about him murdering me for entering your home. Every time I hear you call him Daddy, I just want to run as far and as fast as I can."

"Okay. He won't kill you, though."

Badger grunted, apparently not agreeing with me.

"Hazelnut," he said after a few minutes. "I haven't had a cup of flavored coffee in a long-ass time. And holding onto something might help keep my hands to myself."

Now I was regretting asking about that coffee. I'd much rather have his hands on me than wrapped around a mug. I went to the kitchen and brewed him a cup, taking down the mug I'd bought when my dad gave this house to me, in hopes that one day Badger would come visit. It was a Superman mug, but the cup was a matte charcoal gray and the logo was a glossy black. I'd found it at a discount store and it had immediately reminded me of my very own superhero.

I carefully carried the mug into the living room, where Badger was now standing by the fireplace, and staring at one of the two pictures I'd hoped he wouldn't find. May had given it to me for my sixteenth birthday. It was my mom, Dad, and Badger, their arms all slung around one another as fireworks lit up the sky. Mom said it had been taken not too long before Badger had saved me.

There was another in my bedroom, one I would have hidden if I'd known he was stopping by. It was Badger out in front of the clubhouse, leaning against his Harley with his arms and feet crossed. There was a hint of scruff on his jaw, much like now, and he had a bandana covering his hair. A sexy smirk graced his lips, and I had no doubt that very look had melted panties everywhere. May had framed it for me when she'd realized my infatuation with Badger was getting stronger. I'd kept it in my bedroom when I lived at home, then put it by my bed when I moved into this place. I sometimes wondered if she'd ever hoped we'd end up together once Badger was released from prison. She'd been a hopeless romantic, and I was just like her.

"That was a good day," Badger said, not turning to face me.

"Mom gave it to me for my birthday one year. I was always asking questions about you, wanting to know more about the man who had saved me."

"I didn't do such a great job of that. I got there too late."

I still had nightmares about that night, and probably always would. But despite what Badger said, I knew he really had saved me. The vile man who'd been on top of me had made sure I knew I was going to die. If Badger hadn't come down that alley when he had, I wouldn't have been breathing for much longer. At first, I'd wished that he'd just let me die, but once I came to live with Griz and May, I'd been thankful that I was still alive. They'd given me a good life, and had given me more love than I knew what to do with.

"He was going to kill me," I said, as I studied Badger's profile. "When he was finished, he was going to slit my throat. He told me as much. Said if he'd planned it better, he'd have kept me around a few days, so he could enjoy his time more."

Fury blazed in Badger's eyes as he turned to face me.

"So, you did get there in time. And because of you, Griz and May offered me a home, gave me a family. My life turned out pretty good, and it's all because of you. So don't think for one moment that I'm not grateful for what you did that day."

"You mean murdering someone in front of you?" he asked.

I shrugged. "I never shed a tear over that man's death. I did cry when they sentenced you to prison, though. It didn't seem fair, when you'd only been trying to protect me."

"I could have detained him and called 9-1-1."

"So why didn't you?" I asked.

"Because seeing how damn scared you were, knowing what he was doing to you, something inside me broke and I couldn't stop myself. Once I started hitting him, I wasn't able to stop, not until I knew he wasn't breathing anymore. The justice system doesn't take kindly to people solving problems with their fists. Or killing people, even if they are rapist assholes."

"I'm glad you're home," I told him. "I wanted to go with Demon to pick you up, but everyone thought it would be better if I stayed here. They weren't sure how you'd feel about seeing me."

He reached out and gently tipped my chin up. "I never, not once, blamed you for what happened. You were a victim. A child. It's not your fault I was sent away."

"I'm not a child anymore."

His lips twitched. "I noticed."

I handed his mug to him before I did something stupid. Like kiss him. He accepted the coffee and walked back over to the sofa. He sprawled across the cushions, and took a sip. His eyebrows lifted, and he looked pleasantly surprised.

"This is pretty good."

"I just stuck a pod in the machine. Even a monkey could do it."

He chuckled, and it sounded a little rusty, probably because he hadn't had a reason to laugh in so long. It made me feel good that I'd been the one to bring out that laugh, and I suddenly wanted him to smile more, to laugh more. And I wanted him to do those things with me. Along with some really naughty things I'd read about in books. I wasn't a virgin, not after what had happened to me, but I'd never willingly been with a man before. I'd always wanted Badger to be my first, but if I told him that, he'd probably run so far and so fast he'd be three counties over before I could count to ten.

"I'm glad that Griz and May stepped up to help you," Badger said. "I worried about you while I was inside. Some of the guys from the club came by a few times, but I had to focus on the shit happening inside and not outside. Everyone knew that, so I didn't really get any news about home while I was locked up. I didn't know if you'd ever overcome what happened to you, and maybe I should have asked, but I think I preferred thinking you'd gone on to live happily ever after."

"They've been good to me. Dad's been a little lost since Mom died. I know he stays busy with the club, only going home to crash for the night. I tried to stay over after Mom died, but he sent me back here. I worried that he'd be lonely in that house by himself. As far as I know, he hasn't even looked at a woman since Mom died. He keeps those other women around for the club, but he ignores them."

"May and Griz were together since they were just teenagers, and they wanted kids for as long as I can remember. You made their dream come true."

"What's your big dream?" I asked.

"Never really had a dream except to escape my home when I was a kid. I managed that by joining Devil's Fury. The guys here are my family now. They took me in when I had nowhere to go."

I wanted to know more about his past, about what had sent him running to this club, but I wasn't going to press him. Not right now anyway. Maybe one day he'd open up and tell me about his life.

"So what are you going to do now that you're free?" I asked.

"Try to stay out of trouble for a few weeks. Maybe longer. I'd rather not go back inside anytime soon, and I have parole for the next ten years. I doubt Griz will ask me to handle any jobs for a little while, not if he knows it could send me back."

I nibbled on my lower lip. Was I about to overstep? I didn't think my dad would be angry, but I never really made the big decisions without him. I just answered phones and handled the paperwork at one of the Devil's Fury businesses. One of the only legit ones anyway.

"Any good with engines?" I asked.

He grinned. "I was fixing cars when I was twelve, then started tinkering with bikes a few years later."

"I don't know if you've kept in touch with anyone while you were... gone. The Devil's Fury owns a few legit businesses, one of which is a garage. It stays pretty busy, and Dad makes sure nothing illegal goes down there. We need another mechanic."

"Griz let you hire all the mechanics?" he asked, rubbing a hand across the scruff on his jaw.

It wasn't a full-out beard, but it was still sexy as hell. Made me want to reach out and touch it, see if it felt soft or rough. I'd never kissed a man before, much less one with a beard, and I wondered how it would feel.

Wait. He'd asked me something. Mechanics. Right.

"I work in the office," I said. "And no, I don't usually do the hiring, but we do have an opening, and I know Dad would be thrilled to have you."

"I'll talk to him about it in the next day or two. Right now, I'm just enjoying breathing fresh air whenever I want."

I shifted on the couch, bending my knee and tucking my foot under me. He stopped mid-sip, his gaze dropping to where the shirt barely covered my lap. Badger kept staring even as he took a swallow of coffee, and I had to admit, I'd never felt so feminine, so desirable as I did in that moment. Men never really looked at me. Well, they looked, but not for long. Once I'd become Griz's daughter, a well-placed glare from my new dad, or the Devil's Fury members, made any interested males scatter. And I'd been really grateful for that. I hadn't been interested in boys in high school, and the only man I'd ever wanted was sitting with me now.

"I don't remember that shirt ever looking that good on me," he said, taking another swallow of his coffee.

"I hope you don't mind that I have it. When May and Griz first brought me home, I had really bad nightmares. May gave me this shirt and told me it was yours. It made me feel safe."

"Does it still make you feel safe?" he asked.

I squirmed a little. Should I be honest and see what happened? Or play it safe. I didn't have any experience with guys, especially ones like Badger who could have any woman they wanted. Did he like it when women played games with him? I decided to go for honesty.

"When I can't sleep, I imagine that it's you wrapped around me and not the shirt."

"You imagine me in bed with you?" he asked, his voice dropping a little, sounding even gruffer than before.

"Yeah." I dropped my gaze to my lap before fighting to meet his stare again. I felt completely exposed sitting here, being honest with him. I'd never been all that brave, but if I had a chance with Badger and I blew it, I'd never forgive myself.

"I expected to get out of prison and hear that you were married or at least seeing someone. I'd hoped you'd made a good life for yourself."

"I have a good life," I said. "I don't have to have a man for that. Although, I guess I technically have a MC full of them, just not in a romantic way."

"What do you want from me, Adalia? If Griz knew I was here, especially with you mostly naked, he'd have my balls. You're the President's daughter, which means it's hands off. So, if I'm going to get my ass kicked, I need you to be really clear on what you expect."

I licked my lips. "I don't expect anything. But... What I want is for you to kiss me, to touch me. I want to fall asleep with your arms around me, knowing it isn't a dream this time."

"You're asking for a lot," he muttered. "If I get my hands on you, it won't stop at kissing and touching. I can't lie in bed with you all night and not want to fuck you."

My breath hitched as I pictured us in my bed. My thighs clenched, and I ached in a way I never had before. I wanted Badger, more than anything, and it seemed like he wanted me too. What would it take to make him act on those feelings? I didn't pretend to know anything about men, despite the fact I read sexy books with half-naked men on the covers.

"I'm not asking you to," I said softly. "I want that. I want you."

Badger set his mug on the coffee table and reached for me. He slid his hands around my waist and hauled me onto his lap. His eyes were a stormy gray, and they pulled me in. It felt like I was free-falling, and we hadn't even done anything yet. Gently, he eased his fingers into my hair, cupping the back of my head, and he pulled me closer. He slanted his mouth over mine, in the softest of kisses, but that brief touch was enough to make the dam break. Badger groaned and thrust his tongue between my lips. I melted against him, kissing him back, and hoping he didn't realize I was inexperienced.

Hell, this was my first kiss, and it was everything I'd ever dreamed it would be.

I felt his hand leave my hair and slide down to the front of the shirt. My heart was pounding as he unbuttoned the front, slowly, as if he had all the time in the world. When the last one was unfastened, he pulled back, his gaze dropping as he parted the shirt and exposed my bare body.

"So fucking beautiful," he said, as he lightly trailed his fingers across my stomach.

I shivered, but it wasn't from being cold. I was hot, so very hot. The rough touch of his fingers made me want to beg him to never stop. My nipples were hard, and he lightly brushed his thumb across one. I couldn't hold back the moan that built in my throat, and I knew my pussy was getting wetter by the minute. He moved his hand down farther, teasing me before slipping his hand between my legs. Badger groaned and he laid his forehead against my shoulder.

"Christ, baby. All slick and wet. You make me want you so bad."

"I want you too," I admitted softly.

He lifted his head and stared into my eyes. "Part of me wants to bend you over the back of the couch, and fuck you until we both come. But you deserve better than that. So, I'm going to make you come, and then if you still want me, we're going to move this to the bedroom."

I leaned toward him, brushing my lips against his. Badger deepened the kiss as his fingers rubbed back and forth across the lips of my pussy. The scruff on his jaw was probably going to give me whisker burn, but I didn't care. I'd wear the marks proudly, and remember this moment every time I looked in the mirror and saw them.

"Spread your legs, sweet girl. I want to watch you come apart in my arms."

I could feel my cheeks burning as I spread my thighs farther apart. Badger teased me, his fingers sliding along the lips of my pussy, but never touching me where I wanted it most. I gasped as he plunged a finger inside me, thrusting it in and out a few times before he started to rub my clit with his thumb. Oh, God. This was way better than anything I'd ever dreamed about. After a few more strokes, he added a second finger.

"Damn, Adalia. You're tight as a fucking virgin."

I knew I should tell him the truth, but I worried he'd leave me if he knew. I bit my lip and just focused on the pleasure. Something was building inside me. My nipples hardened even more, and I felt like my body was tightening, straining for release. He didn't stop, not even when it became too much and I squirmed to get away from him.

"Shhh. Let it happen, baby. Just let go," he murmured, pressing a kiss against my temple.

I cried out as the most incredible pleasure I'd ever felt rolled over me. I'd have sworn I even blacked out for a moment, but as I slowly blinked and the room came back into focus, I felt Badger's fingers still thrusting inside me.

"Watching you come like that was the best welcome home gift I could have ever had." He smiled. "If you want to stop, I'll get up and walk away right now."

"Stay."

He didn't say anything for a few minutes, and I was worried he'd changed his mind. Badger pulled his hand away, then helped me to my feet. I wobbled a moment, but he steadied me as he stood up. Without a word, he lifted me into his arms and began striding down the hall. He bypassed the smaller bedroom and entered the room I'd claimed as mine.

A lamp was burning on the nightstand, and my cheeks flushed when I realized his picture was sitting right next to it. He stopped just inside the doorway and took everything in, his gaze scanning the room from one side to the other, then he eased me down onto the bed.

"Last time. Are you sure about this?" he asked.

"I've never wanted anything more."

Badger removed his cut and tossed it onto a nearby chair, then grabbed the back of his black tee and pulled it over his head. I'd always thought guys were sexy when they did that. I'd tried it once and gotten tangled up in my shirt. I licked my lips as he kicked off his boots, removed his socks, and reached for the buckle on his belt. He hesitated only a moment before unbuckling it, then he unfastened his jeans and shoved them down his legs. And holy fuck! He went commando.

"I normally clean things up a little down there," he said, waving a hand toward his cock. "Haven't exactly had access to trimmers and I wasn't about to use a cheap prison-issued razor anywhere near my dick."

I didn't care. I thought he was beautiful, but he probably wouldn't care for that word. Badger kicked his clothes away and stalked toward me. He had that swagger that screamed he knew how to please a woman, and he damn well knew it. My body was still buzzing from the orgasm he gave me in the living room, and I had a feeling it would be twice as incredible when his cock was inside me.

"Stand up, sweet girl," he said, crooking a finger at me.

I rose to my feet and stared into his eyes as he slid the flannel shirt down my arms, and I stood in front of him, completely bare, and extremely turned-on. If he didn't do something soon, I worried I'd combust.

Chapter Three

Badger

Adalia looked like a goddess, her honey-colored hair curling down her back, and those big blue eyes looking at me with complete trust and more than a little desire. Her gaze dropped to my cock, and she sucked in a breath. Yeah, I was big and got that reaction from a lot of women. None of them had ever mattered, though, and Adalia did. I didn't know if the size of my cock scared her or turned her on, and if she asked me to leave I'd get dressed and walk away.

"Will it fit?" she asked in a near whisper.

I bit my lip so I wouldn't laugh. "It will fit, sweet girl. Promise."

Adalia backed up and then lay across the bed, her thighs parted in invitation, and fuck if I wasn't going to take her up on that offer. I crawled up the bed toward her, kissing her soft skin along the way. My weight settled over her, and my cock brushed against her wet pussy, making me go completely still.

"Fuck. Condom," I said, closing my eyes. The two condoms in my wallet were ten years old, and I damn sure knew better than to use them. It would be risky as hell.

"Bedside drawer," she said.

I wasn't sure I liked the fact she brought men back here often enough to keep condoms stocked. The way she'd talked before, I'd thought maybe she didn't really date that much. But only sexually active women kept condoms on hand. At least, I couldn't think of another reason for her to have them. I reached over and opened the drawer, pulling out a strip of three condoms.

"I stole them from the clubhouse earlier when no one was looking," she said. "Are they the right kind?"

I looked at the packaging and grinned. Yeah, she'd gotten magnums. And I liked knowing that she hadn't just had these lying around. "You did good, baby."

I ripped open a package and rolled the condom down my shaft before tossing the other two onto the nightstand. I glanced at the framed picture there and got even harder knowing that she'd wanted to keep me close. I just hoped that being with me tonight lived up to her every fantasy.

"Wrap your legs around my waist, baby."

She hooked her calves around my hips and I felt her ankles cross over my ass. I braced my weight so I wouldn't crush her, then lined up my cock with that pretty pussy of hers and eased inside. I took it slow, giving her time to adjust. As tight as she was, I worried I might hurt her. Her body stretched and welcomed me in, and soon I was balls-deep. Christ, but I couldn't remember ever feeling anything like it.

It took every ounce of control I had not to just pound into her. It was almost like she'd been made just for me, the way she fit me so perfectly. I thrust in and out, slow and steady, trying to take my time and make sure she enjoyed it. Her nails bit into my shoulders and her body started to flush, a rosy tint starting at her breasts and creeping up her neck.

"Damn, sweetheart. Already?"

She whimpered and bit that lip, looking all kinds of sexy. I braced my weight on my knees and one hand, then reached between us to rub her little clit. I could tell she was already close, but I wanted to send her flying. I took her harder, deeper. Her legs trembled around my waist so I pressed a little tighter on her clit, and then she was screaming out my name. My real fucking name.

"Colton!"

Fuck. Just hearing my name on her lips, and her pussy squeezing me just right, was enough to make me come. I didn't stop thrusting until every drop of cum had been wrung from my balls. As much as I wanted to collapse on top of her, I grabbed the condom and pulled out before flopping onto my side. I pressed a kiss to her cheek, then got up to deal with the condom. In the hall bathroom, I tied off the latex and tossed it into the trash, cleaned myself off, and went back to the tempting woman lying in bed.

I pulled the covers down, then we crawled underneath the sheet and quilt. Adalia curled against me, her head resting on my shoulder. I felt... content. Satisfied. It should have scared the shit out of me, but honestly, I was too fucking tired to worry about it too much. I hadn't had a good night's sleep in ten years. As much as I hated to be the guy who fucked, then fell asleep, I could already feel my eyes getting heavy.

"Thank you," she whispered as she snuggled closer. "Will you stay?"

"I'll stay," I told her. Besides, there were still two condoms left.

We both fell asleep for a few hours, but I woke before the sun was rising. Adalia looked so damn young as I studied her features. I knew she was only twenty-three, and at thirty-eight I felt fucking ancient in comparison. Hell, two more weeks and I'd be thirty-nine. I knew that whatever this was between us couldn't last, but I was going to enjoy it while I could. I slid down the bed and crawled between her thighs, teasing her awake with my tongue. It didn't take much to get her nice and wet again. I flicked my tongue against her clit, pushing her thighs wider apart. Her cream coated my tongue as she came, and it was the sweetest thing I'd tasted in a long damn time.

She blinked at me with sleepy eyes and a soft smile curving her lips, then I rolled her onto her stomach and lifted her hips. Nudging her thighs wider, I watched as her pussy opened and beckoned me closer. I quickly rolled on another condom, then gripped her hips and plunged deep. Adalia cried out, but pushed back against me.

"Hold on tight, sweet girl."

I fucked her fast, hard, and deep, giving her everything I had. I felt completely out of control, and watching my dick disappear inside her, only to pull out covered in her cream was enough to make me want to rip off the condom and take her bare. I knew she'd feel like fucking heaven wrapped around my dick without any barriers, and I had this insane urge to fill her with my cum. I wanted to watch it leak out of her and coat her thighs, wanted my scent on her for hours. I'd been tested at the prison a few days before my release and knew I was clean, since I hadn't fucked anyone after that test, but I didn't know if she was on birth control. Taking a chance like that was too damn risky. I was nowhere near daddy material, and probably never would be.

"I can't think of anything I like more than being inside you."

"You feel so good," she said, moaning as I thrust a little harder. "Don't stop. Please don't stop."

Yeah, like that was going to happen. I fucked her until she came, crying out my name again, and then I let loose. I took her like a man possessed, pounding into her, until I shot my load into the condom. Panting for breath, I stayed buried inside her for a moment, wanting to stay connected just a little bit longer.

When I finally pulled out, Adalia collapsed onto the bed and groaned. I swatted her ass before I went to dispose of the condom and clean up. She was already curled up and asleep again when I got back to the bedroom. I wrapped my body around hers and dozed off again. The next time my eyes opened, the sun was shining through the windows. I didn't know what time it was, but I knew I couldn't stay. Not without getting caught. I'd ridden my bike to her house, and it was parked in the driveway for anyone to see. Even if the guys had stayed up all night partying, there was a chance someone would ride past her house and see the bike there.

I wasn't going to slip away while she was sleeping, though. I'd done that before, but Adalia was different. She deserved more than a hard fuck and me vanishing without a word. I smoothed her hair back from her face and marveled at how damn beautiful she was. I knew one day she'd settle down with some nice law-abiding guy, someone who could give her a better life than an ex-con like me. I didn't like the thought of her being in another man's arms, but I knew it would happen sooner or later. Guys like me didn't end up with women like her.

I kissed her until she woke up and gave me a sleepy smile.

"I should shower and get out of here," I said. "It would be pretty bad if your dad showed up and I was still here, especially naked in your bed. Or balls-deep in your pussy."

"Can I join you? I've never showered with anyone before."

Oh, fucking hell. How could I say no to that? "Sure, baby."

She crawled out of the bed, and as I stood up to follow her, I was wishing we had a lot more condoms. Watching her ass as she sauntered down the hall was torture. I hadn't had a chance to do half the things I wanted, but sticking around wasn't a good idea. My ass needed to be as far from her as possible, as fast as possible. The way she'd opened up to me, been so damn honest, it wasn't just her dad I was worried about. If I stayed with Adalia much longer, she might think this was more than just one night. I didn't do relationships. Never had and never would.

Adalia started the shower, and when steam began to billow out of the stall, she stepped under the spray, reaching out to grab my hand and drag me in behind her. I shut the door and watched as the water cascaded down her body, dripping from her pretty pink nipples, and sliding down the curve of her belly. How anyone so damn sweet could be equally seductive was a puzzle, but Adalia pulled it off. She was like this adorable, blonde angel until you got her behind closed doors. The way she'd come apart in my arms would be a memory I cherished the rest of my life. I'd never seen anything so beautiful before, and I doubted I ever would again.

I reached for her shower gel, the honeysuckle scent I'd smelled last night wafting from the bottle as I popped open the lid and squirted a liberal amount onto my palm. Her eyes darkened, and she did that lip biting thing that drove me nuts as I rubbed my hands together, then reached for her. Her skin was soft, and I tried to memorize every curve as I washed her. Adalia pressed her breasts against my palms as I soaped them, my thumbs circling her nipples. She was so fucking responsive that even a monk would have been tempted.

I helped Adalia rinse, and before I could wash myself, she was getting a handful of honeysuckle shower gel and rubbing it across my chest. Fuck. The light touch of her hands on my body was enough to make me hard as granite. When her small hand gripped my cock, I couldn't hold back. I thrust against her palm and claimed her lips in a kiss guaranteed to make her toes curl. It had been a long fucking time since a woman had made me come in their hand, but if anyone could do it, it was Adalia. Even before I'd gone to prison, I'd never gotten off this easy. I could feel my balls drawing up and knew I was going to blow at any moment.

I reached between her legs, stroking my fingers against her pussy and opening her up. I thrust them deep and curled them a little as I pulled back, then thrust inside her again. She whimpered against my lips as I teased her clit, wanting to make her come.

"I want you," she murmured against my lips. "Please, Colton."

Every time she said my name, it did something to me. No one used the name Colton anymore, except for the judge who had sentenced me to jail. But having a woman say it, especially during a passionate moment, was a unique experience. I'd been called Badger for so fucking long, I didn't know if anyone even remembered my name. Except Adalia.

I gripped her waist and lowered her onto my cock. Pressing her against the tiled wall, I took her hard and deep, not holding anything back. My mind was clouded with lust as I pounded into her sweet pussy. She came, squeezing my dick so good I nearly saw stars, but I didn't stop, didn't slow down. I was too far gone to think rationally, and it wasn't until the first splash of cum slicked her channel that I realized I'd just taken her bare. My body shuddered as I thrust deep one last time, staying buried inside her as my cock twitched in the aftermath of the strongest release I'd ever had.

Adalia's fingers played with the hair on the back of my head as she pressed kisses to my chest, shoulders, and neck. All my good intentions, and my sense of self-preservation, went out the window. There was no way I could stay away from her now. I'd never come inside a woman before, not without a condom between us. Maybe it was the fact we were skin on skin that made me feel closer to her, maybe it was because I'd saved her all those years ago. Or maybe it was just because Adalia was the sweetest, most passionate, amazing woman I'd ever met.

My gaze clashed with hers, and the emotion I saw there, the… love… it staggered me. No one had ever given a shit about me, not really. My brothers had my back, but no one had ever loved me. Not even my parents. No, especially not my parents. She hadn't said the word, but she didn't have to. Adalia was an open book, her eyes showing everything she was thinking and feeling. I felt the walls around my heart crack a little, and for the first time in my life, I wanted to let someone in. I wanted to let *her* in.

"We need to clean up again," she said, a soft smile curving her lips.

"Then I'm taking you for breakfast."

"Or I could make something for us here. You've only been out one night, and I doubt you stopped to check your bank account."

I smiled and kissed her softly, my lips barely brushing against hers. "Worried about the state of my account?"

"I just don't think you should spend money if you don't have to. Besides, you'll love my omelets."

"All right, pretty girl. You make breakfast, and I'll look into a few things while you cook. I need to do some shopping later. None of my clothes are going to fit right anymore."

"Is that why you weren't wearing underwear?" she asked, her eyebrow arched.

"Yeah. That and the elastic was shot after rotting for the last ten years."

I hesitated, knowing I should mention the fact I'd just come inside her without a condom. She hadn't stopped me, but that didn't mean anything. With any other woman, I'd be freaking the hell out right now. For some reason, I liked the idea of my cum being inside Adalia. Hell, just thinking about it was making me hard again, but I didn't want her to be sore. I hadn't been gentle any of the times I'd taken her, and I was far from being a small man.

"I didn't use a condom," I said.

She blinked at me but didn't seem bothered by the fact. I eased out of her body and braced her with my hands until I knew she was steady on her feet.

"I'm clean," I said, in case she was wondering. "Got tested at the prison."

"We should talk, but not in the shower. Let's clean up, get dressed, and we can talk about some stuff after I make breakfast."

My breath froze in my lungs at the serious expression on her face. Was going she going to tell me that she had an STD? As tight as she'd been, I didn't think she had sex all that often, but if she was carrying something, that might explain it. She seemed like the type who would have said something before we had sex the first time, though.

We quickly washed and dressed, and as she made omelets in the kitchen, I made a few phone calls. It seemed the club had been taking care of me while I was away, and while I wasn't overly rich, I wouldn't have to worry about money for a few months at least. Maybe longer. The club accountant had been making deposits into both my account and my commissary over the past ten years. But I was a little confused, because the commissary deposits didn't match up. Yeah, the first years the amounts deposited and what I'd received were the same, but about seven years ago, I started receiving a few hundred more than what the club had given me. At the time, I just thought the club had upped the amount they were putting in there, but it didn't look like that's what happened. So where the hell had that money come from?

Adalia was humming as she cooked, and when she placed a plate in front of me, my mouth watered. The biggest fucking omelet I'd ever seen took up the entire dish. I could see chunks of ham, onion, green peppers, and it was smothered in shredded cheese and sour cream. She set a container of salsa on the table, and I poured a little over my food.

"Eat up," she said as she turned back to the stove.

A few minutes later, she joined me with a smaller version of the omelet she'd given me. I hadn't touched mine yet, wanting to do the polite thing and wait for her. Didn't seem right that she was cooking for us and all I'd done was sit on my ass. The least I could do was not eat until hers was finished.

"Oh!" She popped up and ran to the fridge, returning a minute later with a carton of orange juice. Then she pulled two glasses out of the cabinet near the sink and poured us each a glass before returning the juice to the fridge.

"Talked to the bank," I said between bites.

"How bad is it?"

"It's actually pretty good. The club has been putting money into my account the last ten years. Not a ton, since I wasn't here to help with any jobs, but enough to keep my account open and buy me a few months to figure things out. Maybe more than a few."

She smiled. "Well, that's good news. But isn't it part of your parole agreement that you need to find employment?"

"Yeah. I'll ask Griz about the open mechanic position and see what he says. Even if I just work part-time, I think my parole officer will be happy. I need to talk to Griz anyway. My commissary numbers don't match up to what the club was putting into the account."

Her cheeks flushed. "That's not necessary."

I paused, my fork halfway to my mouth. "Why?"

"I put money into your account," she said. "May knew I wanted to do something for you, so she let me get a job when I was sixteen. I didn't really need money for anything back then, so I gave it to Mom and asked her to put it into your account."

"Jesus, Adalia. Why the hell did you do that?" I asked, putting my fork down.

"I wanted to do something nice for you," she said softly. "If it weren't for you, I wouldn't still be here. I can never repay you for what you've done for me."

I closed my eyes and slowly opened them again. She looked nervous, but as I held her gaze, it told me she didn't regret it even a little. I had no doubt if she could do it all over again, she'd do the same damn thing.

"Thank you," I said.

The tension eased from her shoulders and the smile she gave me was damn near blinding. I'd never been good at accepting handouts, but I knew she'd been trying to help. And the funds had come in handy. Little did she realize that the things I'd purchased with most of that money had allowed me to make a few bargains inside, the kind that kept me alive. If she'd wanted to repay me, her account was paid in full. Not that she'd ever owed me shit.

She toyed with her food, and I watched as the joy slipped from her face. "We still need to talk. About what happened in the shower."

"Whatever it is, just lay it on me."

"When I was raped, I suffered for months afterward from pain in my pelvis. The doctors had said that was common for someone in my situation and dismissed it. But it continued for over a year. I didn't get to live with May and Griz until almost exactly a year after the... incident. Mom took me to the doctor and demanded that they check me thoroughly. It turns out, I have endometriosis."

"I have no idea what that is," I said, my hands clenching under the table at the thought of her hurting for so long after what that asshole had done. It made me wish I could bring him back to life and kill him all over again. Slower this time. And her foster family was next on my list, for letting her suffer all that time.

"I could give you the version with medical jargon that I don't understand, but simply put, when I have a period, it's more painful and heavier than it should be. And it can cause infertility. I'm not saying that I can never get pregnant, because there is a chance, but it's harder for me to conceive than the average woman." She fidgeted in her seat. "So, if you're worried about me getting pregnant because of what happened in the shower, it isn't likely to happen."

I didn't know what to say. I hated that she might never get to have a baby, but at the same time, I knew I wasn't ready for fatherhood. Part of me was grateful that it wasn't likely my slip-up in the shower would result in pregnancy. And yet... I couldn't deny a small part was disappointed. How fucked-up was that? If anyone should never be a dad, it was me. I was a longtime offender and more than likely would end up back in prison before my parole was up. That was the last thing Adalia needed to deal with.

"You know this thing between us can't go anywhere," I said. "I'm not the kind of man you need in your life. You deserve better. For whatever reason, you want me, and I'm having a hard time walking away."

"Then don't," she said. "Stay with me. Unless you think I can't give you what you need."

"What I need?" I gave a humorless laugh.

"I know you're used to more experienced women." Her cheeks flushed. "There's something else you should know. I --"

There was a pounding on the front door and I stood quickly, nearly knocking over my chair. Either Papa Bear was angry and was going to rip me a new one for being in his daughter's house, or someone else wasn't too pleased that I was here. Had that been what she was about to confess? Had Adalia been seeing someone? I'd fucked women who belonged to someone before, but never a brother's girl. And I didn't like the thought I might have done that now.

Adalia stood and went to the front door. I followed, hanging back a little. I casually leaned against the doorframe a few feet away from the front door. Adalia swung it open, and a young guy I didn't recognize stood on the other side. He wore a Devil's Fury cut, and judging by his age, he'd likely been voted in while I was in prison. His cut said he was called Twister.

"What the fuck is a bike doing in your driveway?" Twister demanded, pushing his way inside Adalia's home. He froze when he saw me.

"Twister, you shouldn't be here," Adalia said, shutting the door and facing him with her arms folded. "I'm not twelve. If I want to have someone over, I'm allowed."

Twister looked from me to Adalia. "What the fuck, Adalia? You won't go out with me unless your parents make you, but this guy gets out of prison and you immediately spread your legs for him?"

I took two steps toward the little prick, pulled back my fist, and knocked his ass to the floor. He rubbed his jaw, which was already turning red and would probably bruise. Fury flashed in his eyes, but I didn't give a shit. No one was going to talk to Adalia like that, not when I was around. Yeah, I'd fucked her, but that wasn't his business.

"Watch your mouth, boy," I warned. "You treat her with respect."

"Is that what you did? Treat her with respect? Or did you fuck her like she was a common whore?"

I growled and advanced on the little asshole, lifting him up by the front of his shirt. I plowed my fist into his face a few more times. A small hand landed on my arm and looked over my shoulder at Adalia.

"He's one of your brothers. You can't fight him over me," she said.

"I'm not going to stand here and listen to him insult you. He called you a fucking whore. I'm supposed to let that go?"

"I might be Griz's adopted daughter, but I'm not an old lady. I don't belong to anyone, Badger. If anyone is going to defend me, it should be Griz."

I released the ass who had insulted her and gave her my full attention. My knuckles were smeared with blood, so I didn't reach for her. I didn't know what had made her say such a thing. Being the Pres's daughter held more weight than being an old lady. Or was it just that she didn't want me defending her? Knowing I wasn't worthy of her, and her thinking that were two different things. It hurt like fuck that she might feel that way.

Without a word, I pulled open the door and stepped out onto the porch. I left her standing there, left the kid bleeding, and I got on my bike. The engine road to life and without sparing either of them a glance, my tires spit gravel as I tore out of the driveway and down the road. I didn't stop until I got to the gates, and once they were opened, I hit the main road that led into town. If I didn't have to report to my parole officer in a few hours, I might have kept going. The open road called to me. Despite the blue sky above me, I was still in chains. The air was just fresher in my current prison.

Chapter Four

Adalia

Twister was furious. Blood dripped from the corner of his mouth and was smeared across his teeth. His jaw and cheek were already bruising, but it was the fury in his eyes that made me keep my distance. I'd never been afraid of the Devil's Fury members, not once. Not until now. I could tell that he hated me, blamed me for the beating he'd just received. My heart pounded in my chest, and I wished like hell that Badger was still here. I didn't understand why he'd left me.

"I've asked you repeatedly over the years to give me a chance," Twister said. "Every single time you shot me down, claiming you weren't ready to be in a relationship, but it was all bullshit. You just didn't want to be with me."

"I didn't want to hurt your feelings," I said softly, taking a step back. "I like you, Twister, just not like that."

"But you like him like that? You like him enough to spread your legs for him?" Twister sneered and advanced on me. "Well enough to be his little whore?"

"You don't mean that," I said, backing up another step. "We've been friends for years. I like being your friend, Twister. You're like a brother to me."

He laughed, the sound cold and brittle, and I knew in that moment I was in trouble. No one knew he was here, except Badger. I didn't feel very safe, and the crazy look in Twister's eyes told me I had reason to worry. He was a biker, an outlaw, and I didn't know what he was capable of. I never would have thought anyone in Devil's Fury would hurt me, but I wasn't so certain right now.

"Brother?" He sneered at me. "A brother doesn't want to fuck his sister."

The door still stood open. Would I make it if I ran? How far would I get before he caught me, and would I be even worse off then? I'd fought that night in the alley, and I knew I'd fight now if he attacked me. He was so much bigger than me, I doubted I would win, but I had to try. I darted to the right and ran for the front yard, leaping off the porch steps. Our homes were spaced enough that even if I screamed, there was no guarantee someone would come for me.

I heard his roar of fury behind me, then the pounding of his boots. I pushed myself harder and screamed for Scorpion, hoping he was home. I was close to his house, nearly to his yard, when Twister slammed into me from behind. I hit the ground, my chin slamming into the pavement of the road that ran through the compound. Twister flipped me over, then backhanded me, pain exploding through my cheek and eye. I cried out and beat against Twister with both fists. Then suddenly, he was gone, and I heard a roar of fury.

Tears blurred my vision as I struggled to sit up. Scorpion was trying to finish the job Badger started, his fists landing on Twister blow after blow. When there was no fight left in Twister, Scorpion staggered back, his breath sawing in and out of his lungs. He took a step back, then lurched forward and nailed Twister in the ribs with his booted foot. I winced, swearing I heard them crack.

Two more Devil's Fury men came to see what was happening. There was a buzzing in my ears and I couldn't make out what anyone was saying. Someone lifted me into their arms and I tried to focus. Everything started spinning and I knew I was about to be sick. Struggling, whoever held me finally set me on my feet, and I dropped to my knees, losing what little of my breakfast I'd managed to eat. I felt a hand rubbing my back, and that small bit of kindness was enough to make me break. I admit it, I ugly cried.

"Come on, honey," Scorpion said, lifting me into his arms again. As his woodsy scent surrounded me, I started to calm a little. He was like an uncle to me, had always been there when I needed someone, and this time wasn't any different.

He carried me into his house and eased me down onto his battered leather couch. His flavor of the month, Gina, handed me an ice pack. I pressed it to my cheek and wondered what would happen to Twister. He'd attacked me, and I knew he'd pay the price. The beating he'd received was nothing compared to what my dad would do to him once he found out.

It didn't take long for Griz to arrive, and he looked beyond pissed once he saw my face. The biggest badass I'd ever met knelt at my feet, and gently checked my injuries, before cursing so long and loud I wondered if he was inventing some of those words. When he stopped, he sat beside me, taking my hand in his.

"Twister will be dealt with," my dad promised. "What I want to know is where is Badger? I thought he was with you."

"You knew?" I asked.

He smiled a little. "Yeah, I knew. Anyone who passed your house last night or early this morning knew he was there. Did he leave before or after Twister got there?"

"After," I said. "Twister said some things, some horrible things. And then Badger started beating him."

My dad frowned, his brow furrowing. "And he just left you there with Twister?"

"I made him stop," I said softly. "I told him to stop hitting Twister. I didn't realize what would happen, that Twister wasn't the man I thought he was. I didn't understand when he ran off, but I think... I think Badger believed I was choosing Twister over him. He took off without saying a word."

My dad and Scorpion shared a look. Scorpion nodded and headed for the front door. A moment later, I heard his bike start up. It always amazed me when my dad could do that, talk to someone without using his voice. When I'd first witnessed him doing that, I'd asked Mom if he and the Devil's Fury could read minds. She'd been amused.

"I'm taking you to the doctor," Dad said. "Your chin is still bleeding, and I want to make sure that asshole didn't fracture your cheekbone."

"I'll be fine," I assured him.

"No arguments, Adalia."

He led me outside, and we walked the short distance to his house. When I'd come to live with him and May, he'd bought an SUV. Even when I got older, and after May died, he'd kept it. Dad opened the passenger door and helped me inside, making sure I'd buckled up before he shut the door. The ride to Dr. Larkin's office was short, and the minute we stepped inside, a nurse led me into the back. I'd always wondered why we never had to wait like everyone else, and as I'd gotten older, I'd come to realize that Dad paid Dr. Larkin to always be available to the club.

"I hope the other guy looks worse," Dr. Larkin said as he checked me over.

"It was Twister," I said.

Dr. Larkin shook his head sadly. "I'm sorry to hear that, Adalia. I know you considered him a friend."

He pressed on my cheek and I cried out. Tears gathered in my eyes again, but I blinked them back. He also used a light to check my eyes.

"Not broken, but it's going to look nasty for a while. You don't need stitches in your chin. It's going to be sore, and will scab over. Don't pick at it. Just keep some triple antibiotic on it and make sure it stays clean. I think you have a slight concussion. The concussion should get better in the next few days, but you could feel the effects for a few months."

He pulled a prescription pad from his pocket, then stopped.

"Any chance you could be pregnant?" he asked. "I know you have endometriosis, but is it at all possible?"

I started to say no, then thought about the shower this morning with Badger.

"Maybe? It's too soon to know," I said. "I had unprotected sex this morning. It wasn't planned."

Dr. Larkin studied me, and I knew he wondered why after all this time I'd chosen to have sex, and not use a condom. We'd talked in the past about birth control, and he knew I hadn't been seeing anyone.

"I heard Badger came home," he said after a few minutes. "Be careful, Adalia. He's not the kind of man to give you a happily ever after."

I didn't say anything, not knowing how to respond. Did I want Badger to fall in love with me? Of course. Did I think he actually would? Not really. A man had never loved me, not the romantic kind of love, and I didn't think anyone ever would. My past had tainted me, and if that wasn't bad enough, there was my endometriosis and the possibility I would never have children.

"I can't give you pain medication if there's a chance you could be pregnant," Dr. Larkin said. "Ice your cheek for thirty minutes, then remove the ice for an hour. You can ice it again for another half hour after that, if it's still bothering you. Tylenol would be all right in moderation."

"Thank you, Dr. Larkin."

"If the pain worsens over the next few days, you can come back and we'll check it again. Until then, try to get some rest."

Dr. Larkin left, and I went back to the front of the office. My dad was sitting in the waiting room and smiled when he saw me. I didn't know why he was so happy, until I saw him out of the corner of my eye. Badger. He came toward me, slowly, as if he were afraid he'd scare me. When he saw the damage to my face, there was a look of devastation in his eyes. I didn't move, didn't speak. Why was he here? How had he known to come to Dr. Larkin's office?

"If I had known…" He stopped and pulled me into his arms. "I'm so fucking sorry, Adalia. When you told me to stop, I thought you were protecting him. I thought you'd chosen him over me. I never would have left if I thought he would hurt you."

"It's not your fault," I said, wrapping my arms around his waist. "I didn't know he was capable of hurting me. If I didn't know it, then how could you?"

"What do you need from me?" he asked.

"She needs you to man the fuck up," my dad said. "Adalia isn't a one-night stand. If that's all you wanted, you should have stuck with the club pussy we offered you last night."

Badger tightened his arms around me before facing my dad. "I know. I only went to talk to her. I never intended for things to go further."

"But they did," my dad said. "Your bike was seen outside her home all night and early this morning. If you tell me you were talking that entire time, I won't believe you."

"Daddy, leave it alone," I said. "I'm a grown woman."

My dad grumbled and held up his hands, backing off.

"You should ride with your dad," Badger said. "It's probably not a good idea for you to be on the back of a bike right now."

"The doctor said I have a slight concussion."

He reached out and gently touched my cheek, then tipped my head up so he could see my chin. A low growl rumbled out of him and his jaw tightened. Badger looked at my dad and they did that silent communication thing again.

"I'll take you home," Dad said.

"I need to pick up a few things, then I'll come sit with her," Badger said. "I need new clothes and the essentials."

"You won't be able to carry much on your bike," my dad said. "Follow us to Adalia's house. You can write down what you need, and I'll have a Prospect pick it up for you."

Badger looked into my eyes, his touch gentle as he caressed the cheek that wasn't bruised. Slowly, he lowered his head, and kissed me. It was a quick brush of his lips against mine, but it gave me comfort.

"I won't leave your side," he promised. "If there's anything you need, I'll get it for you."

"I'm fine, Badger."

He blamed himself for what happened to me, and I hated that. I didn't want him to act differently around me. Yes, I'd been hurt, but I was still me. I was still the woman he'd been with all night. I might be banged up now, but nothing else had changed about me. I wanted the man back who had made me his in every way last night, the man who had lost control in the shower this morning.

"I'll take you home," my dad said, motioning for me to go out to the car.

"I have one stop to make," Badger said. "I have an appointment with my parole officer."

"David Brant?" my dad asked.

"Yeah."

"I'll call and talk to him," Dad said. "Go straight to Adalia's house. Your appointment will be rescheduled. It's fucking ridiculous they sentenced you to twenty years to begin with, and they damn well know it. Let me handle it."

I felt Badger at my back as I stepped out into the sunlight. His bike was parked next to my dad's SUV. Badger opened the passenger door for me, and I climbed inside, then buckled my seatbelt. After he shut the door, he stared at me through the window a moment before getting onto his bike. I hoped he wasn't going to act like this all the time now. I wasn't broken, and I wouldn't break.

As my dad drove me home, I could hear Badger's bike behind us, and he stayed close until we pulled into my driveway. Dad called the parole officer while we were in the car, but I only half listened. I was far more interested in watching the bike behind us through the side-view mirror. Badger stopped next to the SUV outside my house, and had my door open before I had unfastened my seatbelt. Gently, he reached in and lifted me, holding me close to his chest as he walked up the porch steps. My dad was beside us and pushed open the door to my house, but he didn't enter.

"I'll leave her in your capable hands. Your parole officer said to give him a call later today or tomorrow to reschedule," Dad said. "I'll have a Prospect come by in the next half hour to pick up that list of things you need. If you leave, give me a call. I'll have someone else stay with Adalia. I don't want her left alone for the next twenty-four hours."

Badger nodded, then carried me into the living room. I heard the front door shut as he eased me down onto the couch. When he turned to leave, I reached out and grabbed his hand. We needed to talk, to figure out what was going on in his head. I didn't like the version of Badger that I was seeing right now.

"Talk to me," I said. "What's wrong?"

"What's wrong?" he asked. "I left you. Abandoned you with that asshole. You're hurt because of me."

"Colton, you didn't do this to me."

He snorted. "So now I'm Colton again."

Was that what was bothering him? "I didn't think you'd want me to call you that in front of my dad, or any other Devil's Fury member. I was trying to be respectful and call you by the name you'd earned."

He knelt by the couch and took my hand in his. "Sweet girl, no one has used the name Colton in a really long time. Not until you did last night. I like hearing my name. From you. Anyone else would get their ass kicked. But you're not just anyone."

"I don't want you to treat me differently because of what happened today," I said. "I'm still the woman you took to bed last night."

"Last night, I'd decided I was going to leave, that we would just have the one night together." His hand tightened on mine. "But this morning, I'd decided to stay. I'm not a good man, Adalia, never will be. I don't deserve someone as sweet, or as good as you."

"Shouldn't that be my decision?" I asked. "If I think you're good enough, isn't that what matters?"

"You think I'm some sort of hero. I think I proved otherwise this morning," he said.

"You proved that you're human."

His gaze softened as he looked at me, and I hoped that meant he would give us a chance. He might not think he was good enough, but I knew better. Badger was the only one I'd ever wanted, and being with him last night and this morning had been amazing. I wanted more time with him. Not just the intimate moments, but even sharing a meal together, or curling up on the couch to enjoy a movie.

"I should make that list so it's ready when the Prospect comes by," he said, releasing my hand.

"There's paper in the kitchen. I have a tablet and pen in the drawer next to the fridge. I use them to make my grocery lists."

Badger left the room and I reached for the remote, finding something to watch that I thought might interest the both of us. He came back a few minutes later, set his list down on the coffee table, then disappeared again. When he returned a second time, he had a glass of sweet tea in each hand.

"Thought you might be thirsty," he said. "I didn't see any soda in the fridge."

"I usually drink tea or water during the day. I have juice or coffee for breakfast, and sometimes have a cup of hot tea at night before bed."

"I think I drank enough water the last ten years to last me a lifetime," he said.

I glanced at the list on the table and wondered if I should add some groceries. I didn't know what Badger liked, or what he'd missed while being locked away. If he was going to stay here, I wanted to make sure I had the things he liked or wanted.

"You can add soda to your list, and anything else I don't have that you want to eat or drink. I know you've missed out on a lot the last ten years."

Badger left the room and came back with the pen. He added some more items to his list, and just in time. The odd knock at the door was familiar. I smiled and called out for the Prospect to enter.

Badger glared at me. "You just welcome people into your home without seeing who's there?"

"It's Max. He's the only one who knocks like that."

When Max came to the living room, I could tell that Badger was looking him over and sizing him up. Max wasn't as tall as Badger, nor as broad, but he was far from weak. He'd asked to join the Devil's Fury when he'd been released from the military. An IED had taken the lower part of his left leg and he'd been medically discharged, not that anyone could tell when he was wearing jeans. We'd talked when he'd shown up at the gates that first night, and I'd learned a lot about him. I admired Max, and I knew he was a good guy. A little rough around the edges, but so were the other Devil's Fury.

"Max, this is Badger," I said.

Max held out his hand to shake, and Badger took it. The tense lines around Max's mouth told me Badger was giving him more than a simple handshake. I rolled my eyes, wondering why men felt the need to act so childish.

"Will the two of you stop?" I asked. "Why can't men greet each other without getting into a pissing contest?"

Max smirked, and Badger released his hand.

"I'm not after your girl," Max said. "Anyone who talks to her for five minutes knows she's taken. You're about all she's talked about as long as I've known her."

Badger glanced at me before focusing on Max again. "My girl?"

Max shrugged.

"The list is on the table," I said. "Feel free to make yourself scarce, Max."

He chuckled, grabbed the list, gave me a salute, then walked out.

"The two of you are close?" Badger asked.

"He's a nice guy. He started prospecting here about six months ago. I have no doubt that he'll be patched in. I think Dad already has a name picked out for him."

"That didn't answer my question."

"I consider him a friend," I said. "Max is easy to talk to. I think you'd like him if you gave him a chance."

He stared at me, but I could see he was considering it.

"Would it make a difference if I told you that I've never been romantically interested in Max?" I asked. "I've never once pictured him naked, or wished he was lying in bed with me. I save those thoughts for you."

He smiled a little and sat next to me. "Good to know."

"I thought you might like this movie. It's on Netflix so we can stop and start it if we need to. Did you have Netflix before…"

"No. It was around, but I didn't have it."

"Then you're in for a treat," I said with a smile. "You can watch hundreds of movies or TV shows without having to buy DVDs or pay for cable. I've gotten rather spoiled with all the streaming services around now. I have Netflix, Hulu, and Amazon Prime, so we have tons of choices. Although, I admit I have a slight online shopping addiction so I really have Prime to save on shipping."

"I'm amazed you ever leave the house."

I glanced his way. "I could think of other reasons to stay home."

"Sweet girl, if you think I'm taking advantage of you hours after you were attacked, then you'd be wrong. I might be an asshole, but I'm not that much of one. What you need is rest."

"You're really going to sit here and watch TV with me, and not touch me?" I asked.

"That's the plan."

Great. I wondered what it would take to change his mind. Yes, my face hurt, but surely an orgasm or two would take my mind off the pain. It was a good theory anyway. Now that I'd had a taste of Badger I wanted more. I didn't know how long he'd stay with me, but I was going to enjoy every last minute of our time together. And hoped a lot of that time would be spent in the bedroom, or anywhere else he wanted to get naked.

Chapter Five

Badger

I didn't think much of it the first time Adalia's hand drifted up my thigh. The second time, I began to suspect it wasn't an accident. By the third time, I knew she was trying to cause trouble. How she could possibly want sex after that asshole Twister had hit her face and she'd cut her chin open? She needed to rest, and heal, but it seemed Adalia had something else on her mind. And I was only human. Every brush of her hand against my cock made me harder. Hell, sitting next to her had me semi-hard before she'd started touching me.

I wasn't used to fighting temptation. I'd always been the guy to take whatever I wanted, but I didn't want to treat Adalia like a club slut. And fucking her while she was injured was an asshole thing to do, even if she was asking for it. There were two choices. Either give in and fuck her, or put some space between us. Knowing I needed to do what was best for her, I got up and took a few steps away. She looked confused and a little hurt, her brow furrowed and her mouth tipped down at the corners.

"Colton? What's wrong?" she asked.

"I need to make some calls. I should reschedule my meeting with my parole officer. It's one of the conditions of my release, and not reporting could send me back to prison."

Her gaze softened. "I hadn't thought of that. You know where I keep the cordless phone. If you want some quiet to make your calls, I won't be offended if you sit in the kitchen."

I breathed a little easier, knowing she wasn't mad, even if I hadn't been completely honest with her.

Yeah, I did need to make that call, but the other call was just as important. If I was even going to think about having sex with her, I needed to find out from her doctor whether or not it was safe. Just because she said she was okay didn't mean she really was. I'd had a concussion before and knew the side effects could be a pain in the ass. She might not realize just how badly she needed rest right now, but I did.

My parole officer wasn't as much of a dick as I'd feared he would be. He actually seemed nice and wasn't upset that I was rescheduling. He'd even given me an extra three days to come in, even though my parole agreement stated I needed to meet him today. It made me wonder just how well he knew Griz and what the story was there. I knew the club had people they relied on, like my lawyer, Dr. Larkin, and even a warden at one of the state prisons. Unfortunately for me, it hadn't been the prison I was sent to. Hell, I thought even our town mayor was one of Griz's contacts. Griz had tried to get in good with the local judges, but it hadn't happened, at least not that I knew of. A lot had probably changed over the last ten years.

I hated to call Adalia's doctor behind her back, but I needed to know for sure if I would hurt her if we had sex. I wasn't going to take any risks with her.

"Dr. Larkin's office," a chipper woman said as she answered.

"I need to speak with Dr. Larkin or his head nurse. It's about Adalia."

"Oh, that poor girl. Dr. Larkin is in his office on a break. I'll put you through."

The line clicked and then started ringing again.

"Dr. Larkin," the man answered.

"This is Badger with Devil's Fury. I'm watching over Adalia and I need to know what she can and can't do while she's recovering."

The line was quiet for so long I'd thought he hung up on me.

"She needs to rest, if you can get her to. She can even go to sleep if that's what she wants. For the longest time, it was believed that sleep was bad when you have a concussion, but now we're being told the opposite is true."

I cleared my throat. "She, um, wants to have sex."

"I see." Dr. Larkin cleared his throat. "Well, her head bouncing around wouldn't be a good idea right now. At least not for a few days. She'll likely have headaches off and on over the next few months, maybe some dizziness, and she might be tired more often than usual. If I had to guess, I'd say she has a headache now."

"Should I give her something for it?" I asked.

"A cold compress might help, but if she needs more relief she can have Tylenol. Until we know for certain if she's pregnant, I don't want her to take anything else."

I felt like the floor had fallen out from under me, and I collapsed onto the nearest chair. Pregnant? Adalia had told me she didn't think she could get pregnant. Had she lied?

"Pregnant?" I asked.

"Yes. With her condition, it's not as likely, but it's still a possibility. I don't want to take any chances. If Adalia is pregnant, this could very well be the only baby she ever has, and it might not even make it to term. I've had several patients with endometriosis who tried for years to get pregnant, and none of the babies made it past the first trimester."

Holy hell. My chest felt tight, and the room spun a little. Adalia pregnant, with my kid. I had no doubt she'd be an awesome mom, if she ever had the chance, but just thinking about her carrying my baby made it hard to fucking breathe.

"In a few weeks, we can do a blood test," Dr. Larkin said. "If she skips a period before that, she can come in, but she's never been regular. She might not know when her next one is due."

I pulled the phone away from my ear and stared at it a moment. Was he seriously telling me about Adalia's periods? What the fuck? All I knew about that time of the month was that you threw chocolate at the woman and ran as fast as you could, unless you wanted to be missing a few limbs. The sweetest woman in the world could be a raging bitch when it was that time of the month, and I'd always made myself scarce during those times.

"Thanks, Dr. Larkin," I said. "I'll keep an eye on her."

"If she loses consciousness at any time, seems confused, or has memory problems, or starts vomiting, take her to the ER. Don't wait."

I swallowed hard, hoping none of those things happened to Adalia. I knew brain injuries could be fatal, and I hoped that wasn't the case with the woman I cared about more than I should. I thanked Dr. Larkin again and hung up. There was a knock at the door once more, and this time I recognized it. Before Adalia could call out, I went to answer it. Max stood on the other side, several bags in each of his hands, and a grin on his face.

"I got everything on your list," he said, stepping into the house. "Well, I got all the clothing and stuff. The groceries are being picked up by another Prospect and will be delivered within the hour. Griz called while I was out and needed me to take care of something, so I had to come back sooner than I'd planned."

"Thanks." I reached for the bags, surprised they felt as heavy as they did. Then my eyes narrowed when I saw two of the bags were from the Harley Davidson store. The others were from department stores at the mall. What the hell? I'd figured he'd just go to one of those cheap twenty-four hour places. Should I have been more specific? I wasn't exactly hurting for money, but I didn't need to drop a grand on this shit either.

"Griz said all this stuff was on the club. You saved his daughter, and he said it's the least he could do." Max paused. "I've come to care about Adalia. She's like a little sister to me, and for what it's worth, I'm glad you beat the shit out of that guy. He deserved what he got, and you got a shit deal when they sent you away."

Fuck me. Why the hell did everyone around here act like I was some sort of fucking hero? I was just an asshole ex-con who got into trouble more often than I walked the straight and narrow. There wasn't a fucking thing that was special about me.

"Thanks," I said.

Max nodded and stepped back out onto the porch. "Adalia has my number programmed in her cell. Call me if you need anything. Unless I'm on club business, I'll be here as fast as I can."

Max slapped my shoulder and took off down the steps toward one of the club trucks we used for hauling anything from furniture to some of our more not so legal things. He waved as he pulled out of the driveway and I shut the door, not sure what the hell to do with all the bags I was holding. I'd just needed a few changes of clothes to get me by for right now, and some bathroom shit like shampoo.

Adalia appeared in the doorway. "Was that Max?"

"Yeah, he was just dropping off this stuff. Said someone else would bring the groceries. Your dad is sending him off on some errand."

She nodded. "Want me to help you put that stuff away?"

"Put it away?" I stared at the bags in my hands before looking up at her.

"I was hoping you might want to stay here," she said softly. "With me."

Was she…

"You want me to move in?" I asked.

Adalia's gaze darted off to the side, and she shifted from foot to foot. "If you don't want to, then…"

I dropped the bags and reached for her, pulling her close. Tipping her chin up, I kissed her softly.

"If you want me here, sweet girl, then I'll stay. But the minute I think you'd be better off without me, I'm out of here. I was serious when I said you deserved better than me. I'm not the hero you seem to think I am. I'm just a fucked-up ex-con with a really long rap sheet."

"You're my hero," she said. "And you always will be. Colton, I wouldn't be here if it weren't for you. Stop painting yourself as some villain and accept the fact that other people don't see you that way."

"You don't understand, Adalia. Even when I was a kid, I was all kinds of fucked-up. I've done things you never want to hear about. Dark things. My parents…" I swallowed hard. I always tried not to think about that part of my life.

She reached for some of the bags in my hands. "Let's put your things away, then you can tell me what has you running scared. And don't deny that you are. Something in your past has scared the shit out of you. Maybe talking about it will help. I promise not to judge you."

"All right." My heart ached because I knew she was just telling me what she thought I needed to hear. Once she knew who I'd been, what I'd done, she'd never look at me the same way again. She'd be disgusted by me. No one knew about the shit in my past except our ex-Pres, and he'd taken it with him when he'd left the club to Griz and decided to travel in his last years on earth.

She was quiet while we put my new things away. She cleared out some closet space and two drawers for me to use. It felt so damn domestic, putting my things in that closet next to hers, the new boots Max had bought lined up next to her small, dainty shoes. I stared at the closet for a few minutes, wondering why I wasn't panicking. Anytime a woman had tried to get close in the past, I'd shut that shit down fast, and booted their ass to the curb. Adalia was different, though. I wanted her acceptance, wanted all of her, even if I didn't feel deserving of someone so pure, so sweet.

I sat on the bed, and she eased down next to me, reaching for my hand. She laced our fingers together and stared up at me patiently. When I didn't say anything for a few minutes, she nibbled her lower lip.

"Will it help if I tell you something about me first?" she asked.

I shrugged. I wasn't really sure if that would help, but I did want to know more about her.

"You were my first," she said.

My brow furrowed. "First what?"

"The first man I've ever kissed." Her cheeks flushed. "The first man I've slept with. I might have lost my virginity when I was thirteen, but I haven't been with anyone since then. The only man I've ever wanted was you."

It was hard to breathe as I absorbed her words and what they meant. She'd waited for me, all these years? No one had ever wanted me that much before.

"My birth mother was a rape victim," she said softly. "She signed me over to the state the day I was born. I found one of the nurses who was working that night. My mom never even wanted to hold me, and refused to look at me. If I'd had a baby as a result of what happened to me, I'd never have been able to do that. I would have loved that baby regardless."

My throat tightened and my eyes burned as I stared at her. I hated that so much evil had touched her life, and it sickened me that I would only add to it once she knew who I really was.

"When I was in the system, I thought I had it pretty good. I'd only had three foster families in thirteen years. All of them were kind enough, I suppose, even if they weren't all that loving. But I never knew what it felt like to belong, to be part of a family, until May and Griz adopted me. And I know they did that because of you. They knew you'd want to take care of me."

"They wanted a kid," I said.

"Maybe. But they would have never known I existed if you hadn't been in that alley that night. Because of you, May came to find me. She wanted to check on me and see how I was faring. When she found out my foster family was about to get rid of me, she and Griz asked to adopt me."

"I'm not who you think I am," I said, looking anywhere but at her. "I'm not who anyone in this club thinks I am. I've done things none of them know about, and I've kept it a secret for a reason."

I felt her hand slip into mine and she squeezed lightly. "I won't tell anyone, Colton. Not even my dad. But maybe talking about your past will help you heal. I went to therapy when May and Griz adopted me. And talking to someone about what happened to me helped, more than I'd thought it would."

"My parents weren't good people. They lived in another town, about two hours from here. They were mixed up with some really fucked-up people, and had no problem using me to get what they wanted." I swallowed hard. "When I was fourteen…"

My chest felt like someone was squeezing it tight and I couldn't breathe, couldn't speak. I sometimes still relived those horrors in my mind, but I hadn't put them into words since I'd told the old Pres why I wanted to prospect with the Devil's Fury. He'd listened and hadn't judged, but we'd agreed that it would be best if no one else knew about my past.

"If you can't talk about what happened then, what was your childhood like before you were fourteen?" she asked.

"Got into trouble with the law a lot. In order to escape my parents' house, I often boosted cars. Got caught twice and went to Juvie. I got out the last time when I was fourteen, and my parents decided I owed them something."

I closed my eyes, trying to block the images that battered my mind. The things my parents had made me do before I got the courage to run away, and had ended up here. If the old Pres hadn't taken me in, there's no telling what would have happened to me. I wasn't good for much back then. Mentally and emotionally damaged from being forced into what amounted to prostitution, my father nearly killing me anytime I refused. I didn't want to share that part of myself with Adalia, or anyone else. Shame still burned inside me from those days. I might be a big guy now, but I'd been a small, scrawny kid until I'd hit sixteen. I tried to tell myself that I was defenseless, but a voice always whispered that I should have fought harder, run away sooner.

Maybe that's why I still felt like I'd failed Adalia. Even though I'd killed the man who had raped her, I hadn't gotten there soon enough to stop it from happening. Even after all these years, I was still damaged from what had happened to me, and it was possible that I always would be. I should have gotten help sooner, like she did. Despite what Adalia had been through, she seemed like she was doing well.

"Whatever they did to you, whatever they made you, that isn't who you are," Adalia said. "It doesn't define you. It's a part of your past, and something that happened to you, but it's not... you. If that makes sense," Adalia said. "You have to forgive yourself. What happened wasn't your fault. You were a kid, and those people were supposed to protect you, to love you."

"You don't understand, Adalia."

"You were sexually abused, weren't you?" she asked softly. "That's part of why you reacted so violently when you found me in that alley."

Maybe she understood more than he'd given her credit for.

"Colton, I don't know the details of what happened when you were a kid, and I don't have to. What I do know is that you're a courageous, honorable man. You're loyal to this club, and you saved a young girl when you could have just walked away. Do you think you're the only person who walked past that alley that night? Because you weren't. The other people kept walking, didn't even hesitate when I cried out. But you stopped. You did something. And you paid the ultimate price for your sacrifice. Not just anyone would do that."

I didn't say anything, just processed her words, and took comfort in her soft touch.

"If you're worried the guys would look down on you, if you think they would feel like you're less of a person because of what happened, then you should know that this isn't the same club from ten years ago," Adalia said. "One of your new brothers was a male prostitute before Griz found him, got him cleaned up and off the hard stuff, and let him prospect for the club. His past was probably similar to yours. Parents who didn't give a shit and used him as they saw fit. Dagger is bi-sexual, and no one here cares. He has everyone's back, and that's what matters. One of the current prospects is gay, and the club accepts that without question. They don't give him a hard time because of it."

"For someone who doesn't exactly know what happened to me, you sure know just what to say," I murmured. Yeah, I'd been worried that if my club found out I'd been forced to service men when I was a kid they would sneer at me, think I was garbage. It wouldn't be the first time I'd ever been wrong. I should have opened up to them sooner.

"We've both had darkness in our lives, Colton. Most of this club has, if not all of them. But we're fighters, we're survivors. We're still standing, and we have each other. This is a family, even if it is a bit dysfunctional. It's time to let go of the past, let go of the darkness inside, and learn to be happy."

I smiled a little. "You're awfully smart for someone so young. Are you sure you didn't get a degree in counseling while I was gone? I think you'd be good at it."

Her cheeks flushed at the compliment, and she ducked her head before looking up at me again, a slight smile on her lips.

"You work for Griz as a way to pay him back, don't you?" I asked, everything suddenly becoming very clear. "It wasn't your dream to work in the office at the shop. You feel you owe it to him, to the club."

She shrugged.

"Adalia, you're smart. Way smarter than most guys in this club. You should have gone to college, gotten a degree. Do you think Griz would be happy to know you held yourself back on purpose?"

"No, and you're not going to tell him. I'm content. And as unconventional as it is, he told me that one day the garage would be mine. Although, I think he's honestly hoping some car savvy guy will claim me before that happens because I can run the office well enough, but I know shit about cars."

I chuckled and pulled her into my lap.

She gave me one of those sexy looks with sultry eyes that women seem to be born knowing how to do. Her tongue flicked out and slicked her lower lip, and I knew she was about to try manipulating me. And I was probably going to let her.

"Maybe you could teach me about cars," she said, her voice husky as she wet her lips. "For every car lesson, I could pay you. Any payment you'd like."

She wiggled on my lap, her ass pressing against my hardening cock, and I knew she meant the sexual type of payment. I wasn't certain if I was pissed that she'd do that to herself, or amused that she'd try her feminine wiles on me. We both knew all I had to do was kiss her, touch her, and she'd turn to putty in my hands. I'd be willing to bet that just sitting in my lap was making her wet. Her nipples were showing through her shirt, hard and begging for attention.

The doctor's words of caution were all that kept me from bending her over the kitchen table and fucking her until neither of us could stand. If I wasn't worried about her, I'd pull her jeans down, smack that fine ass of hers, then take her hard and deep. We both needed it, but I could be patient. Her health was more important than dealing with blue balls.

She squirmed again and I could tell she was doing it on purpose, trying to get me to lose control. Such a naughty little minx. When she was better, I'd definitely have to punish her. Just the thought of that was enough to make me even harder. Oh yeah, my hand swatting that fine ass of hers, alternating between making her ass cheeks sting and making her pussy beg to be fucked. I'd have her worked up so good that she'd be begging me to take her.

Christ, I needed to think of something else. I still remembered how fucking good she'd felt on my bare cock as I took her in the shower. We needed to be careful and not slip up like that again, but I didn't like the thought of having to wear a condom again. Now that I'd tasted paradise, I didn't want to go back.

Her legs parted a little and she rubbed herself against me. "Please, Colton. I need you so bad."

"Sweet girl, your doctor said you needed to take it easy. And trust me when I say easy isn't even remotely possible when I'm inside you. All I want to do is pound into that sweet pussy until you feel me for days after."

"I need to come," she begged. "Make it stop hurting."

Fuck me. How the hell was I supposed to deny her when she said that? Of course, the doctor had said sex wasn't a good idea. He hadn't said anything about me giving her pleasure without taking my own.

"Stand up," I told her. "Take off your clothes. All of them."

Her eyes widened and she slowly stood and began stripping off her clothes. When she stood naked in the middle of the kitchen, I spread my legs a little to brace her weight and pulled her down across my thighs. Her legs splayed and I could see how slick she was, my poor angel. Oh yeah, she wanted me, and while I couldn't give her my cock, I could still make it good for her.

I wrapped my arm around her back and she leaned against it, her breasts thrusting upward, just asking for attention. I bent my bent my head and took a rosy tip between my teeth, giving it a gentle nip before sucking on it. Adalia trembled in my arms as I sucked and licked her hard nipple. I reached across her and teased the other side with my fingers, pinching and rolling the rosy peak until she was crying out for more. I almost wished I had a third hand, so I could tease that sweet pussy at the same time. Maybe we should have taken this to the bedroom so I'd have both hands free.

I released her breast and slid my hand down the slope of her belly. I didn't stop until I'd reached that pretty pussy, and used my fingers to open her up. Releasing the nipple still in my mouth, I looked down between her legs and nearly groaned at how fucking beautiful she was. All slick, pink, and swollen. Yeah, my baby needed me, and I was going to make sure she had an orgasm that would satisfy her at least for the rest of the night. Or so I hoped. I really didn't want to push it while she was healing.

I brushed her clit with my thumb, just lightly stroking it. Her eyes were dark with passion as I kept rubbing, each stroke getting a little harder, until she was moaning and trying to fuck my hand. I slipped a finger inside her, but I knew it wouldn't be enough. She'd taken my cock like she was born to it, and a single finger wasn't going to satisfy my hungry girl. Keeping her still was more of a challenge than I'd anticipated, but I gripped her tight as I fucked her, adding a second finger, then a third.

She was getting hotter and wetter with every thrust of my fingers, and I knew she wouldn't last long. Suddenly, the thought of her coming on my hand wasn't enough. I abruptly pulled away and lifted her onto the edge of the table. She gasped, then waited to see what I would do next, her legs still parted, her pussy on display for my viewing pleasure. I could look at her like this all day. I'd be hard as fuck the entire time, but I wouldn't mind looking at her like this for hours.

I kicked the chair out of the way and knelt next to the table, gripping her thighs with my hands. Then I latched onto her pussy with my mouth, my lips pulling on her clit and making her squirm before I thrust my tongue into her tight channel. I wanted her to come, needed her to. While I fucked her with my tongue, I stroked her clit with my fingers, using quick, hard strokes in hope she would come fast. I didn't know how much longer I could torture myself.

I felt her thighs tense a moment before she screamed out my name, her thighs clamping down on my head. I kept thrusting my tongue in and out of her sweet pussy until the last of her orgasm had ebbed and she was left trembling on the table, her breaths coming out more like pants.

"Colton, I..." Her fingers tunneled through my hair and she moaned as I kept pleasuring her with my mouth. I'd thought I'd wanted it over quick, now that I had her cum on my tongue, I wanted her to come again. She lifted her hips, and I kept rubbing her clit with my fingers, kept fucking her with my tongue, and soon enough I was rewarded with a second orgasm from my beautiful angel.

I drew away and wiped her juices off my face.

"I want to do that to you," she said.

Oh hell. "Sweet girl, you're supposed to be resting. I think the doctor wants you to keep your head as still as possible."

"Then hold my head still and fuck my mouth. You can have complete control."

Jesus. Did she have any idea what she was asking? If she knew how fucking turned-on it made me, just to think about gripping her hair and fucking her mouth, shoving my cock down her throat until I came... I shuddered and my cock throbbed in my jeans.

"Not tonight, baby. Soon, but not tonight. I'd lose control and I don't want to hurt you."

She pouted, but didn't argue.

"You should get dressed," I told her, and nearly froze at the evil glint that entered her eyes.

"Or I could stay naked," she said. "And you could get naked. We could lounge on the couch and watch TV together. Naked. And if your cock just happens to slip and end up inside me…"

If she weren't injured, I'd have pulled her off the table and spanked her ass for that one. As it was, all I could do was narrow my eyes and growl at her, which she found funny if her giggle was anything to go by. Maybe I needed to work on being scarier. If one pint-sized female wasn't afraid of me, how was I supposed to strike fear in any assholes who came up against me?

"Clothes, Adalia. Put some on. I'll get us some food while you're doing that."

"Fine." She poked her lower lip out, which should have looked ridiculous on a grown-ass woman, but I just found it endearing. What the fuck was happening to me?

She slid off the table and I quickly moved to the other side of the kitchen, not trusting her to keep her hands to herself. And if she touched me, then I couldn't promise my cock wouldn't end up inside her, just like she wanted. Adalia was going to be trouble, but it was the kind I enjoyed. I smiled as she sashayed out of the room, swishing her ass more than usual, likely in an attempt to get me to change my mind. She was something else. A handful and then some.

Life certainly wouldn't be dull with her around. Maybe I could do this. Lead a mostly legal life, with her at my side… do the committed relationship thing. I'd never been a one-woman kind of man, but then I'd never had a woman like Adalia. She made me want to be a better person. Oh, I was still an outlaw biker, and I always would be. But maybe I could still be part of this club, stay out of trouble for the duration of my parole, and give Adalia what she wanted.

For the first time, I finally wanted to give it a try, see where things went. I wanted that happily ever after women were always reading about. And fuck if that didn't scare the shit out of me.

Chapter Six

Adalia
Three Weeks Later

The first thing I noticed when I opened my eyes was that it was still dark outside, or maybe that was the room-darkening curtains Colton had added when I'd started having daily headaches from my concussion. The second thing I noticed was that Colton wasn't in bed with me anymore. And the third was that I didn't have a headache for the first morning since Twister had slammed me into the pavement.

A smile curved my lips. I knew exactly what that meant. Colton had kept me at arm's-length. Oh, he'd given me orgasms, as long as I held really still, but he hadn't let me touch him in all that time. He had to have blue balls from hell, especially since he got hard every time I was naked, or bent over, or sat too close to him. Pretty much if I breathed in his direction. Poor guy had been suffering, and while I might have enjoyed it a little bit at first, now I just wanted to put him out of his misery. If that meant he fucked my brains out for twenty-four hours, I was okay with that.

I got out of bed and padded over to the window, pulling the curtain back, then frowned when I realized it really was dark out there. I fumbled for my cell phone on the nightstand and saw it was only three in the morning. So where was Colton? I checked each room of the house, and found him in the kitchen, a cup of coffee clutched in his hand as he stared out the window over the sink. The lights were off, and his expression was pensive at best, from what little I could see in the moonlight. I didn't know what made him leave the bed, unless he'd had a nightmare. Ever since our discussion about his past, he'd woken during the night several times, reliving those moments. I hated it, hated that I'd pushed him. I'd thought talking would make it better, but maybe it had only made things worse for him.

"Colton, is everything okay?" I asked.

He didn't acknowledge me, just took another swallow of coffee. It wasn't like him to ignore me, and my stomach clenched as I wondered what that meant. I moved closer and pulled out the chair next to him, sitting down and reaching for his hand. He didn't pull away, which was nice. I hadn't been certain, not with his present expression and quietness. It unsettled me, seeing him like this, and I didn't know how to fix it. If he wouldn't talk to me, how could I find out what was wrong?

"Bad night?" I asked, trying again to draw him out.

"Your appointment is this morning," he said after a few more minutes of silence.

"And it's going to go great. No more headache!"

He took another swallow of coffee, then pushed the mug aside.

"That's not what you're worried about, is it?" I asked.

"I've been sitting here the last two hours thinking. The last three weeks have been the best of my life. Griz hired me at the garage just like you said he would, I get to come home to you every night and see you at work when you venture out of the office. I don't remember a time before this I was ever happy. Guess I'm just waiting on something to come along and trash everything."

"And you think my appointment will do that?" I asked. I didn't understand, unless… "Are you worried I might be pregnant? I know I haven't started yet, but I told you that doesn't mean anything. I'm late all the time."

"The thought of you being pregnant scared me a few weeks ago. Now, I'm not so much worried about screwing up my kid's life, but more that you'll decide I'll be a shit dad and ask me to leave. You wouldn't be wrong. I never had a good example of what a dad should be like."

I squeezed his hand and moved my chair closer. "Colton, if I'm pregnant, and that's a really huge *if*, then I know you're going to be an amazing dad. You might not see it, but you're kind and caring. You've watched over me since I got hurt without once thinking about yourself."

His lips twitched. "Oh, I thought about sex. Thought about your lips wrapped around my cock, thought about pounding into that sweet pussy of yours. But I didn't want to make your headaches worse."

"I don't have a headache now," I said, leaning in closer. "And we still have five hours until I need to see Dr. Larkin. I'm sure we could find a way to pass the time."

"You should rest."

"All right." Obviously, my sexy biker was going to play hard to get. So I'd see just how hard I could make him.

I slowly stood and took a step back. His gaze was focused on me as I began stripping out of the tank I'd slept in, then shimmied out of the matching shorts. My fingers dipped under the waistband of my panties and I worked them down my hips, then let them fall to the floor. Colton didn't move, but every line of his body was tense. I reached up to cup my breasts, pulling at my nipples in what I hoped was a sexy come-and-get-me kind of way. I'd never tried to seduce someone before and had no idea if I was doing it right.

I let my hands drift down my belly and one slipped between my legs. I was already wet, and I parted my thighs to make sure he could see what I was doing. Spreading the lips of my pussy, I felt the cool air coast over my heated skin. He made a low, growling sound and his hands clenched into fists. I stroked my clit, slowly. My gaze was locked on Colton, waiting to see if that iron control of his would snap.

"Feels good," I murmured. "Know what would feel better? Your cock."

I could have sworn I heard him grinding his teeth, and still he didn't move. I didn't know what would make him break, but I had an idea. Easing down onto the chair, I spread my legs wide and leaned back so that my breasts thrust upward. I toyed with my pussy with one hand, while I cupped my breast with the other. I teased my nipple and my clit at the same time, letting my eyes slide halfway closed. I rubbed, pinched, and flicked as my pleasure grew. Soon I was coming, my hips lifting off the chair. My eyes opened all the way when I saw Colton reach for the button on his jeans as he slid his chair back a bit. He eased the zipper down and worked his jeans down a little ways, until he could pull out his cock.

"Come here," he said, crooking a finger at me.

My heart raced in anticipation as I stood on trembling legs and approached him. He pointed to the floor and I dropped to my knees. Colton reached out and threaded his fingers through my hair, then dragged me closer to his cock.

"Open," he demanded.

I whimpered and licked my lips before opening wide. He used his grip on my hair to control my movements, dragging my lips down his hard shaft. He didn't stop until I'd taken every inch, my eyes watering as I fought not to choke. Then he pulled me away, only to drag me back down again. His pre-cum coated my tongue and he groaned, his cock flexing in my mouth. It was almost like he lost control at that moment. His grip tightened, and he began fucking my mouth, deep strokes that I fought to breathe through.

More pre-cum coated my mouth and he began grunting with every thrust. Soon, he erupted, and I struggled to swallow all of his release. He didn't stop thrusting into my mouth, not even after he'd stopped coming. Colton was semi-hard, but he seemed determined to keep fucking my mouth. Not that I minded. I hadn't been expecting this side of him, and I certainly hadn't been expecting him to flood my mouth with cum. His cock hardened even more, and then he pulled me away.

"Stand up and bend over the table," he said.

I stood and turned to face the kitchen table. There was barely any room since Colton hadn't moved his chair much. I knew my ass had to be in his face, and my cheeks flushed at the thought. I felt his hands as they slid up the backs of my thighs, then spread my ass cheeks.

"You've been very naughty," he said. "Lean forward and press your breasts to the table. And don't fucking move."

I heard the chair scrape back farther, then his footsteps as he left the room. He wasn't really going to leave me like this, was he? My hands tensed against the table, but I slowly relaxed when I heard him returning. I heard the rustle of material and wondered if he was removing his jeans, then there was the sound of something opening. What the hell was he doing?

"Reach back and spread those ass cheeks for me," he said. "And hold them open."

My heart took off at a gallop. He wasn't going to… Was he? I did as he commanded, finding it hard to breathe as I waited to see what he would do next. I squeaked and flinched as cool liquid dropped in the crack of my ass. Colton used his finger to rub the lube around my tight hole, then eased the tip of his finger inside me. I gasped and froze. He'd mentioned before how much he liked my ass, but he'd never tried anything back there.

"Relax and breathe, sweet girl," he said.

"Is this the punishment you were talking about?" I asked, feeling breathless as his finger sank farther into me.

He chuckled, a deep, husky sound that sent chills down my spine.

"No. You're going to like this part too much for it to be a punishment."

If I didn't trust him completely, I might have worried what he meant by "this part." Just how many parts were there to what we were doing?

Colton slid a hand up my thigh, then his fingers teased my pussy. As he stroked across my clit, I couldn't hold back the moan that built in my throat. The finger in my ass stroked in and out, then he added a second one. My ass burned, but at the same time, it felt really damn good. Forbidden and naughty, but good. I'd read books where the couple had anal sex, but I'd never thought I'd be in this position.

He added a third finger and stroked my clit faster. I didn't think I could handle much more and I wanted to beg him to let me come. Colton removed the fingers that were in my ass and I heard him open the lube again. More cold wetness, and then I felt his cock pressing against the tight hole.

"Breathe out and let me in, baby," he said, pressing deeper. "So fucking tight."

"Colton." I bit my lip, not sure if I wanted to ask him to stop or keep going. It pinched and my ass still burned from being stretched, but I kind of liked it.

He added even more lube as his cock pulled out, then slowly slid back into me. I heard him set the bottle aside, then he gripped my waist with both hands.

"Hold on, sweet girl."

His thrusts were slow and steady. My clit throbbed and begged for attention, but he hadn't given me permission to move yet. I still held myself open for him, and it made me feel a little dirty, but in a good way. A warmth was starting to spread through me as he took his time.

"Beg me for it, baby."

"B-beg?"

"Beg me to fuck this ass," he said, going still with just the tip of his cock inside me.

My eyes slid shut and I shuddered at his tone.

"Please, Colton. Fuck me."

"Not what I said."

I whimpered and squirmed in his grasp. "I want you to fuck my ass, Colton."

"You want it hard and deep?" he asked, his voice a purr in the darkness.

"Yes."

He growled softly and thrust deep. I cried out as he fucked me, no longer holding back. It was like he was possessed as he pounded into me. I could feel myself getting close, but before I could come, his cock flexed and soon he was filling me with his cum. Colton stopped, his cock buried inside me.

"Now that was your punishment," he said. "Does my baby want to come?"

"Yes," I nearly wailed. It was so unfair. I'd been close, like really close, and then he'd finished without me. He hadn't done that in all the times we'd been together.

"I'll let you come."

Colton reached around me and started rubbing my clit again. I wanted him to do it harder and faster, but gave the little bud lazy strokes that only made me want to come even more. His cock was still hard, and as he teased me, he started fucking my ass again. I knew I'd be sore later, but I didn't care right then.

"More," I begged. "I want more, Colton."

"Want me to fuck my cum into this tight ass again?" he asked.

"Oh God." I whimpered and knew I wouldn't last much longer. The combination of him fucking me, playing with my clit, and talking dirty was going to be my undoing. I could have withstood one of those, maybe two, but not all three.

He was relentless, fucking me deep and hard as he toyed with my clit. He pinched the little bundle of nerves and I screamed out my release. He kept stroking and kept thrusting, and one orgasm turned into two.

"Come for me again, baby," he said softly.

I didn't think I could, but he proved me wrong. When I screamed out his name, I felt him slam into me three more times, grunting as his cum filled my ass.

His fingers eased away from my clit and he placed his hands over mine where I still held myself open for him. Colton thrust a few more times, slow and easy, before pulling out. I could feel his cum slip out of me. When I tried to stand, he pushed me down again.

"Not just yet, sweet girl."

"I can't take any more."

He chuckled. "I just like looking at you, all spread open for me, my cum leaking out of you. Let's get cleaned up and we head over to the diner and get some breakfast. If you think you can sit down."

I glared at him over my shoulder, but he just smirked at me. I released my ass cheeks and slowly stood, wincing at the discomfort. His smirk just grew and he swatted my ass as I passed him. The man could be insufferable, but I wouldn't kick him out of bed. Not with as many orgasms he could wring from my body. And maybe it had a teensy bit to do with the fact I was in love him.

And you know what they say... Love can make you do stupid things. Like letting a badass biker fuck your ass while you're bent over the kitchen table, just hours before your doctor appointment.

Chapter Seven

Badger

I don't know what I'd been expecting from Adalia's doctor appointment, but lots of sitting wasn't it. The waiting room was packed, and the chairs were fucking torture devices. If you didn't need medical attention before you arrived, you did after sitting for hours in the ass-numbing chairs. They'd called Adalia immediately, but it had only been to take some blood. The nurse had escorted us right back to the waiting room. And here we sat. A mom a few seats over had a little kid with her, who thought it was hilarious to throw blocks at people. The kid had hit me twice, but after the glare I'd leveled at the mom, it had quickly stopped.

"Is it wrong I'm suddenly hoping that pregnancy test is negative?" I asked Adalia.

She snickered and looked at the kid who was now running in circles around the room pretending to be a plane. The mother didn't even look up from her magazine, a bored expression on her face. I figured that was her coping mechanism, because if I was faced with that all day, large quantities of alcohol would be required. She had a water bottle with her. Maybe that wasn't water. Maybe she had vodka stashed in there, in which case she needed to share with everyone she was subjecting to her kid.

"It's not that bad," Adalia said.

The kid let loose with a squeal that rose in pitch the longer he drew it out until I wanted to cover my ears. I narrowed my eyes at Adalia, and she put a hand over her mouth, but it was too late. I saw that smile and she would pay for it later.

"Okay," she conceded. "Maybe it's a little bad. He just has a lot of energy."

"What he needs is a spanking," I grumbled.

The kid went chair by chair, kicking the person sitting down. Everyone shot glares at the mom, but she didn't pull her nose out of her magazine. He stopped in front of me, drew his foot back, and I leaned forward.

"Do it and I will toss you out the nearest window. Can you fly?"

The kid's eyes went wide and he froze. Adalia nudged me with her elbow, but I didn't look away from the rotten kid.

"How would you like it someone kicked you? You wouldn't like it, would you?" I asked. "So don't kick other people."

The kid's lip trembled, but I didn't soften my glare. If anything, I turned it up another notch. I wasn't about to be manipulated by this three-foot terror. It was obvious the mom never disciplined him. He was a terrorist in the making, or at the very least a criminal in the making. Not the hard-core kind, but the "I should get what I want because I want it" kind. A good swat on his behind every now and then would help straighten him out. So would hearing the word "no" on occasion, but mom over there looked like a "yes" type of person.

I crooked my finger for him to come a little closer and he hesitantly took a step, then another.

"I want to say something that I want you to remember. Can you do that?" I asked.

He nodded, his eyes even wider.

"If people always give you things but you never earn them, then you'll never appreciate the things you have. Do you know what's more important than things? Friends. And if you go around throwing things at people, kicking them, or hitting them, you're not going to make many friends. If you don't have friends, who will stand beside you when you're in trouble?" I asked.

The little boy blinked a few times.

"Why don't you pull one of your toys or books out of that bag by your mom and sit down quietly the rest of your visit," I said.

He nodded and scurried over to his mom. He promptly dug around in the tote by her feet, pulling out a book, and sat in the chair next to her. The kid opened the book, but kept casting me furtive glances. After a few minutes, he closed the book and scooted over until he was on the chair next to me. With a quick grin up at me, he opened his book again and started reading.

Adalia rested her head on my shoulder. "That was pretty damn impressive, Colton. I think you're going to make an excellent daddy, just don't throw our kid out a window, okay?"

I bit my lip so I wouldn't laugh and just winked at her. Let her make of that what she would. If my kid ever acted like that, I wouldn't promise not to threaten them with a flight through a window. When I'd been in Juvie the first time, the cop had said maybe he could scare me straight. I hadn't understood it at the time, but now I did. I doubted the kid next to me would forget me any time soon. I just hoped he remembered to behave everywhere he went from now on. It would suck if his life went down the wrong path just because his mom couldn't be bothered to deal with him.

Adalia's name was called and I stood, then followed her into the back. We were led to a room a few doors down, and Adalia hopped up on the padded table, the paper crinkling under her. The nurse assured us the doctor would be in soon, then shut the door. Great. We went from waiting in one room to now waiting in another room. Didn't seem like much progress.

"Have you never waited at the doctor before?" she asked, watching me pace the small area.

"Never been," I said.

She blinked slowly. "You've never been? Like you've never, not ever, seen a doctor?"

"Nope. They had medical care in prison, but I wasn't ever sick. When I'm on the outside, if something happens, I either stitch up myself or get a brother to do it."

"For the record, you're not ever stitching me up."

"You'd damn well better not need stitches to begin with. But if you do, we're going to the ER. Getting stitches would hurt you, and I could never do that to you."

Her gaze softened. She parted her lips like she was about to say something when the door swung open. The doctor wasn't quite what I'd expected. The man looked to be in his early fifties, but had a thick head of hair that only had a sprinkling of silver threaded through it. I wasn't sure I liked someone like him being around my girl.

"Adalia," Dr. Larkin said, looking up from the tablet in his hand. His eyebrows rose when he saw me. "And you must be Badger."

"Yeah."

He nodded. "Well, I'm not sure what news you were hoping for, but the pregnancy test is positive. I know that's probably a bit shocking with Adalia's medical history. I've never treated a patient with endometriosis who was able to get pregnant on the first try. Most try for years and still don't have success."

It felt like the room was spinning and I leaned against the wall. Pregnant. I glanced at Adalia to see how she was taking it, but her expression was blank. That didn't tell me shit and I hated it. Did she want this baby? Was she happy about the pregnancy? I needed some clue from her how I should respond to this.

"I'm going to call in a prescription for prenatal vitamins," Dr. Larkin said. "You'll need to schedule an appointment your OB-GYN, Adalia. They'll treat your pregnancy from this point forward."

"Thank you, Dr. Larkin," she said softly.

"Do you have any questions for me?" he asked.

Adalia shook her head.

"I don't think I have to tell you this, but you need to be careful, Adalia. It's still quite possible you'll lose the baby before the first trimester is over. Have you had sex since the last time I saw you?" Dr. Larkin asked.

"No," she said.

"Then I think it's safe to say you're three weeks along."

"I thought a pregnancy test couldn't be done until a month after?" I asked.

"That's often a misconception. I actually confirmed a pregnancy a few months ago within a week of conception, using the same blood test we performed on Adalia. We didn't realize that at the time, but the OB-GYN was able to narrow it down a bit," Dr. Larkin said.

I watched Adalia, hoping she'd give me something. Anything. She was too quiet. The fact I couldn't see any emotion on her face scared the shit out of me. The doctor said we could leave and I helped

Adalia off the table. She released me immediately and walked out the door ahead of me. With no other option, I followed her to the parking lot, stopping beside the truck we'd borrowed from the club. I hadn't fit in her tiny ass car, and no way was I going to let her ride on the back of the bike, not with a possible pregnancy hanging over our heads.

I helped her into the truck, then went around to the driver's side. I hesitated before I got in, and just watched her through the window, wondering if she'd crack and show me something if she didn't know I was watching. Nope. Still impassive.

I got in and cranked the engine. Then I reached for her hand and lifted it to my lips, kissing the back of it.

"Sweet girl, I have no idea what's going through your mind right now and it's fucking killing me. You being pregnant is a good thing, right? I mean, isn't this like a once-in-a-lifetime chance for you?" I asked, not really knowing anything about endometriosis. I needed to do some research, though.

"You don't want kids," she mumbled. "You hated that kid in the waiting room."

"I didn't hate him," I said. "He just needs a good ass whooping. If his mom gave him some boundaries, he'd probably be a good kid. Right now, he's a rotten little shit."

Her lips twitched, but she refused to smile.

"I'm not going lie, Adalia. The thought of being a dad scares the shit out of me. But there's one thing I know for certain."

She turned to look at me, waiting for me to continue.

"You're going to be an awesome mom," I said. "You're patient, kind, and you're the sweetest person

I've ever known. If our kid is half as awesome as you, then we'll be the luckiest parents on earth."

I could see the wheels turning in her head, but she still didn't give in. She was worried and she had every right to be concerned. I wasn't dad of the year material by any means, and I'd likely fuck things all to hell sooner or later. But as long as she was there to help me stay on the right path, then we'd be fine. Where I was all heat and a react first ask questions later type, she was calm and thought things through. We balanced each other nicely.

"We need to tell Griz," I said.

"Not unless you want to die," she said. "You knocked-up his only daughter."

I chuckled. "Yeah, I did, didn't I? And it was all kinds of awesome. Maybe we should do that night over. There are a few more things I'd like to try with you."

She looked up at me with wide eyes. "Are you serious? I just told you my dad is going to murder you and you're thinking about sex?"

"Sweet girl, I just went three weeks with my mouth attached to your pussy every night and my cock only had the relief of my hand. Not the same by far. So yeah, I'm fucking thinking about sex. A lot."

She snorted and then started giggling.

I ran my hand up the inside her thigh and slid it under the edge of her sundress. The giggles died off and the heated look in her eyes told me she was thinking about sex now too. Good. I wouldn't be the only one worked up until we got home. I rubbed the outside of her panties, feeling how damp she was, then smirked. Adalia narrowed her eyes at me, then slammed her thighs together, trapping my hand.

"Is that your way of asking to get off?" I asked. "Because we're in the middle of the parking lot, baby. And these windows aren't tinted enough that people won't know what we're doing in here."

Her cheeks flushed and she released my hand, then squirmed in her seat. "Just get me home."

"In due time. We need to get your prenatal vitamins first. Then we'll need to get some lunch. We probably should stop by the store…"

She smacked my arm. "Not funny, Colton. You have me all hot and bothered over here. You're not leaving me like this for hours, damn it."

"Baby, I've been worked up for weeks." I winked. "The anticipation will make it even better."

The look she gave me said she was ready to murder me. I tried not to smile as I pulled out of the parking space and headed to the pharmacy. I loved winding her up. She was so fucking cute when she narrowed her eyes at me and gave me what she probably thought was a fierce glare. It was like being threatened by a fluffy bunny. Someone probably should have warned me bunnies have claws and really sharp fucking teeth.

Maybe then I could have prepared myself.

When we got home, Griz was waiting on the front porch, hands in his pockets and an expectant look on his face. We got out of the truck and Adalia stalked up the steps, sounding more like an elephant than the dainty little female who cried out my name in the dark.

"Appointment not go well?" Griz asked.

"Ask Casanova over here," she said as she stormed past her dad and flung open the front door. "He knocked me up."

My jaw dropped as she slammed the front door. It rattled on the hinges as Griz tensed, his expression going from doting daddy to "I'm going to fuck you up" in a matter of seconds. I held up a hand, but refused to back down. If he was going to beat the shit out of me, I'd take it like a man. Wouldn't even take a swing at him.

"Now, Griz. It wasn't planned."

"Your dick accidentally slipped into her without a condom?" Griz said as he came down the stairs.

"It happened before the incident with Twister," I said.

He stopped. "You mean she was pregnant when he did that to her?"

"Um, yeah. I guess? Not sure how long it takes a sperm to fertilize an egg. I was shit at school crap."

He closed his eyes a moment. "If I hadn't already beat the shit out of him and banished him from this club, I'd kill the bastard right now. He not only hurt my daughter, he could have killed my grandkid."

"Adalia is fine," I said.

"Is she? Or is she going to be raising this kid on her own?" he demanded. "Or do you think you can keep your ass out of jail long enough to be a parent?"

Well, fuck. He wasn't holding back, was he?

"I'm working at the garage and staying clean. I haven't done anything illegal since I got out. I've even obeyed every traffic law," I said.

"That girl has been in love with you for as long as I can remember. You may not know it, but you have her heart, and now you're having a kid with her. Don't fuck this up, Badger."

"I don't plan to."

Griz sighed. "Look. I know you're part of this club, and we aren't exactly law-abiding citizens. The garage is one hundred percent legit, which is the only reason I've let Adalia work there. We're turning a profit, even after everyone is paid and all the other expenses are covered. I'll make a deal with you."

I folded my arms over my chest, not certain I liked where this conversation was going.

"You do right by my daughter and grandkid, and I'll sign the shop over to you and Adalia. It can be a wedding present, and a way for you to stay legit. You can still live here in the compound, but I don't want you anywhere near anything that's not one hundred percent legal. You got me?" he asked.

"You're bribing me to be with her?" I asked, fury spiking inside me. My blood nearly boiled at the thought. "You think you have to pay me to stay with her?"

"Don't I?" he asked. "Everyone knows you don't do commitment."

"I moved in with her," I pointed out. "She's not like the others. She's had me by the balls since I set eyes on her at that welcome-home party. And you think I'd do anything to hurt her? To fuck up what we have? I fucking love her, asshole."

He smirked and the front door slowly opened. Adalia peered out at me with wide eyes.

"You love me?" she asked.

I glared at Griz. "You really are an asshole. You knew she was listening, didn't you?"

"I thought it was likely," he said, then slapped me on the shoulder. "Welcome to the family, son. I'll have Magda get started on a property cut."

"I would have told her when I was ready," I muttered.

Adalia came down the steps and slowly approached me. "Did you mean it? You love me?"

"Yeah, sweet girl. I love you. I think I fell for you the moment our gazes locked at that party. I was going to tell you when the time was right."

Her lips pursed. "And you don't think the time was right when we found out we're having a kid?"

I shrugged.

"I swear to God, you can be so infuriating, Colton."

I leaned in closer, my lips brushing her ear. "Want me to kiss it all better? As I recall, you like my kisses... on your pussy."

She gasped and I chuckled. Throwing her off balance for the next fifty years should be fun. Of course, she hadn't exactly said she loved me back. I pulled away and looked down at her.

"So?" I asked.

"So what?" She looked flustered.

"Do you love me too? Or are you going to make me look like a jackass for telling a woman I love her when she hates my fucking guts?"

"Like I could ever hate you."

"Guess you'd better prove it."

"Or you could save that shit for when I'm not in hearing distance," Griz said.

Fuck. I'd forgotten he was there.

"Sorry, old man," I said.

"Do I need to kick your ass to remind you I'm not fucking old?" he asked in a bored tone.

"You can't kick his ass," Adalia said. "He's the father of your grandbaby. Which means no fighting between you two."

Griz gave her a warm smile. "Anything for my girl. Even if it means I have to get along with this asshole."

She rolled her eyes. "Like Mom didn't tell me about all the times you and Colton hung out. You're friends, and now you're family. Real family, not just part of a brotherhood."

"You're not married, so he's not family yet," Griz pointed out.

Adalia blinked up at me. "Colton?"

"Yeah?" Did she expect me to drop down on one knee?

"I'd kneel, but you might get other ideas." Her dad sounded like he was choking. "Colton, will you marry me? Be the love of my life, my partner in all things, and the daddy to any children we might be blessed with? Will you buy me chocolate and ice cream when it's that time of the month, rub my feet when I'm all fat and pregnant, and find fun ways to punish me when I'm a bad girl?"

Now I was choking.

"Um, are you proposing to me?" I asked.

"I thought I made that obvious," she said.

"Too much like her fucking mother," Griz muttered behind me, and I remembered that May had proposed to him when they were younger.

"Yeah, sweet girl. I'll let you make an honest man of me," I said, smirking.

She leaned in close. "Just for that, you owe me four orgasms."

I roared with laughter and pulled her in close. Yeah, the next fifty years were going to be fun. I could already tell there would never be a dull moment with Adalia in my life, and God fucking help me if our kid was anything like her.

"On that note," Griz said, "I'm out of here. Call me when you want to set up the wedding."

I heard his bike start up, but my attention was focused on the amazing woman in my arms. I didn't deserve her, and I fucking knew it, but I would be thankful she was part of my life for however long I lived.

"You know my parole officer has to give the okay for us to get married," I said.

"You just leave him to me," Adalia said.

"Maybe I should go ahead and apologize to him early. I have no idea what you have planned, but he's probably going to end up on his ass."

"I would never…"

I kissed her softly, slowly. "I know, baby. I was kidding. Come on. I owe you four orgasms, then we can figure out how to handle my parole officer. You want a wedding; I'm going to give you one. Fuck the state if they don't like it."

"I better be the only one you're fucking from now on," she said as she entered the house.

"No worries there, angel. You're the only one I want."

Adalia took me by the hand and dragged me to the bedroom.

I couldn't predict our future, couldn't even predict would happen later today, but I did know one thing. As long as she was by my side, then nothing else mattered. If they wouldn't let us get married, then we'd wait. I was completely devoted to her whether I wore a ring or not, and I knew she felt the same.

Who'd have ever thought an ex-con like me could be reformed?

Not me. Probably not the state. And anyone who had seen my rap sheet definitely wouldn't have believed it.

Saving Adalia had sent me to prison, but loving Adalia was what saved *me*.

And I was going to spend the rest of my life giving her all the orgasms she wanted, all the chocolate she could handle, and give her every bit of love I had to give. Because the gorgeous woman currently unzipping my pants was my world, my life, my heart, and there wasn't anything I wouldn't do for her.

Harley Wylde and Paige Warren

Paige Warren:

Award-winning author Paige Warren spends her days weaving tales about alpha males and the women who love them. There's nothing hotter than a man in tight Wranglers, dog tags (especially if he's ONLY wearing dog tags!), or bad boys covered in ink. When Paige isn't creating romantic tales, she enjoys reading and watching movies -- romances, of course. If you see her out in the wild, you'll most likely find her at Starbucks, sipping a white mocha with a distant look in her eyes as she figures out the right wording for the next scene in her latest book.

Paige at Changeling: changelingpress.com/paige-warren-a-202

Harley Wylde:

Short. Erotic. Sweet.

Harley's other half would probably say those words describe her, but they also describe her books. When Harley is writing, her motto is the hotter the better. Off-the-charts sex, commanding men, and the women who can't deny them. If you want men who talk dirty, are sexy as hell, and take what they want, then you've come to the right place.

When Harley isn't writing, she's thinking up naughty things to do to her husband, drinking copious amounts of Starbucks, and reading. She loves to read and devours a book a day, sometimes more.

Harley at Changeling: changelingpress.com/harley-wylde-a-196

Changeling Press E-Books

More Sci-Fi, Fantasy, Paranormal, and BDSM adventures available in E-Book format for immediate download at ChangelingPress.com -- Werewolves, Vampires, Dragons, Shapeshifters and more -- Erotic Tales from the edge of your imagination.

What are E-Books?

E-Books, or Electronic Books, are books designed to be read in digital format -- on your desktop or laptop computer, notebook, tablet, Smart Phone, or any electronic ebook reader.

Where can I get Changeling Press e-Books?

Changeling Press ebooks are available at ChangelingPress.com, Amazon, Barnes and Nobel, Kobo, and iTunes.

Changeling Press LLC

ChangelingPress.com